THE DEATH ROW VAMPIRE

THE CRADLE OF ALL KIND BOOK 1

IM ZONO

Book Cover Design: Miblart

ISBN: 978-1-7764653-0-9

ikagengzono@gmail.com

To all the dreamers, adventurers, and lovers of fantastical worlds. This book is dedicated to you—the seekers of magic, the voyagers beyond reality's borders, and the ones who find solace in living multiple lifetimes within the pages of the books we write. Your passion for the fantastical, your hunger for escape, and your willingness to journey alongside characters through realms unknown inspire every word penned.

Thank you for your support, for embracing these tales, and for allowing your imagination to soar alongside mine. May these pages be a gateway to countless adventures and a refuge from the ordinary.

Please take a moment to visit my socials and sign up for my newsletter so you don't miss out on any updates.
Links are below.

Follow me on Book Bub: @imzono

Social Media links

Instagram & Tik Tok: im_zono_author

PART ONE

THE LAST MEAL

CHAPTER ONE

SOUL FOOD

"Soul food. Now this is what I call a special last meal," the guard murmured, his voice barely audible among the mesmerizing aromas wafting from the dish. The scent is so alluring he can't resist lifting the dish to his nose. His nostrils flare as he takes in the delicious aromas, and his chest swells with excitement for the meal he will never taste. The self inflicted temptation makes his stomach grumble.

In her cell, Mariah sits on the bed, her hands resting gently on her knees as she assumes a lotus position. Despite the guard's noisy arrival with clanking and jingling keys, she remains unbothered, showing no sign of curiosity. The prison walls fade into the background as her mind is consumed by a realm beyond.

The guard places the food on the table, stands with his hands on his hips, and gazes at Mariah, trying to read the emotion on her face. "Your daughter asked if she could prepare your last meal for you. We would never allow this under normal circumstances." He pauses, expecting a reaction. "There is always the risk that death row inmates may use the opportunity to ingest poison and die on their own terms. Lucky for you, the Police Commissioner called in a special favor."

Mariah finally turns to look at the guard. Her eyes, bloodshot and weary, are the remnants of many sleepless nights that even sleeping pills from the prison medic could not remedy. A lonely, long overdue blink sends a tear drop running down her left cheek. She doesn't bother wiping it away. "The Police Commissioner? Is this his way of saying -

no hard feelings?" She scoffs with bitterness in her tone.

The guard wrinkles his brow. "I don't follow."

Mariah lazily moves from her bed and takes the food from the table, holding it with both hands. She cradles it on her lap as she sits. "Forget about it. Even if I had some poison, I would never take it." She looks up as if imagining something. "An old woman in her bed dying peacefully in her sleep. Those are the only terms under which I'm prepared to kick the bucket."

"Unfortunately, none of us get to choose how we go. Try to enjoy the meal, Mariah. It's your daughter's last act of love to her mother." The guard can tell by the way she fixates her gaze on the tiled floor that her mind has once again drifted to another realm in her head. She remains silent and doesn't even blink. He clears his throat. "Will you be adding your name to the wall? Everyone who came before you did."

When Mariah looks up, the guard raises his eyelashes to direct her attention to a particular white wall in the square death-watch cell. It stood in stark contrast to the brown tetris bricks adorning the other sides, while the cell bars and iron door completed the prison's grim enclosure. The white wall of the cell is covered in the names of numerous death row inmates who spent their final day here, along with their age and the date of their execution. Each prisoner that came before inscribed their name with their unique handwriting.

"I want to leave my name, too. But not in black like the rest of them," Mariah asserts. Her voice was firm, yet tinged with vulnerability.

"A unique color for a special lady? I can hook you up. Be right back." The guard walks out, locks the cell and returns moments later with a green marker. He hands it to her through the cell bars. "Unfortunately, I don't have a pink one."

"Good. I hate pink." They both smile. Mariah walks up to the wall, finds a space in the bottom right corner and writes her full name. *Mariah Pepper Jenkins- 9th June 2022. Age: 50.* She draws a sad emoji, and a broken heart to finish it. She and the guard take a moment to admire the writing as if it were a precious work of art in a museum. When they feel content with the writing, the guard takes the marker and returns to his station.

Mariah returns to her seat, unwraps the plastic cutlery and digs in. The tin foil that covered the food kept it warm. Memories of the time she taught her daughter the fried chicken, mac and cheese recipe that is now her final meal playback in her mind. Indeed, if she has ever regarded any meal as soul food, it is this one. Maybe the meal will be the reason her soul can rest in peace. "She went crazy with the salt. I always tell her not to go crazy with the salt. My blood pressure can't handle it." A giggle accompanies her murmurs. "Not that it will matter in a few hours," Mariah chuckles while talking to herself. Still, she savors the meal. Her facial expressions interchanging between a smile, a grin, and a frown with every spoonful. A result of the diverse plethora of memories and emotions triggered by the meal prepared by her only child. "Too salty," she let out a whisper as she finished her last spoonful with a lone tear streaming down her right cheek.

"Salt is a symbol of purity." A deep voice resonates from within the room and spooks Mariah. Startled, she jerks in her seat, causing the empty dish to tumble and the orange juice to spill, staining her pristine white prison overalls.

"What the? Who the hell are you?" Mariah asks as she steps backward till she feels the cold iron bars pressed against her back. The stranger grins but offers no explanation. Moments ago, there was no sofa in her cell. Now she is looking at a man sitting legs crossed on a brown leather sofa that matches his skin. He has a captivating look with a medium-sized afro and a classic Panama hat sporting feathers tilted slightly backward. His voice seemed to carry an air of authority and mystique, exacerbated by the fact that he now occupies a room he never entered. "Guard! Steven! Help! Someone is inside my cell." Mariah's desperate voice echoes through the dimly lit prison corridor. She strains to squeeze her horrified face between the unforgiving metal bars of her cell, hoping for a better view of the guard's desk. From her position, she could see the guard and a Sergeant nonchalantly seated at their desk. They are engrossed in their card game, seemingly oblivious to her impassioned cries for assistance. Determined to make them hear, she summons every ounce of strength and screams even louder.

"Here, let me help you." The man flicks his finger, and the guard abruptly rises from his chair and marches towards the cell.

Relief washed over her as she saw the guard approaching. "Oh, good. Finally, Steven! Look!" she exclaimed, pointing at the mysterious man. "There's someone in my cell! I have no idea how he got in here!" Yet, despite her urgent plea, Steven's eyes seemed distant and unresponsive, as if gazing through her rather than at her. Frustration welled up within Mariah, wondering if he had heard her at all.

"Steven, did you even hear what I just said?"

"He cannot hear you or see me. I have limited his senses to what I choose to reveal to his mind. So, as far as he is concerned, you are still sitting comfortably on that chair, enjoying your meal. And even though his body is here, his mind remains fixated at that desk, engrossed in a game of cards with his colleague." Another snap of the fingers and the guard obediently retraces his steps, returning to his desk. The stranger continues as he elaborates on the extent of his power. "The same applies to every person in this entire building and within a three kilometer radius of this facility."

A bead of sweat trickles down Mariah's forehead. She brushes her tongue against her lip and struggles to swallow saliva. "Who are you?"

The stranger allows a moment of suspense before he replies. "My name is Gundo. It's a pleasure to meet you, Mariah."

"Unfortunately, I can't say the same. What do you want from me? How did you get in here?"

"Actually, I am here because of what you want. And to get you out of here. You prayed, asking for deliverance. And now here I am."

"You're an angel? An angel of death?"

Gundo chuckles. "Angel? Me? I wish. Contrary to popular belief, there are only four angels in this entire world, and regrettably, I am not one of them. As for the angel of death, well…let's just say he is a collector of rare souls. I don't believe he considers yours to be worth collecting."

Summoning her courage, Mariah takes two cautious steps forward, her eyes blinking repeatedly, trying to make sense of Gundo. Her movement abruptly halts. She stands frozen in place. Her voice trembles as she seeks clarification. "I prayed for deliverance, and yet you are not an angel sent to rescue me. So, who or what are you exactly?"

Another moment of suspense. Gundo raises his chin and regards Mariah. "I am a vampire." Mariah shifts her weight to one leg and plants her hands on her waist. "A powerful vampire," he says.

The words hung in the silence that followed until Mariah's laughter erupted to break it. "Yep, I knew it. I must be losing my mind," she chuckled, her eyes dancing with amusement. "What on earth did Gwen put in that food?" She shrugs her shoulders as she reaches for her chair and places it back in its position. As soon as her bum touches the seat, the room starts spinning, gaining speed with each passing moment, until the walls became a blur around her in a whirlwind of motion. She felt panic washing over her and her heart racing as she was caught in the middle of a chaotic hurricane of hazy bricks and concrete. As abruptly as it had started, the commotion came to a sudden halt. And now, Mariah found herself seated at a table in a quaint diner, with Gundo sitting across from her. Steam billowed from a cup of coffee positioned in front of her. Her eyes are widened with astonishment. "What just happened? How did you...?" She wheezes.

"You are right. For now, you and everyone else in this facility have all lost your minds. To me. But fear not. You are all in safe and capable hands. Take a sip." Gundo offers, but Mariah hesitates. "Go on." He encourages her. Reluctantly, Mariah wraps her trembling fingers around the coffee mug and takes a sip. The coffee was calming.

Its warmth partially melting her anxiety. At least enough for her racing heart to slow down to a normal beat. "Is it good?" Gundo asks. Mariah confirms with a nod. "It's also in your mind. I put it there. It's called psycho telepathy. My specialty. And I intend to use this wonderful power to help you escape death. Maybe even bring you some justice."

Mariah scoffs. "Young man, as much as I find all of this amazing and confusing, I have no intention of becoming a fugitive."

A playful smirk curved the corners of Gundo's lips. "I am actually fifty-five years old and since you are only fifty, I should call you a young lady."

She rolled her eyes and waved him off with her hand. "Boy, shut up. You look at least twenty five."

"I became a vampire at twenty-nine. And if I turn you today, you will always look much younger than you do now. Maybe even thirty if you feed well."

"Turn me?"

"That's the plan. The best way to cheat death is to gain immortality."

A shudder rippled through Mariah's body. "I don't know much about vampires but last I checked, they suck blood from people. Now I'm sure as hell not ready to spend eternity sucking on people's blood."

"And I am pretty sure you are not ready to die." Gundo leans forward. "Mariah, I can assure you, once you turn, you will be ready to suck blood like a leach."

"Hell no," her response is quick.

"Your reasons to accept this gift and live far outweigh any reason for you to give up and die tonight. I know you are innocent. Your heart is pure, like salt."

"What good is my innocence if I can't prove it? Death row inmates can spend a decade and sometimes even two decades waiting for execution. It's only been one year." She holds up her index finger. "Only one year since they sentenced me and they are ready to execute me," Mariah sobs.

Gundo hands her a napkin. "Here, your tears are not part of my illusion. Neither is this napkin." Mariah takes the napkin and dabs the tears from her eyes. She wishes this entire ordeal was an illusion. That the room could spin again so she can wake up from her bed at home and thank God that it was all just a bad dream. With the appearance of a mythical creature claiming to be a vampire that wants to save her, she began to believe that it was all indeed a bad dream. *Let me play along until this nightmare ends*, she thought to herself. She watches as Gundo takes a sip of the coffee. "Did you just drink from a cup of your own illusion?" she sniffs.

Gundo smiles. "No, there is actually a diner within this facility. I am currently sitting there and enjoying a cup. All I have done is bring your mind here. I assure you I am real. What you are going through is real."

"Well, I've never had a dream or nightmare where a single person I dream about, including myself, has ever admitted it was just a dream. I still hope it's all a horrendously long nightmare. Every minute of it. A nightmare I will wake up from so I can back to my normal life again." She takes a breath. "That night when our lives were turned upside down has played out in my head so many times."

Leaning in, Gundo narrows the gap between them. "Can you fill me in on what happened?" asked Gundo. A mix of understanding and compassion softens his demeanor.

Mariah wipes her tears and snot away with her wrist and looks around the diner. She takes a moment to compose herself as best as she can. "We were driving home after a beautiful evening." Mariah began, her voice trembling with emotion. "Gwen's friends and I had organized a bridal shower for her. It was two days before her wedding. We were both a little buzzed from the wine, but we figured we could make the short drive. Gwen, however, exceeded the speed limit. She was driving sixty miles per hour in a forty miles section. That's when a traffic officer pulled us over." She lets out a deep sigh. "He checked her license and registration and asked her to step out of the vehicle. Things got tense when Gwen failed the breathalyzer test and other stupid tests he had her do. I am still not sure how she failed them. She didn't drink that much. I sat in the car and watched as they argued for some time. Eventually, my daughter walked back to the car and collected her purse while the officer got into the back seat of his patrol vehicle.

"Gwen told me the officer threatened to arrest her unless she paid a bribe. She said she begged him and told him she was getting married in two days, but he was having none of it. I said well go on and pay the bribe then. We certainly did not want her spending her wedding day in jail. My daughter walked back to the patrol car with the money in her hand. After a brief discussion with the officer through the rear passenger window, she also jumped into the back seat of the car. I thought maybe he didn't want to risk us recording him taking a bribe.

"My eyesight is not so good, but moments later I could see them struggling and wrestling in the back seat of that patrol vehicle. The car door flung open, and I saw the money as it fluttered out of the car and got carried away by the wind. That's when I quickly jumped out of the car and rushed to help my daughter. That monster was trying to rape her. He had already torn her shirt open. Money was not the only bribe he wanted. I punched the back of his head as hard as I could and tried to pull him off my daughter. He somehow turned and pushed me back with his legs. The next thing I knew, I was on the ground with a thousand volts of electricity from his taser gun coursing through my body. I was about to pass out. The sound of a single gunshot was enough to send adrenaline pumping back into my brain and jolted me back to consciousness.

"I thought he had shot my baby. I don't know when or how my daughter got hold of his pistol, but she shot him right in the chest. He crumpled to the ground, gasping for air and choking on his own blood. Eventually, he died. When the cops showed up, we had wiped Gwen's prints from the gun and I took the fall. We told the cops that he tried to rape her, but they were having none of it. All they cared about is that I had killed one of their own. They charged me with the first degree murder of an officer of the law. From then on, nothing made sense. Police vehicle footage and body cam footage went missing.

"Turns out the cop we killed was the Police Commissioner's son. We had upset powerful people, and they made sure we paid dearly for it. Never had I imagined it would end with me being executed by lethal injection. I still hope it's all a dream. Once the injection goes into my veins and I lose consciousness, I hope to wake up in my bed, sweating and with my heart pounding, and then rush downstairs to tell Gwen about the long nightmare I had." Tears began to stream down her face.

Gundo allows her a moment. "I am sorry you went through all that, but now it's your turn to have power on your side. Supernatural power."

Mariah slowly lifts her head. "Power means nothing to me." She sobs. "I want justice and to get my life back. I protected my daughter that night, like any good mother wood, and I have no regrets. I sure as hell would do it again. But I don't deserve to be punished for being a loving mother."

"That's the problem with heroes. They love saving others, but they hate it when it's them that need saving. Right now, you don't have the power to save yourself. Let me save you, Mariah." The room spins again till everything is a blurry hurricane. When it stops, Mariah and Gundo are back in the death row cell. Police commissioner Grimshaw and eight members of the jury that sentenced her to death are standing in the same cell. Mariah jumps to her feet, and moves back, recognizing the telltale signs of Gundo's mind control on their blank faces.

"Are they really here or is this another one of your mind games?"

"They are really here, but also under my spell," Gundo confirms and points to the clock with his eyes.

"12:30AM. It's almost time for my execution. I have 30 minutes left to live," Mariah whimpers.

A jury member steps forward, picks up the black marker and writes his name on the white wall. All the jury members take turns doing the same before walking out. The Police Commissioner is last to write his name before he also walks out. "You wanted justice. That is exactly what I intend to give you."

"Are you going to kill them? If you are, I want no part of it. This is not the type of justice I want." Mariah watches as the room spins into a disorienting blur yet again. When it stops, she is at her daughter's house, standing in the middle of the living room. There's a shrine in her memory by the fireplace where her daughter, son-in-law, and granddaughter are huddled together. Even amidst the warmth of the flames, they still tremble from the bitter void Mariah left in their hearts —the frigid dread of facing a tomorrow without her. "Is this real?" She murmurs.

"No?"

"Then it is heartless of you to paint such a picture in my mind at a time like this." Mariah's lips tremble as she chides Gundo. Her eyes blur with tears once more.

"If I let you die, this will be your family's reality for the rest of their lives. Justice is you going back to your family and spending the rest of your life with them. I brought you here so you can see that you have so much to live for. You do not deserve to die. They do not deserve to lose you. Let me save you." Mariah releases the torrent of tears she has been struggling to hold back. She hides her face with her wrist as she weeps. Gundo allows her a few minutes within the illusion. "Take your time, Mariah. The guard and sergeant are now escorting you to the execution room. I think it's better if I keep your mind here."

After a few minutes, Mariah finally recollects herself and breaks her silence. "Is Gwen here?"

"No. I placed a hypnosis on your daughter to make sure she stays home. She thinks the execution has been postponed."

Mariah's mouth opens in an attempt to speak, but all that escapes are short gasps. She hesitates for a moment, but eventually, the words roll from her tongue. "I want to live. I don't want to die. Not like this." She shakes her head. She blinks, and the illusion vanished instantaneously, leaving her in the stark reality of the real world. Unsure whether Gundo was real or her mind and the hope in her heart had colluded to play a cruel trick on her.

Mariah's heart raced as she took in the sterile scent of the execution chamber and felt the leather restraints on her wrists as they were tightened. She lay in the execution bed with the IV's and heart rate monitor already attached to her. A medic, chaplain and sergeant are in the room with her. "Gundo!, Gundo!" she calls out twice, lifting her head to search around the room. Her reflection in the two-way mirror left her feeling a sense of horror as she continued to question the reality of Gundo's existence. Was it just her anger and fear of dying causing her to lose her mind and conjure up illusions in her head? Or even better yet, maybe it is all just a long nightmare as she has always hoped.

"We are now ready to begin," the Sergeant confirms. His voice is authoritative and stern draws Mariah back to reality once again.

Her heart races as she desperately struggles against the restraints that hold her to the execution bed, but her efforts prove futile. Every pore on her body releases beads of sweat. "Try to relax, Ms. Jenkins."

"Are you serious right now?" She protests.

"Any last words?"

"Wait. I'm not ready. Is Gwen here? Is Gwen behind that glass as well?" Desperation seeps through her words as she lifts her eyebrows to point to the two way mirror.

"Your daughter couldn't make it. We tried our best to get in touch with her but failed to get through to her. Unfortunately, we will have to proceed without her," The Sergeant says.

The hypnosis? The vampire? Was he real? Maybe that is why Gwen is not here. Or maybe she could not bare the thought of watching me die. The thoughts continue to race through her mind as she struggles to make sense of her predicament. The heart monitor beside her beeps wildly, its shrill sound echoing her racing pulse. Tears welled up in her eyes, blurring her vision and the world around her. The chaos in her mind drowned out the words of the people in the room, even though their lips were moving, she could hear nothing. *Oh Mariah, Mariah, Mariah. Don't be stupid. Vampires are not real. None of it was real. It's all just a long nightmare. A horrendously long and cruel nightmare.* And with that thought, her heart rate slows. She never even noticed when the medic pieced the vein in her palm and injected her with a calming drug.

"The governor has issued permission for us to commence with the execution," are the next words she hears from the Sergeant. His voice carries a weight of finality. "Mariah Pepper Jenkins, you are hereby sentenced to death for the cold-blooded murder of Billy Grimshaw, who was a Police officer of the law, a father, a husband and a beloved son." The Sergeant reads the charge sheet before concluding with the chilling words; "May the Lord have mercy on your soul."

In the adjacent room, two executioners stand poised, their hands hovering over the buttons that would administer the lethal injection. Only one button actually triggers the injections, however, neither of the two executioners know which one it is. As the executioners push their buttons simultaneously, the tension in the room grows palpable.

A faint hissing sound can be heard as the anaesthetic is released from the first vial. The transparent liquid snakes its way into the IV tube, slowly infiltrating Mariah's trembling body. Her eyesight, already blurry with tears, blurs even further. Her heart rate slows to normal as her eyes shut and release tears that run down the side of her face before she falls into a deep sleep. Next, the second injection, a paralyzing agent, surged through the tube, its insidious effects gripping Mariah's muscles. Her chest rose and fell in shallow, faltering breaths as her body succumbed to its numbing grasp. The final vial, brimming with a toxic, lethal agent, completed the lethal trio. In a matter of minutes, the heart monitor emitted a shrill, unbroken beep, its steady line reflecting the absence of life.

The medic, dressed in sterile white scrubs, walks over to the bed and checks her vitals. Upon confirming that she has passed, he solemnly nods his head. "Time of passing is 1:25 AM. Well, that's all, folks. Thank you, everyone." The silence in the execution chamber is so profound it seems to stretch on for an eternity. Even though it is done, nobody is in a hurry to leave the room, as if they are waiting for an end of credits scene at a movie theater. The occasion does not disappoint.

BEEP. The piercing sound reverberates through the room, breaking the heavy silence. There is not a single heart that did not skip a beat. Their nervous glances bounced around the room, never settling on one spot for long. The straight line on the monitor shows one wave and reverts to the straight line. "That was weird," the warden remarks. They all dismiss it as a glitch and brush it off. Exactly sixty seconds later, a second beep punctuated the air, shattering everyone's composure. Another wave appears on the monitor. Doubt has crept into the heart of every person in the room like an unwelcome intruder.

"Hey Doc, are you sure she is dead?" The sergeant asks. The people on the other side of the two-way mirror are all on their feet, trying to make sense of what is unfolding in the room.

"Hang on. Something is not right," the doctor exclaimed. A frown of concern marred his face. Retrieving his trusty stethoscope, he leans in, pressing the cold instrument against Mariah's chest in search of a flicker of life. Praying he does not find it. As soon as he places it on Mariah's chest, the heart rate monitor produces another beep and a wave. This time, the doctor picks it up through his stethoscope. His face contorts as he furrows his brow. "This can't be right."

"You know what Doc? We need to fix this. I have no intention of making the morning news for being involved in a botched execution," the sergeant pointed out.

"Perhaps we should prepare another dose of Lethal injection," the warden suggests. Now there are beeps and waves every thirty seconds.

The doctor takes a medical torch, lifts Mariah's eyelids and exposes her eyes to its probing light. "Hey Sarge. Didn't she have brown eyes?"

"She sure as hell did," the sergeant confirms.

"Well, now they are blue, and glowing."

"Is that a good or bad sign?"

"How the hell am I supposed to know?" the Doctor snaps.

"You are the medic. Aren't ya?"

"And you and your team are the idiots that botched this entire execution. For Pete's sake," he yells. "She has a heartbeat every ten seconds. This woman is literally resurrecting and is probably going through hell, but can't express it because of the paralytic agent."

"Well, what would you have me do? Should I blow her head off?" the sergeant yells.

"Shut up, both of you. Your bickering won't solve anything," the warden interjects. "Doc, please prepare another lethal dose so we can end this poor woman's suffering."

"Hey Doc. Her chest is moving," says the sergeant.

"My word. She is breathing," he uttered, his voice scarcely above a whisper. "This should not be possible. Her heart rate is seventy beats per minute." All eyes turned to Mariah's chest. It was rising and falling rhythmically in a steady cadence.

Mariah's eyelids flicker before her eyes finally snap open with a sudden jolt. The men surrounding her instinctively leap backward. An icy chill runs down their spine. The doctor, in his hasty retreat, collides clumsily with desks and equipment as his balance fails him. Sinister black veins form around Mariah's eyes and on the white of her eyes. Her gaze shifts sideways to focus on the Doctor, the noise he makes in his stumble drawing her unwanted attention. He attempts to swallow a large gulp of saliva, but he is too terrified to manage it. He clears his throat. "Ms. Jenkins? Are you alright?" he asks with a trembling voice.

"You idiot. Is she alright? She's supposed to be dead. Just what kind of doc…." Before the sergeant can finish his sentence, Mariah snaps the straps that restrain her as if they were elastic bands. First, her hands are free, and as soon as her legs and the rest of her body are free, she moves into a frog-like crouch position on the execution bed. A hiss. Then she launches herself towards the Doctor, wraps her legs around his torso and lunges her fangs into his neck. The medic screams as the warden and sergeant try in vain to pull her off. After draining the doctor of his last drop of blood, she finally releases him and throws his lifeless body to the ground like a rag doll. Within a second, she has the warden in a bear hug, with her fangs planted deep into his jugular. His screams fill the room until the silent grip of death smothers them. Like a predator that has not fed for months, she drains him quickly and entirely, leaving behind a hollow still shell resembling a manakin.

The jury members, consumed by panic, make a desperate dash towards the exit. One jury member has her hand on the door handle but struggles to command it to turn the nob and open the door. Mutiny by her own hand.

"What the hell is wrong with you? It's just a doorknob," another jury member berates her as he dashes forward, pushes her aside and gives it a go. He too fails. They all take a turn. All of them can hold the door but cannot command their hands to carry out the task at hand.

"Turn, turn, turn," the sergeant shouts from within the execution chamber. He faces the same door knob dilemma as the jury members. His hand is on the door handle, but his mind refuses to turn the handle and open it. The jury members watch and scream as Mariah takes hold of him from behind and plants her fangs into his jugular. The jury members watch in horror as the sergeant changes skin color like a chameleon, from pink to pale in no time. When Mariah has finished with him, the jury members watch in silent terror as she steps over the sergeant's body and approaches the door attached to the far end of the two-way mirror that partitions the two rooms. Slowly, she opens the execution chamber door and walks into the observation room. Blood dripping from her mouth.

"Don't hurt us please," a man whimpers. Mariah bares her bloodied fangs, lets out a hiss, and begins the massacre. One by one, she sucks them dry. When she is busy with one, all the others can do is watch, scream, tremble and soil themselves. When there is nobody left alive in the room, the black veins around Mariah's eyes recede. Finally, Mariah comes to her senses and is horrified by the aftermath.

"What have I done?" She exclaims.

"You executed justice."

She turns and sees Gundo standing behind her.

"You've been here all along?"

"From the moment the execution started."

"I killed them. Some of them were good people," she cries.

"Trust me. Every person who is here deserves to die."

"No, the sergeant, he was a good man. He was good to me."

"The Sergeant, he is a cold-blooded killer. The Doctor, he has drugged multiple patients and raped them. The Chaplain, he is a pedophile. I can go on, but time is not on our side."

Mariah takes a moment to take another look at her victims before she turns back to Gundo. "What the hell am I?"

"I think you already know the answer to that question. You just refuse to believe it. But you will. For now, I need you to trust me. My power does not work on vampires, so I have to ask you to please follow me."

"No, I don't want to kill anyone else."

"You've fed enough to keep your cool. But if you stay here, you will grow hungry and end up feeding on innocent people and killing them. If you really don't want to kill anyone else, come with me. I will take you somewhere safe." Gundo holds out his hand. After much suspense, Mariah reluctantly places her hand in his. She is covered with so much blood the few clean patches that remain on her clothes look like white stains on red overalls. The blood that dripped from her mouth soon disappears as it is absorbed into her skin. A vampire's body does not waste blood. Even the smallest drop on the skin is absorbed.

"I don't see the Police Commissioner. Where is he?" The door that everyone failed to open creeks as the Police Commissioner walks in. He has a butcher's knife in his hand. Mariah hisses and lunges towards the commissioner.

Gundo stops Mariah, restrains her and pins her against the wall.

"Stay calm Mariah. He is still under my spell." She tries to struggle more, but realizes that he is much stronger than her and stops.

"What will you do with him?" She asks. Gundo releases her from his hold. They both turn their attention to the Police Commissioner who walks up to the dead bodies and starts stabbing them. He repeatedly strikes the areas where Mariah sunk her teeth during her assault, hiding all traces of the bite marks. There is barely any blood coming out of the wounds. "You are framing him?"

"This is justice. And a taste of his own medicine. Don't you think? Let's go." Mariah casts one last, long glance at the scene behind her as they slowly walk out and close the door behind them. Two personnel who work in the building walk towards them. "Don't worry. We are as good as invisible to them." Mariah breathes a sigh of relief when the two men walk past them as if they do not exist. "I also compelled the security staff to switch off all surveillance cameras. They will switch them on once we are clear of the area."

The facility has very few people working the night shift. Gundo and Mariah walk out without a hassle. When they reach the gate, a taxi is waiting for them. Gundo pulls the door handle and holds it open for Mariah. She hesitates. Gundo stares at her and waits without saying a word. His lip bends into a slight smile. After wrapping her arms around her shoulders and rubbing them, she finally gets in. Once Gundo is inside, the taxi drives off.

CHAPTER TWO

TURBULENCE

The air outside was crisp and cool, signalling the start of a new day as the taxi cruised towards the airport drop off point. Mariah remains seated silently in the car while Gundo rushes out, circling around the vehicle before heading towards her door. Her eyes follow his every move. She sat with a rigid body, her arms tightly folded against her chest. "Let's go. We have a plane to catch," he hurries her.

"Look at me. I can't walk into an airport in these bloodied clothes looking like Jack the ripper. And what if I suddenly get hungry? I could hurt someone."

"I already told you. Nobody will notice us. I control the surveillance and people wherever we go. Trust me," Gundo patiently assures her. Mariah hesitates before stepping out of the car. Just as she exits, she feels a sharp pain on her face and arm from the intense heat of the sun. The sun's warm rays, once longed for, now feel like an assault on her skin. As if she and the sun are enemies.

Tendrils of smoke are still wafting from her skin as the pain quickly subsides and her skin heals. Gundo's chuckle grabs her attention. "What just happened?"

"I'm so sorry. I thought it's a good opportunity to prove to you that you have changed. Just in case you still don't believe you are not human anymore."

"In that case, I'm staying in the car."

"Here, put this on." Gundo hands her a bracelet made with

colorful African beads.

"What's this?"

"A talisman that protects you from getting toasted by the sun." Gundo opens the trunk, pulls out a backpack and swings it onto his shoulder. Mariah puts on the bracelet before extending her hand into the rays of the sun to test if they will affect her. When she feels the familiar warmth she was expecting and longed for, she gingerly exits the car. The blood stains on her clothes have dried up and turned black and yellow. Gundo notices how she restlessly tugs at her afro and smiles. "Don't worry. Even the bloodstains that were in your hair were absorbed. Like I said, a vampire's body does not waste blood. In fact, your hair looks better than ever." Gundo places a two hundred dollar note on the front passenger seat of the taxi before compelling the driver to drive off. "Let's get going. We don't want to miss our flight."

Mariah peered intently at her reflection, studying her face through the car's rear window. Even though the reflection is not as good as a mirror, she notices that the once prominent streaks of gray in her hair have vanished completely. Even the wrinkles she had embraced as part of her old age have vanished. Her brown skin is smooth and soft like that of a newborn baby. She only stops playing mirror-mirror on the car window when the taxi drives away along with her makeshift mirror. "Gundo. I still feel like I could harm somebody."

"You won't. I made sure you are well fed before our flight. What did you think all those people at the execution chambers were for?"

Mariah's eyes water as a wave of nausea hits her, causing her to bend forward and cover her mouth. Despite her best attempts to expel the contents of her stomach, all she can manage are a few droplets of saliva. "I can't believe it. I drank human blood," she says, wriggling uncomfortably. Her palm muffles her words.

Gundo rolls his eyes. "You won't vomit it out. A vampire's body…"

"Does not waste blood. You've said it a million times already." Mariah interjects. Placing her hands on her knees, she tilts her head up to meet Gundo's gaze. "You seem to be enjoying this?"

"Maybe I am. Come. I have blood bags in case you get hungry." He taps his backpack. Mariah gags again. She stumbled forward as Gundo yanked her hand. She scurries alongside him, her teeth bared in a snarl to reprimand him.

They walk into the airport shoulder to shoulder. Despite the early morning hour, the terminals are already abuzz with activity. As they climb up a flight of stairs, Mariah braces herself for the familiar ache in her knees that comes whenever she has to deal with stairs. It never comes. Her body feels so light and movements that used to feel like olympic feats are now effortless. They move faster than the people using the escalator. After a few minutes, they reach one terminal where the last passengers for the flight are boarding.

"The information board says the flight is going to England."

"Yes, but not before dropping us off in New York."

"Are you taking me home?" Mariah asks.

"Not yet. But when you are ready, I will," Gundo replies. They confidently walk past the security checkpoint undetected, and board the plane.

Mariah's nerves get the best of her as she becomes acutely aware of the people around her while walking down the aisle. Even though she knows the passengers are under Gundo's spell, their presence is overwhelming. Her heightened senses kick into overdrive, transforming the ordinary sounds of the cabin into a symphony. People's heartbeats are drumming in her ears like a stampede. The sound of their lungs expanding as they push air in and out feels like she is standing in the middle of a waterfall. Normal conversations between multiple people sound like protests and battle cries. She freezes on the spot. Her breaths become heavy as her eyes grow wide. Each breath escapes her lips in quivering bursts. "Look at me. Calm down," Gundo places his hands on her chicks and locks eyes with her. The warmth of his palms is calming and helps her recollect her mind. When her pulse slows, the cacophony of sensations fades away. "There you go," Gundo whispers. He smiles when he hears her heartbeat slowing. "Good girl."

She sank into her seat with a heavy sigh, feeling the weight of her mental exhaustion settling over her. From their position, they have a clear view of the plane's wings. "It's going to take me a while to adjust to this," Mariah said as she settled into her seat.

"And I will help you. I will be with you every step of the way." Gundo assures her. "Also, you are a fast learner." His words of encouragement are met with a smile. With a newfound sense of calm, Mariah takes a moment to reclaim her senses, savoring the familiar sensation of her faculties operating close to normal but still slightly enhanced. It grants her a silver of self control and soothes her. She starts to process everything that has unfolded so far. "Alright. I am sure you have a lot of questions. Now is the time," Gundo invites her.

Mariah pauses thoughtfully, taking a deep breath before speaking. "The cops. They won't find my body. They will know something is wrong."

"There is an in-house crematorium at the execution facility. They use it for people who are executed and have no family to bury them. After we left, I compelled the in-house coroner to take one of the bodies at the execution chambers and cremate it. He will tag the ashes with your name and keep them ready for your family and anyone that has questions about your whereabouts to discover them."

"And the Police Commissioner?"

"I promised you justice. We will have to wait for the news to see how that one unfolds. I'm pretty sure they will suppress the story till midday at least." As the plane begins to taxi away from the boarding bay, the air hostess guides the passengers through the standard safety procedures. The engines roar to life, their symphony filling the cabin. A few words from the Pilot, then the plane accelerates on the runway and takes off. Once it reaches the right altitude and levels out, Gundo unzips the backpack full of blood bags and passes one to Mariah. "Here. Eat."

A wistful smile graces Mariah's lips. There is a hint of melancholy in her eyes. "My goodness, Maria Pepper Jenkins. Drinking blood to stay alive. My mother would have poured holy water on me by now."

"For the safety of the passengers on this plane, it's best we keep you fed. Also, it was either this or joining your mother six feet underground."

"Oh, my mother ain't dead. She is in a mental institution. The whole drama of me going to jail and getting sentenced to death was too much for her. Us black people don't normally put our old folks in old age homes and institutions. We stick with them till the very end. But it hit her so badly, Gwen and I couldn't cope. My Father on the other hand, couldn't handle it. He had a heart attack in the courtroom the moment he heard the Judge pass down the death sentence."

Sympathy tugs at Gundo's heartstrings. "I am sorry to hear that."

Mariah wraps her lips around a straw-like tube that protrudes from the blood bag. She makes fish lips as she sucks. Now and then her eyes involuntarily blink slowly. With or without her consent, her body enjoys every drop of blood and her expressions show. She doesn't even notice Gundo glaring at her with a smile on his face. Without pausing for even a breath, she consumes the contents of the bag, her lips smacking with satisfaction once she's finished. "I know you saved me, but there are some things I have lost that can never be found again, or saved. I would give anything to travel back in time and fix this mess." She licks her lips.

"If you were to go back in time, you would find yourself in this mess again. Like you said, you have no regrets and you would do it again to save your daughter. I don't believe any of us can fix our mistakes by going back to the past. Unless we can carry the knowledge we gained from the future with us back to the past, which is impossible. But we can always carry the knowledge we gained from our past into the future and do our best to make tomorrow a better day. We all want to create a better future for ourselves and the ones we love."

"Why me? Why did you decide to save me?" She quivered.

The plane banks left, trembling in the grip of turbulence. Gundo inhales deeply, stealing a fleeting glimpse outside the window before responding. "When you save some people, you are not saving just them, but the people connected to them. People whose lives would be hell without the person. I lost both my parents, and since that night the trajectory of mine and my sisters' lives has been towards hell."

"I'm sorry to hear that. But since my family will think I am dead, what's the point of all this?"

"They will eventually know that you are alive. As soon as you are ready. And as soon as we have found a way to prepare them for what you have become. Living forever is not worth it if it means being separated from the ones we love the most." Gundo notices a teardrop escaping Mariah's eye. He tenderly wipes it off with his thumb. "Now you're just being a girl."

"No, Im being human."

"Yet you are not. Not anymore."

"It doesn't feel that way," Mariah replies, her voice tinged with sadness. Gundo peers out the window as Mariah watches the air hostess approach with a trolley. The hostess gives the passengers who occupy the seats in front of them their choice of replenishments before skipping them as if they do not exist. She knows Gundo has a hand in it. "Hang on, you are 55 years old."

"That's right, young lady."

"This is so weird."

Gundo chuckles. "Look. I know you still have a lot of questions, but I need you to take a nap."

"Ok, you may be older than me, but I am not a baby," Mariah retorted.

Gundo's lip curled into a sly smirk, his eyes glinting with amusement. "I know you are not a baby, but as a vampire, you are still a newborn. That means your metabolic rate is off the charts. You've already used up most of the blood supply I brought for the trip." Gundo holds the backpack open, exposing the four remaining blood bags.

"But there is still plenty left," Mariah points out.

"These are for me. Using my powers to keep us from being noticed and controlling essential people wherever we go takes a huge toll. You have consumed enough blood for now and sleeping is the best way to preserve your fuel. We still have about an hour and thirty minutes before we get to New York. So it will just be a quick nap."

"I don't even feel sleepy."

"Vampires never feel sleepy. But we can sleep. When we need our bodies to perform at their peak, we accelerate our heartbeat. When we need our bodies to relax, we can slow our heartbeat. I'll teach you. Close your eyes," Gundo said, but Mariah just stared back at him. "I need you to Trust me," he pleads gently. Mariah pinches her eyelids, lets out a sigh and rolls her eyes as she lowers herself into her seat and lays her head back in a reclined position. "Good. Close your eyes and listen to your body. You should be able to feel your heartbeat and the blood moving in your veins. Feel every part of your body where there is a pulse. The same powers that allowed you to sense the chaos in this plane when we walked down the aisle are the same powers that can allow you to listen to the signs of life inside you. Once you find them, you can control them and find peace."

Two hasty breaths later, Mariah sighs. "I don't feel anything."

"Start by listening to your own breathing and slow it down."

Mariah takes another deep breath in and listens to the sound of her breath as she lets it out. She gradually slows her breathing. After a few seconds, she can hear the rhythmic thump of her heartbeat. Soon she feels the pulse on her neck, her wrist and other parts of her body. "I can feel them," she whispers. There is a hint of amazement in her tone.

"Good," Gundo whispers. "See, your breathing is automatic, but you can still take over and slow it down or accelerate it. You can even take deep breaths if you want. Vampires can control their heart rate in the same way. Now, slow your heart rate to about thirty beats per minute and think happy thoughts."

After a few minutes, Mariah gets the hang of it. She has a library of happy thoughts to refer to. All of them revolve around her family. A life before it all turned upside down. A life that a few hours ago she was convinced was all but over. She imagines her granddaughter in her arms. Sunday's spent preparing meals and passing on family recipes to her daughter. Helping her granddaughter with homework and plating her beautiful hair while she sits between her legs. A sense of tranquility washes over her, lulling her into sleep. She falls asleep, not from counting sheep, but from counting her blessings. Her heart filled with hope that she will be reunited with them soon.

When he realizes that she is asleep, Gundo compels an air hostess to bring a blanket and cover her with it. *Not that the cold will ever bother her again.* He thinks to himself, as he pulls out a blood bag and starts sucking on it. He looks out the window and takes in the breathtaking view above the clouds. His mind swiftly takes him on a personal odyssey into the depths of his past. It has been so long since he last saw his family. Their faces are a blur in his memory. Or rather, his memory of them is marred. The last time he saw them, their faces were covered with blood and horror because of him. Every time he tries to conjure their faces in his memory, his mind fails to put together any other image except the horrific last moments when they died. He is not counting blessings; he is counting regrets. If only he could see them again.

Immortality is great, but when your loved ones have lost their lives because of you, there will always be a voice inside you saying you should also die. He yearns for the opportunity to apologize to his family and hear them say they forgive him.

Just as the weight of regret threatens to drag him into the abyss of despondency, Gundo senses a gentle pressure on his shoulder, drawing him back to reality. Mariah has tilted her head sideways and uses his shoulder as a pillow.

What is the point of living forever if the things you live for do not last forever? Gundo does not bestow immortality upon those who seek it, but rather upon those who possess something worth living for. But now, he himself feels he has nothing to live forever for. He feels only death can connect him to that which he has lost. He wonders if he is not cruel for giving Mariah hope, only to take it again because he himself has lost hope. He had hoped other people's reasons for living could be an anchor for his own desire to live. That if many lives depended on his own, it would be enough to fuel a desire to live on within himself. And now he wonders if it was not irresponsible of him to turn Mariah into an immortal when he himself no longer has a desire to live forever. After all, he has sired her. If he dies, she dies.

CHAPTER THREE

BREAKING NEWS

"Welcome to the 12:00 PM news hour. Our top story this afternoon has sent shockwaves throughout the city of Indianapolis and the country. The city of Indianapolis's Police commissioner is under the custody of the FBI after he was discovered in the execution chambers of the state correctional facilities in the horrendous act of stabbing multiple bodies. Officers say the commissioner seemed confused as they took him into custody and refused to speak without his lawyer present. Among the victims were a medic, three correctional services officials and what investigators confirmed to be seven members of the jury that sentenced convicted cop killer Mariah Pepper Jenkins..."

"Convicted cop killer? That just breaks my heart," Mariah protests as the reporter continues to read the news in the background. She has not taken a seat since they arrived at Gundo's house. Though it lacks the familiarity of her own home, the walls provide a sense of enclosure that she finds comforting.

The taxi ride from the correctional facilities was not bad. The airport and flight, on the other hand, were difficult environments to be in, with the bustling crowds overwhelming her supernatural senses. The forty-five minute train ride from New York's Grand central station to the quaint village of Larchmont was the worst. Even though she knew Gundo's spell concealed their presence and movements, she still found the experience unsettling. Throughout their commute, her eyes darted nervously around the train, scrutinizing every face. She realized how different she was from everyone else. She had noticed a woman relishing a taco, her mouth watering not for the savory delight, but for the pulsating blood coursing through her veins. The gnawing hunger clawed at her, an internal predator yearning to be unleashed, while she fought desperately to restrain it. A sigh of relief escaped her lips as Gundo handed her the last half-filled blood bag, its contents just enough to tame her. When they were in the cab on the way to Gundo's house, she was a lot more calm and even enjoyed the scenery the village of Larchmont offered through the car window.

Larchmont in New York City is an enchanting village that exudes a timeless elegance, nestled along the serene shores of Long Island and capturing the essence of small-town charm. The tree-lined streets are a picturesque sight, with Tudor and colonial-style homes adorned with ivy-clad walls and blooming flower gardens. The sound of seagulls fills the air as the sun casts its golden glow over the idyllic marina, and sailboats gently sway in the whispering breeze, reminding visitors of Larchmont's deep connection to the sea. Amidst this idyllic backdrop, Larchmont remains a cherished haven, a place where time slows down, and its tranquility is just what Mariah was hoping for.

As Mariah continues to listen to the midday news, she finds herself grappling with the whirlwind of events that had transpired over the past twelve hours. She wonders if they will ever lead to her seeing her family again.

"You made an incredible sacrifice to protect your daughter. Had they not been reading your name, it would have been hers," Gundo gently reminds her, his words a balm to her troubled mind.

"Gwen will be so confused when she sees this news report."

The news reader continues, "Meanwhile, in New York, passengers that were on an Airbus A380 which was scheduled to fly to England were left anxious, angry and confused. Originally bound for Heathrow Airport, their journey took an unexpected twist as the massive aircraft descended and landed on the runway of John F. Kennedy International Airport. Air control officers alerted the authorities when they realized that the Airbus was flying the wrong direction and were concerned that it may have been hijacked by terrorists. The Pilot and co-pilot insisted that there was no terrorist threat and simply needed to make an emergency landing. Officials were left with no choice but to take safety precautions and evacuate sections of the airport and landing strip. The Airbus landed on the airstrip with special police units waiting to take control of the situation. All passengers were safely escorted from the plane and investigators have confirmed that there was no terrorist threat. Preliminary investigations have also indicated that there was no technical issue that justified the emergency landing. The Pilot and Co-Pilot have been suspended and will both undergo psychometric evaluation. It is highly unlikely that they will be allowed to pilot a passenger plane again."

"Wow," Mariah exclaimed, her eyes wide with awe. "You really lit up the news with your mind games. You sure we won't get caught with all this clout you are generating?"

"Trust me, nothing points to us ever being there. Nobody saw us. No camera recorded us. And as far as the world is concerned, you are dead." Gundo assures her. "Come, join me." He gestured towards a seat and observed as her delicate hand brushed against the supple brown leather, marveling at its exquisite quality and craftsmanship. With a nod and pursed lips, she took her seat. "Leather works best for us. It's easier to clean blood stains from its surface," Gundo explains.

"Speaking of blood," Mary interjected while rubbing her palms together nervously before tucking them between her thighs. Her legs fidgeted up and down in an inconsistent rhythm. "You wouldn't happen to have any more of those blood bags stashed somewhere around here would ya?"

Gundo's face switches to a serious demeanor. "I do. But I can't give it to you yet."

"Why is that?"

Gundo lifted his wineglass, its crimson contents swirling gracefully within. He brought it to his nose, inhaling deeply to savor its aroma. "You might find this hard to believe," he began, a note of intrigue lacing his words, "but this, my dear, is not blood. It is wine. Exquisite wine, I might add. If it wasn't for the blood I consume, I would not be able to enjoy this fine wine."

Mariah leaned forward, her posture more intent, seeking a direct connection with Gundo's gaze. "What do you mean?" she inquired.

"Do you remember how back in the day, when television used to be only black and white and now we have color tv in ultra hd definition, 4K and all that?"

"Yes?"

"As a vampire, you will always experience two sides of life. While you have been feeding, you have been experiencing the colorful ultra hd side of a vampire's life. Now I need you to experience the black and white side of a vampire's life."

A shudder runs through Mariah's body. "Ok, now you are scaring me."

Rising from his seat, Gundo gracefully moved through the open plan lounge, making his way to the kitchen. He opened a drawer, retrieving something mysterious, and tossed it to Mariah, who caught it with a mix of curiosity and apprehension. "A chocolate bar?" she said, her voice laced with confusion.

"Go on," Gundo encouraged, a hint of mischief dancing in his eyes. "Take a bite." Mariah unwrapped the chocolate bar and hesitantly took a small nibble. As she chewed, a puzzled expression washed over her face. Something was amiss.

"I can't taste anything," she remarked, her words muffled by the half-eaten bar in her mouth. Determination etched across her features, she took a larger bite, hoping to unlock the familiar flavors she knew so well. Yet, to her dismay, the taste continued to elude her. This was her favorite chocolate bar, one she had savored countless times before, and yet on this occasion, it offered no sensory delight. She rushes to the fruit bowl in the kitchen and grabs a lemon, sinking her teeth into its peel. Still, there is no taste—not even a hint of flavor, as if her senses had been stolen. *What has he done to me?*

"Catch," she turns just in time, her hands snapping out to catch the blood bag Gundo has tossed in her direction. With a fluid, hasty motion, she brings it to her lips and starts consuming its contents. Within a minute, she had already devoured two bags. "Slow down, girl.

Try taking another bite of the lemon."

Mariah pauses to lick the blood from her lips before she obliges and takes a huge bite of the lemon. As the tangy sourness hits her taste buds, she quickly spits it out, a grimace crossing her face. "I hate lemons," she mutters, her focus already shifting to the remaining piece of chocolate. She cramps the delectable treat into her mouth. There it is. Sugar, wafer, caramel, and all the goodness she was looking for a moment ago. She is all smiles and giggles.

Gundo can't help but smile at her reaction. "Vampires feed on humans so we can experience life in color. When you stop feeding and hunger creeps in, you stop experiencing the world in color. You can't smell flowers or taste food. Even sex will feel like you are making love to a rock. No emotions. But when we drink blood, we gain the ability to experience life. It is the elixir that restores our humanity. Otherwise, we would be like zombies. That's why they call us the living dead or undead. That is how precious blood is to us. We already have eternal life, but we feed on humans so we can experience life."

"Good heavens. What have I become?" Mariah places her trembling hands on her bloodstained lips. "Is there a cure?"

"Cure? Mariah, this is not a disease that needs to be cured. It is a gift." Gundo speaks with conviction. "If you do not embrace it and learn to have self control, you will become a danger to people. If that were to happen, the responsibility to stop you is mine."

"You mean…you would kill me?"

"Would you rather I let you kill innocent people?"

"I asked if there is a cure?" Mariah snaps.

Gundo is unwavering in his response. "There is no cure. Self control is the only cure. It's also your best chance of ever seeing your family again."

"This is just a lot. A lot of things which you should have told me before you turned me." Mariah starts pacing around with her hands on her hips.

Gundo steps forward, pressing deeper into her personal space till he is close enough for her to feel his hot breath against her skin. His eyes are locked with hers. "Before your parents brought you to this world, they never told you how rotten it was or gave you a chance to choose whether you want to be a part of it. The same applies to the birth of a vampire. You are brought into a new world as a new creature and you must embrace it. There is no cure. This is a gift." He takes a step back as the sound of his heavy breath dominates the silence in the room. "I want to hear you say it. This is a gift. Say it," he demands, his voice is elevated.

"Okay, first of all, step back and show some respect, young man. Who do you think you are, speaking to me like that?" Mariah retorts, pointing her finger directly at Gundo's face. Her eyes are ablaze with defiance as he rolls his eyes in response. "Secondly, don't stand there and pretend you never questioned the possibility of a cure when you first realized you had lost your humanity. Any sane person would have."

A flicker of vulnerability passes through Gundo's gaze. "I did. I even searched for a cure until I finally accepted that the human Gundo had perished. We cannot cure dead things. We must bury them in the past. And unless you bury Mariah Pepper Jenkins, you will never truly live as a vampire," he declares. Gundo grabs Mariah's hand and pulls off the Luna bracelet before he storms off as he makes his way upstairs.

"Hey, wait!" Mariah calls out, panic lacing her voice. "Didn't you say I'd need that for protection from the sun?" She takes a few steps towards the staircase and stops.

"We ain't going for a walk in the sun anytime soon. Just keep the curtains closed. I'm going to sleep. You should also take a nap and preserve your blood. We don't want you getting hungry and running out to eat my neighbors." Gundo's voice echoes from above as he disappears from sight.

"Oh, so I'm your prisoner now?" Mariah's voice reverberates through the room, but no response comes. Left to her own thoughts, she stands defiantly, hands firmly planted on her hips, wrestling with the weight of her new existence and everything she just learned about life as a vampire.

CHAPTER FOUR

"ME AMIGO"

An FBI agent strides purposefully into the dimly lit interrogation room, located deep within the confines of the imposing Indianapolis Metropolitan Police headquarters. The heavy door swings shut with an ominous thud, sealing off any glimpse of the outside world. Devoid of windows, the room exudes an air of claustrophobia and isolation, heightening the psychological tension that permeates its walls. The hands on a clock that hangs on the wall are stuck at twelve o'clock. All part of a psychological game the Police play with suspects they interrogate. Not knowing what time of day it is can cause anxiety and make suspects easier to break. Especially when they are kept in the interrogation room for long periods of time.

The agent approaches a stainless steel rectangular table that is bolted to the floor. The screech of the chair reverberates through the room as he pulls it back and eases himself into the seat. A wispy trail of steam rises from the takeaway cup cradled in his hand. The scent of the piping hot coffee within it permeates the room. With a fluid motion, he places the cup on the table's surface, sliding it across to Police Commissioner Adam Grimshaw.

The agent leans forward, resting his elbows on the cold table, his hands pressed together and fingers interlaced with a practiced precision. His steely gaze meets Commissioner Grimshaw's. "Alright Commissioner. My name is Special Agent Kenneth Folly. I must say, things are not looking good for you. I hope you can help me, so I can help you. Tell me, what happened?"

"You people disgust me. Throwing me into my own interrogation room at my own headquarters," Grimshaw seethes, his anger palpable. He slams his hand on the table. The impact jolts the agent's cup, causing rivulets of coffee to spill. The agents' steely composure wavers for a fraction of a second. "I have served this city my entire life. My son even lost his life while serving this ungrateful state. I deserve a little more respect."

"The fact that you are not in cuffs already speaks volumes about the respect we have for you, and the officers in this station that have been working under your command. But if you can't keep calm and cooperative, that may very well change."

Grimshaw reclines back in his chair and lifts his chin. "I'm not saying anything until I speak to my lawyer."

"The video footage already says a lot. We are not here to determine whether you killed those people or not. We just want to understand why you did it."

A smug expression crosses Grimshaw's face. "They should have assigned my own detectives to this case. They are way smarter than you glorified FBI clowns."

"How the hell did you overpower all those people? Including trained officers who were physically in better shape than you. The only weapon we found in the room was the butcher knife you used. How did you do it, Grimshaw? Were you working with someone?"

"Well, I think you just cracked the case there, detective."

"That's Special Agent Folly, thank you very much," the agent retorts. "Also, a significant portion of last night's footage is inexplicably missing. What we have is footage of you stabbing those victims repeatedly, even after they were dead. You kept stabbing them like a madman."

Behind the special agent there is a two way mirror, the Commissioner stares at his own reflection on the mirror. He knows he has seen better days. He is still wearing his white evening robe with the name Police Commissioner Grimshaw inscribed on the back as he shifts his attention back to the agent. "I remember how the crime scene looked. There wasn't enough blood on the floor, blood spats on the walls or even on my robe. It simply defies logic that such a horrific event, as you describe it, could have unfolded without leaving blood all over the scene and on the perpetrator."

The agent clears his throat and leans back into his chair. "Only a man in your power and position is capable of making hours of security footage vanish. Even though you would never admit it, you and I both know you've made it happen before. That is why body-cam footage from your son's murder case was missing. You are a man that will go to great lengths to protect or even avenge people close to you. So, somebody must have helped you. Who are you trying to protect?"

A creak pierced the tense atmosphere as the door swung open with a forceful thrust. The agent turns to check who it is. He lowers his gaze and sees a dwarf sized Mexican man stepping into the dimly lit interrogation room. In his hand is a black wooden walking stick with a golden wolf's head forming the handle. Flanking him on either side are two imposing figures, akin to bouncers, their black suits exuding an aura of silent protection as they stationed themselves outside the door, vigilant and resolute. "Can I help you? We are in the middle of an interrogation."

A sly smile tugged at the corner of the dwarf-sized man's lips, as if he held a secret that could unravel the entire situation. "Actually, amigo, I can spare you the trouble of a lawsuit. My client already made it clear, he does not wish to speak in my absence."

Was he listening in on our conversation? How could he have heard that? The Agent thinks to himself. "Well, little man…" the agent mocks with a grin on his face. "Since you've finally joined us. Why don't you grab a seat and we can carry on in your presence?"

The dwarf drew a deliberate breath, his exhale slow and measured, as if mustering his composure. "No. I would like to have some privacy with my client. We are well within our rights to demand this. Big man."

The officer cast a calculating gaze on the lawyer, his eyes studying the man's demeanor for a few fleeting seconds. Eventually, he rose from his chair, his movements reluctant. "You have ten minutes only," he conceded, signaling his decision with open palms, as he exited the room and firmly closed the door behind him.

The attorney gracefully places his polished cane on the table, its golden handle glinting in the dimly lit room. He maneuvers himself onto the chair, using it as a stepping stone to climb onto the table. Once he has ascended, he retrieves his cane once again, takes three steps forward and stands right in front of the seated commissioner. He plants his cane firmly in front of him, leaning upon it with an air of authority. From this elevated vantage point, he stands above the

Commissioner and gazes down into his eyes, exuding a commanding presence. On the other side of the two-way mirror behin, him he can hear the observing officers jesting and laughing at him. He is unperturbed.

"Took you long enough," the Commissioner complains.

The attorney's discerning gaze sweeps over the disheveled appearance of the commissioner. "You look a mess mi amigo."

Leaning back in his chair, the commissioner tilts his head sideways, his weariness evident. "I am in a mess. And you, Xavi, need to get me out of it."

"Have you seen that video footage? You need a damn good attorney. I'm not a damn good attorney. I am no attorney at all. So, why did you call me?"

Grimshaw slams his fist on the table. "This is not a game, Gonzalez. I know how resourceful you can be. There is no attorney that is good enough to help me." Grimshaw draws in a deep breath. "Look. I am certain that there was a supernatural influence involved and you need to find out who, what, and why. You need to get me out of this mess."

"In that case, whoever put you in this mess is clearly powerful. In fact, I am not sure I want to mess with them."

As he leans in, the commissioner's tone grows hushed and bristles with aggression. "Oh, you will mess with whoever you need to mess with to fix this. Otherwise, I will expose all the activities we keep under the carpet for you and your werewolf friends. That will be the end of your sick, twisted prey versus predator games." The words hang in the air in prolonged silence.

Xavi closes the distance between them until his presence loomed over the commissioner, his hot breath wafting onto the man's forehead. His once black eyes transform into an incandescent red. Baring his fangs, he emits a deep growl that resonates from the depths of his stomach, amplifying through his chest and reverberating across the room. The low rumble caused the coffee within its cup to ripple, sending tremors through the commissioner's hand as he rests it on the table. He is frozen and attentive as Xavi addresses him in a much deeper voice than the one he is accustomed to.

"Jeez Grimshaw. Look at you suddenly growing some kahunas and resorting to threats." Xavi replied, his words melding with the continuous growl that now underscored his voice. "Speaking to me as if I were your enemy. Are we enemies, Grimshaw?"

Veins pulsed on Xavi's forehead and hands. A bead of sweat rolled down Grimshaw's brow, landing on Xavi's glossy black leather shoe. Droplets cascaded down the commissioner's anxious face, reminiscent of raindrops on a fractured windshield. Despite his unease, Grimshaw maintained a stern countenance. "You tell me, Xavi. I thought we were friends. Allies."

"I did not put you in this mess. It is disingenuous of you to place the responsibility of getting you out of it on my shoulders. Most importantly, it is stupid to threaten me." Xavi takes a step back, arrogantly lifting his chin. "But, I like you Grimshaw. You have been very useful. So, mi amigo. I will see what I can do. But you will have to be patient and wait a few days. We are hosting a big hunt this week.

Time for distractions and side missions, such as your predicament, is a luxury we do not have." Xavi jumps off the table and gracefully plants his feet on the floor. He walks towards the door.

Grimshaw slaps the cup of coffee, a sharp, resounding smack that propels it from the table, sending it hurtling toward the wall. The hot, dark liquid erupts from its container, splattering across multiple surfaces and staining them. He kicks his chair backward and rises to his feet in a jolt. "To hell with your hunt. I am not just a side mission you can set aside for later. Xavi, if you know what's good for you, you will make this your number one priority."

Xavi halts in his tracks and responds without turning to face Grimshaw. "Listen carefully, because I will only say this once. My pack will always take precedence. And if you threaten me again, I will definitely make you my number one priority. But it won't be to help you." He pauses and taps his cane against the door twice. "Don't forget Grimshaw. You can't expose us without exposing yourself and many other people that are way more powerful and dangerous than you. Don't do anything stupid. Be patient." The door creaks as one of his men opens it from the other side. "And Grimshaw, never forget your place," he concludes as he walks out.

"Xavi, Xavi, get back here, you stinking dog!" Grimshaw shouts. Xavi ignores him.

Special Agent Folly crosses paths with Xavi as he returns to the room, shutting the door behind him. "If that is your attorney, I'd say your chances of getting out of this mess are short. I mean, slim," he chuckles.

Grimshaw picks up his chair and sits. "I want a phone call."

"You already used that privilege for today. If you want another phone call, you will need to earn it. The best way to earn it is to talk."

"To hell with you."

The agent ignores the insults and presses on with his interrogation. "Before your so-called attorney rudely interrupted, you mentioned something about the blood."

Grimshaw points a finger into the agent's face. "That should be the first sign that this was a setup. And I hope you are good enough at your job to locate that missing blood, and you may locate the person or whatever did this."

"And the video footage of you stabbing those people?"

"I don't know. Maybe a moment of madness. I recall nothing about last night except the moment I realized I was in those execution chambers with cops surrounding me. What I know for sure is those people were already dead."

"The agent scoffs. "Is that the plan, Grimshaw? Pleading insanity?"

"Make of it what you want. But I will not say another word until I get my phone call."

"Very well. Suit yourself. One thing I won't tolerate is you instructing me on how to perform my job and insulting my competence. As far as I'm concerned, this is an open-and-shut case. Any judge who views the footage will comfortably sentence you to death." The agent closes his notebook, pushes his chair back and rises to his feet. "You need to remember, you are no longer the Police commissioner. Stop barking orders at everyone and start giving me answers. Maybe then, things can improve for you. You know how to find me when you are ready to talk." Grimshaw flips him a bird. Unfazed, the agent displays his watch and taps it three times as he and walks out. "Tick Tock Grimshaw. Time is not on your side."

CHAPTER FIVE

AN OPEN WOUND

"What's up Zendaya nation? It's your girl, Zendaya. Today I am at Federoff's Roast & Barbecue, taking on the legendary three burning musketeers chilli cheese steak roll challenge. This is the hottest and biggest chilli cheese steak challenge in all of New York, maybe even the country. Hell, maybe even the world." Zendaya makes multiple gestures with her hands as she speaks like a rapper dropping bars. "I have ten minutes to finish all three cheese steak rolls. Afterward, I have to endure a ten minute after burn before I can drink milk or anything to alleviate the spicy heat." She places a portable timer next to the table and casually flips her cap backward. A beautiful, curly ebony afro unfurled beneath the cap like a cascade of coiled secrets, her ears barely visible under it. As the crowd counts down from three, her vibrant energy transforms into focused intensity. After the countdown, the audience shouts, Go!

She picks up the first cheese steak roll and stuffs one end into her mouth, chews three times, and swallows like a python. A minute later, the first cheese steak is gone. A minute and thirty seconds later, the second is no more. Two minutes afterwards, the last cheese steak is done and the first part of the challenge is complete. She opens her mouth wide and sticks out her tongue to show that it is indeed empty.

Five minutes into the challenge and the countdown for the after burn begins. The large glass of milk next to her seems like a mirage in the desert. A cooling spring that seems to move further whenever she tries to approach it for relief. She sticks out her tongue and just lets the saliva flow as tears roll down her eyes. The once-amber hue of her skin now bears a reddish tinge, a testament to the fiery assault she has to endure in her mouth. Snort runs freely down her nose as she unleashes a torrent of sniffles, hoping to regain control. "I hate it when this happens, she exclaims."

"One more minute Zen, you can do it," Jabu cheers her on as he grabs a napkin and wipes away the snort, temporarily restoring her dignity. She fidgets and taps her feet on the ground as a coping mechanism and is thankful when she hears Jabu giving her the final countdown. The audience joins him as they shout, "Three, two, one! You smashed it." A chorus of applause erupts from the onlookers, showing their collective admiration.

Zendaya gulps down the glass of milk and holds the last of it in her mouth, savoring the relief it grants her. Jabu unwraps a chocolate coated ice cream on a stick and gives it to her. She swallows the milk and takes a big bite of the chocolate coated vanilla ice cream. She uses her free hand to catch a piece of chocolate coating that breaks away as she bites and almost falls to the floor. Her mouth looks like a battlefield. Sauce, grease, ice cream and snort all in one place as if they were ingredients in the same stew. Even her red crop top and blue jeans have food stains from the challenge.

"Oh wow, that was by far the hottest food challenge I ever attempted." Zendaya rises from her seat, preparing to wrap up her video as she catches her breath. "But you know what, we smashed it," she shouts and raises her fist into the air, drawing another cheer from the crowd. "We have a new record. The meal is free, plus I get my name and picture up on the wall of fame. A big thank you to Federoff's Roast & Barbecue and everyone that showed up. Your support means the world to me. We are now plus minus one hundred subscribers away from hitting the one million mark. So, please, like, share, and if you are new on my channel, hit subscribe and the notification button. See you next time." She blows a kiss to the camera.

Patrons at the restaurant approach Zendaya and offer their congratulations. With a playful tongue sticking out, she strikes a pose for a photo with the restaurant manager.

"Great work Zendaya. This photo will look great on our wall of fame," says the manager.

"Much appreciated Bill. I'll definitely be coming back for another challenge."

"Oh, for sure. We are busy creating a new challenge. I think we should partner with you to launch it."

"Music to my ears. You know that's what I live for." Zendaya hugs the owner Billy and his wife before she leaves the restaurant with Jabu. They walk closely side by side with their hands entwined around each other's waists. As they saunter away, Zendaya's playful voice drifts toward Jabu. "Kiss me."

Jabu obliges with a peck on the lips before licking his own lips. "I can still taste the hot peppers on your lips. No, wait, your lips are always this hot."

Zendaya giggles. "Flattery will get you everywhere."

"Good, because I am trying to get you some place far, far away."

"Oh yeah? And where is that lover boy?"

Curving his brawny arms around Zendaya's waist, Jabu effortlessly lifts her and gently places her on the boot of his sedan. She wraps her legs around his waist as her hands tenderly caress his neck. They pull each other into an embrace that tells a love story to anyone that is looking. Jabu rubs his hands together to warm them before placing them on her hips and massaging the skin under her crop top. She is still wearing her cap backwards with the sun shining through her hair, casting golden highlights like liquid gold. Their eyes are never empty when they gaze at each other. Their eyelids move in sync. They only break the connection to accommodate a rare blink.

A splutter of kisses before Jabu explains. "How does a week in the Bahamas sound to you?" Jabu proposed, his voice brimming with excitement. "I'm talking about a five-star hotel, a beautiful beach, couples' massages and a lot more."

"Mmm, that sounds like heaven," Zendaya purred.

"Isn't that what every goddess deserves? A heaven of their own?" Zendaya placed her hand tenderly against his cheek and caresses his dark skin, drawing him closer before planting a long, passionate kiss on his lips. "I take it that's a yes," Jabu gasps.

"Oh yes. Only a fool would say no to that." they both giggle. Whenever they should take a breath in their conversation, they share a kiss instead. Long and short ones and a peck on the lips here and there.

"Detective Zendaya Zabalaza." A voice pierces through the moment, interrupting them just as they are about to kiss again. A uniformed officer steadily approaches them, his hands gripping the buckle on his belt. He strides purposefully from the other side of the street, drawing their attention like a magnet. Jabu moves back, allowing Zendaya the space to jump off the boot.

"That's former Detective Sir," Zendaya coolly corrects the officer. "What can I do for you?"

"My name is Officer Mckelly. Commissioner Grimshaw of the city of Indianapolis has been trying to get in touch with you. It seems your contact number is no longer operational."

"The last time I checked the news, it was former Police Commissioner Grimshaw. And yes, I changed my number. In fact, he is one of the reasons I changed it. That man is a part of a past I want to leave behind. I was hoping he would never find me again." She shrugs her shoulders.

"Well, consider yourself found. The Commissioner has requested a meeting with you. He is currently in the custody of the FBI and has requested your presence."

"No."

The officer clears his throat. "Ms. Zabalaza, please."

"I want nothing to do with Grimshaw. That bastard ruined my career and made sure I never got closure for what happened to my brother."

"Well, that's the thing. He said he has information regarding your brother."

Jabu steps forward. "Now you listen here, officer. It took every ounce of strength in her soul for Zendaya to accept that she will never know what happened to her brother and move on with life. What you and your stupid Commissioner are doing is opening and aggravating a wound that never healed and was very difficult for her to learn to live with. Now, with all due respect, please leave us be."

"Get your finger out of my face, son, before you get yourself in trouble," the officer warns Jabu.

"Or what?" Jabu moves in closer, their noses almost touching.

"Jabu, wait," Zendaya interjects, tugging him back gently. "What exactly does he want to discuss? Shouldn't he be focusing on his own predicament?"

"He wants to make an offer. One that can bring you the closure and healing you need. Provided you give him the assistance he needs. He said I should tell you he has concrete information that will lead you directly to the answers you need." Zendaya's breath quickens, and she narrows her eyes.

"Babe, you don't have to entertain these stooges," Jabu said.

"I think my work is done here. Based on the look on your face, I will tell the Commissioner he will be seeing you soon." The officer takes three steps back. "A lovely day to you, mam." He gives Jabu one last look from head to toe as he turns, walks across the road, and enters his police vehicle. The officer winks at Zendaya as he speeds off.

Zendaya's teary eyes meet Jabu's gaze. He pulls her into a comforting embrace. "Are you alright, babe?" he whispers.

"I can't ignore this, babe. I have to go see him," Zendaya said, with a note of sadness in her voice, it is a mixture of resolve and nervousness.

"No, you do not. It will only open old wounds."

"Like you said, it's an old wound that never healed. I simply learned to live with it."

"So live then. Just like you have been doing all along. And you have been so happy." Jabu's fingers intertwine with hers, his touch both comforting and pleading. He raises her hands to his lips, planting a tender kiss on each one. "I say we get on a flight to the Bahamas and we put all this behind us."

Zendaya gently shakes her head. "Please, babe, I am begging you. Let's just go and hear what he has to say. If whatever he says sounds like nonsense, I promise we will leave it all behind. At least then I will know that I am entirely focused on us, mind, body, and soul. If there is a chance for me to find closure and heal, I want to take it so you can have me without any baggage."

"Babe, I love you with all your baggage and imperfections," Jabu affirmed. "Don't get me wrong. It's not that I don't want you to heal. I am just afraid that whatever that man has to say, or whatever we discover when we dig deeper into this, will only make your pain worse." Jabu strokes her hair back with his hand. "But if you are confident that you want to do this, and you think this will help you heal, let's do it. But please promise that after this, we will never have to open this chapter again. I mean, I know your brother will always be a part of you and I don't expect you to forget he ever existed. But we can at least put all this Police commissioner nonsense behind us for good."

She places her hands on his cheeks as they draw closer and lock eyes. "You have my word. In fact, when we book the flight to Indianapolis, let's also book a flight to the Bahamas seven days from now. No looking back."

"You sure?."

"Oh yes. I want you to know I am totally committed."

Another flurry of kisses. Their lips are like two magnets constantly attracted to each other. They wrap up with a passionate hug.

"Well, come on then? We have a flight to catch." Jabu pulls her by the hand and leads her back to the car.

CHAPTER SIX

KING

In South Africa, the sun casts its golden hues upon the rolling landscape of Midrand, Johannesburg, as if bestowing a divine blessing upon the earth below. Nestled amidst this captivating scenery is the gated Steyn City. A luxurious gated community occupying a vast amount of acres where some of the wealthiest people in South Africa have created their own exclusive utopia. Meticulously manicured gardens adorn every house. If you make it past any of the three access controlled gates, you can follow the winding road that leads deeper into the heart of Steyn City, lined with opulent mansions that seemed plucked from the realms of fantasy. A private golf course and vast stretches of parkland are the cherry on top.

In one of the exquisite houses nestled deep within the opulent enclave of Steyn City, a striking African woman, adorned in a sleek black two-piece suit lined with a colorful ankara fabric that accentuates her graceful curvaceous silhouette, confidently strides up a grand staircase. Passing by two magnificent pillars, meticulously crafted with intricate African artistic details on either side of the entrance. She enters the large door as she navigates through the hallway; her determined gait underscored by the resounding echoes of her heels against the polished marble floors.

As she reaches the door at the end of the hallway, she pauses momentarily, her slender fingers delicately clutching a mobile phone, displaying an ongoing call on hold. With a measured grace, she removes her stilettos. With a firm grip, she pulls the double-sided wooden door open, revealing the allure of the next room. Her eyes, adorned with a hint of subtle eyeshadow that complements her rich complexion, blink slowly, savoring the luxurious sensation of the plush Persian carpet beneath her feet. Every step she takes, the fibers beneath her feet mold perfectly to the shape of her soles. The room that unfolds before her is a captivating blend of elegance and extravagance. A long, rectangular dining table made from oak occupies the center of the room, decorated with immaculately arranged candlesticks that cast a warm and inviting light.. Each flickering flame dances in harmony, painting the room with a soft, mesmerizing radiance.

A shirtless, hairy-chested African man with a black garibaldi beard, adorned with silver-gray hairs on its edges, sits on a throne-like chair at the far end of the table. The magnificent beard, so huge that his lips are barely visible under it, is meticulously braided into a single resplendent strand, cascading from his chin all the way to his waist. A constant sharp gaze emanates from his eyes. His skin, reminiscent of aged vintage leather, boasts a deep hue of dark brown. A donut shaped traditional Zulu headband rests on his head, exposing a bald patch on the top of his scalp.

A few meters behind the man, a short staircase ascends to a grand stage. Upon it, an ornately adorned chair rests, its opulence evident in the lavish covering of leopard skins. Crowned skulls of ancient African kings dangle like sacred artefacts from the corners, paying homage to the ancestral heritage that permeates the atmosphere. The lion skin, stretched beneath the chair, serves as a magnificent carpet, its majestic head poised as a focal point, almost guarding the legendary portrait of the King Shaka Zulu that hangs above. The portrait, vast in its proportions, is as if the legendary King himself overlooks the room. Its width extending halfway across the expanse, while its height reaches from the floor to the lofty ceiling.

As the woman approaches, she gracefully descends onto her knees. She lowers her head, avoiding any direct eye contact. Long braids cascade over her face, serving as a veil to shield her eyes from his scrutiny. "Ndabezitha. Your Majesty," she greets and reverently extends her hand, proffering the phone to the King.

"Thandi, who is…" The King's words trailed off as he paused to lick the blood from his fingers. "Who is so important that it is worth disturbing my meal?"

"Forgive me, my Lord. He said I must tell you he is the Alpha. He is so discourteous and said you would be displeased if you discovered I did not allow him to speak to you." The King's stare lingers on Thandi for a moment before finally accepting the phone and placing it on his ear but does not say a word. He lets his heavy breathing speak for him, conveying to the person on the other end that the phone had indeed reached its intended destination.

"Lord Shaka. It's been a long time since we spoke."

"Xavi Gonzalez, I was hoping we would never have to speak again."

"Ouch, that breaks my heart. Alas, the fault is on your side. It seems a powerful vampire, one of yours, has interfered in the business of very important stakeholders in my business. This is proving to be quite an inconvenience for me."

Shaka arched his brow. "Why do you assume he is one of mine?"

"I will even give you a name. The crime scene reeks of Gundo and his psycho telepathic abilities. It is the only explanation that makes sense. Fetch your boy, Shaka, and make sure he fixes this mess. I know he is an important asset to you. But if I have to fetch him myself, you will never get him back." He drops the call.

The phone landed with a thud next to Thandi's knees after Shaka tossed it. With a knife in hand, he cuts another piece of meat and quickly devours it. His forehead is creased with wrinkles, and his eyes began to radiate a tense glow that resembles a rare blue moon. With her head bowed, Thandi crawls backwards on her knees as she retreats. She rises to her feet only after she's put a good distance between herself and Lord Shaka. With a final bow, she makes her way towards the exit.

Moments later, the door bursts open, and the sound of hurried footsteps filled the room as three men and one woman stormed in.

With a swift movement, Shaka points his knife towards the door. His eyes are still locked on his steak. "Take off your shoes," he commands. The group lose their thunder as they scurry out the door and remove their shoes. They reenter the room, their heads bowed low like a congregation of devoted nuns. They fall on their knees and crawl towards Shaka until they are a meter away from him.

"Oh great elephant, chief of immortals, mighty spear of the nation. You who say die and we perish. We humbly request an audience with you," one of them petitions.

"Sit down. All of you. I was about to summon you." Shaka commands.

They all take their seats. Dabula, who has just pacified the King with his clan praises speaks on their behalf. "My King. Forgive us for the manner in which we barged into your presence. However, this is a matter of utmost importance. Life and death."

"Immortals such as yourselves worried about death? Why is that?"

"Even though we are immortal, we can still make the choice to die. However, it feels like that choice is about to be made on our behalf, without our consent. Our brother Gundo has once again been showing signs and expressing a strong desire to die." Dabula's voice rises with every sentence he speaks. "It was better when he was here where we could monitor him. Now that he has vanished, we constantly live with the anxiety of knowing that we could perish at any moment. He sired all three of us. There are probably others out there he has sired. If he dies, we all die," he shouts, his hand stabbing toward his companions.

Ramsey picks up where Dabula left off. His voice was tinged with a mix of resentment and despair. "Dabula is right. Yaya and I never asked for immortality. Gundo decided to save us when the people of our country, Uganda, were determined to execute us just for being gay. He saved us at a point when we had already made peace with death. Now, after giving us the gift of eternal life and an opportunity to enjoy our freedom, to fall in love, he wants to take it from us. Like a cat playing with its prey only to devour it. Yet he calls himself our brother. What kind of cruelty is this?"

"My King," Yaya adds his two cents' worth. "Five years ago, back in Uganda. My beloved Ramsey and I were about to be burned alive. They wanted to make an example of us because we were children of high-ranking politicians. Do not forget. Our parents paid a great tribute to you in exchange for the promise that you will shelter us and protect us. You selected Gundo to act on your behalf and made us his responsibility."

"Because his abilities are well-suited for such circumstances," Shaka replies.

"I understand that my Lord. But his suicidal tendencies are inconvenient for those of us who were sired by him. It feels like we are back in Uganda and on death row, not knowing when our lives will end."

"Great elephant," Dubula takes over. "Let me remind you. I was also not a commoner when Gundo turned me. I am Dabula Mafu, the breaker of skies, the sixth son of the current reigning King of the Zulu nation. I am also your direct descendant. Gundo on the other hand is just a commoner. Yes, he is an important asset to you, but I am your family." Spit accompanies the words out of his mouth.

Shaka raises his head and looks at them for the first time since they walked in. The stake that used to be on his plate has been reduced to a pool of blood. He shifts his gaze to the only woman in the room. "And you, Lupita? Do you agree with what they say about your brother?"

Lupita swallows before she answers. "Gundo forfeited his right to be called my brother the day he shed the blood of our parents and that of our elder brother. "These men here," she declared, "are now my true brothers. Moreover, Dabula is my only love. Gundo is as selfish as ever. He has taken everything I love. Now he wishes to take Dabula from me as well. I say he has taken enough. Save my brothers from him, my King, and I will forever be indebted to you. Save them and punish him for his ingratitude for the immortality you gifted him," she growls.

No one spoke after Lupita, and the silence that followed was heavy with expectation. "We await your judgment, great elephant," Dabula said, with his head bowed. He spoke slowly and carefully, with a calm and measured tone.

It takes more than a minute, but eventually the King speaks. "Gundo is not a commoner." All around the table raise their heads and listen intently. "He is my greatest asset. When you are a vampire, your value is not determined by your proximity to politicians, money or royal blood. It is determined by the power you wield." A palpable shimmer of disappointment fills their eyes. "If it were possible, one of you would drink him dry so you can take his power. Unfortunately, the legacy of a power gained from drinking the blood of a witch cannot be passed from vampire to vampire. His gift has allowed us to achieve so much and build this guild to what it is today. Also, his power is extremely rare. I have not come across anyone else who possesses it. Even among witches. This makes him all the more valuable. Without Gundo, it will be difficult to achieve the greatest purpose of my immortal life. Ending our reliance on human blood and making the vampire a self-sufficient being. Only then can we be considered truly immortal. When this dream is realized, I will wield a power to change our very nature. I will ensure a vampire's life will no longer be anchored to that of their sire. Such squabbles as the one you bring before me will no longer be an issue."

"But my King," Dabula interjects.

"I am still speaking," Shaka silences him. "Nevertheless, your cries are justified, and I have heard them. You are not the only ones Gundo has offended. If we do not get him under control, there will be a lot more people barging into my house and disturbing my peace. I know of his whereabouts. I received a call from a stinking werewolf in America. Thandi will give you the details of the location. Gundo is older and more powerful than all of you, but together you can take him. Also, you have Lupita. She is the leash on which I have kept him since I turned him. Lately, it seems even that is not enough. You are not to bring harm upon him. It is in the best interest of everyone if Gundo can be put to sleep until such a time that I need him to fulfill my purposes. It takes a thousand years for the sire bond to be broken. He will only be released when I need him or when a thousand years have lapsed." The look of disappointment fades from their faces as they struggle to hide their smiles. "Perhaps during his time in hibernation, he will learn to appreciate the value of eternal life. More importantly, for all of you, he will not be able to end his life along with yours. You have my assurance that I will never again allow him to have the power to decide whether you all get to live or die. I have spoken. Now, go, my children."

They stand and begin to recite clan praises to the King in unison. "Great elephant, chief of immortals, mighty spear of the nation. You who say die and we perish." They walk backwards with their heads bowed low as they leave.

As soon as they step outside, Ramey and Yaya jump up and high-five each other in celebration. Dabula and Lupita celebrate with a passionate kiss and a hug.

"It's up to us now. Lord Shaka is giving us the opportunity to reclaim sovereignty over our lives," Ramsey said. There is a flicker of determination in his eyes.

"We need to book flights to the USA immediately," Dabula adds.

"Flights will take too long," Thandi interjects as she walks up to them with a tablet in hand. "I have arranged for you to fast-travel using the Ironwood train. You can be in America when the moon rises there. All essential details will be sent to your emails. You better hurry."

"We can always count on you, Thandi. Thank you," says Lupita. Thandi acknowledges her compliment with a smile as she walks away, leaving them to their preparations.

CHAPTER SEVEN

DETECTIVE ZABALAZA

All of the FBI's efforts to extract information from Police Commissioner Grimshaw have thus far proven fruitless. They tried to soften him up with tacos. He said he had no appetite. Instead, his only request was for a steady supply of cigarettes to soothe his nerves. Eventually, they stopped supplying him with the cigarettes, hoping he would talk, but it just made him grumpier and harder to reason with. So they let him smoke. They promised him leniency if he confessed and gave up the names of officials that assisted him. He said he would talk provided they allow him to make a call first. There was a brief standoff before they folded. Once he was done with the phone call, not a word came out of him. Of course, the FBI tapped the phone they had given him. He was aware of this, but did not care. They listened in on the conversation. It was futile. It went something like, "My case is in the hands of bumbling FBI agents and lazy detectives. That's right Agent Folly, I know this phone is tapped, you imbeciles. Get me former Detective Zendaya Zabalaza," he had said to someone he has faith in on the other side of the phone line. They took him back to the holding cells and decided to keep him there until they could come up with another strategy.

After some hours, the commissioner finds himself in the interrogation room again. This time, it's not for interrogation, but for the meeting he requested. Normally, he would have had to use the visiting area, but his officers allow him to use the interrogation room out of the respect they have for him. They even made sure they arranged for him to use a different room in case the FBI tried to tap the previous one.

The commissioner raised his head and perked up at the creaking sound of the door. For the first time since his ordeal began, there was a smile on his face. With his parched, cracked lips, the smile looks borrowed. Especially since the rest of him looks like what he is going through. His constant perspiration had rendered his gray hair damp and clumped together, casting a disheveled sheen upon his otherwise bald head. Even his face looked more wrinkled due to his brow being folded with worry for most of the time.

Zendaya stood at the threshold of the room. She crinkled her nose as a noxious blend of cigarette smoke and the acrid tang of sweat hanging heavily in the air assaulted her. The once towering and authoritative figure under whom she used to be a subordinate now appeared diminished, reduced to a mere shell of his former self, perched precariously upon the chair. Grimshaw folds the sleeves on his white shirt before gesturing towards the seat opposite him, a subtle attempt to establish a sense of control and authority. "Please come in, detective." He clears his throat, rubs his nose, and taps his feet.

With her arms crossed, Zendaya held maintained her position by the door. "Oh wow. In all the years I worked for you, it's the first time you smiled at me," she murmured softly, her words laced with a bittersweet tone.

"Please detective, have a seat," the commissioner's voice cracked as he released one last puff and extinguished his cigarette. The smoky haze lingered, obscuring the table. Zendaya patiently waited for it to dissipate before carefully pushing the door shut and easing into her chair. A flick is enough to move her naturally curly, honey colored hair away from her face, revealing her amber skin behind a chin-skimming afro. A high neck, black sleeveless vest exposes her toned arms. A tight blue jean skirt and black stockings completed her look. All the colors she wore were talking to each other. Her long purple nails make a crackling sound as she taps her fingers on the table. "Well?"

The commissioner sniffed. "Thank you for coming, detective."

"I am not a detective anymore. You made sure of that. Remember?" she retorts.

"I know. But…It was nothing personal."

"Like hell it wasn't."

"You know I can get you your career back. You know that, right?"

"That lie wouldn't have sold well even if you were still the Police Commissioner," she scoffs. "Anyway, I didn't come here because I want my career back. Your message boy said you have information about my brother."

"That's right. I do. But nothing comes for free."

"What do you want, Grimshaw?"

"Pretty sure you've seen the news. I am in a bit of a pickle and I need your help."

"A mini massacre is not exactly what I would consider a bit of a pickle."

"I'm innocent. And I need you to help me prove it."

"They have video footage of you stabbing those people."

"They were already dead," Grimshaw shouts and stabs his finger towards Zendaya's face.

"So what were you doing to those people in the video when you repeatedly stuck a knife into their bodies? Checking for a pulse?" Her question lingered in the air as a brief silence passed. "You have an entire army of officers, detectives, and unlimited police resources. Why do you need me?"

"The FBI won't let any of my men anywhere near this case. Also, this is not an ordinary case. If you take a closer look at the evidence, you'll notice the unmistakable presence of supernatural forces at play. The FBI cannot investigate something they do not believe exists. This entire case and whatever I tell them appears nonsensical to them. However, we both know and have experienced the supernatural world firsthand. More importantly, you are part of it. Everyone in this precinct grew up with the notion that witches are ugly, old hags with large pimples on their pointy noses and fly around on brooms in the middle of the night. Little do they know that a bombshell of a witch just walked into the building and is sitting right in front of me."

Zendaya leans back, folds her arms, crosses her legs and lifts her chin. "Alright Grimshaw. Whom or what exactly do you believe got you into this mess?"

Grimshaw shakes his head. "All I remember is retiring to bed that evening. I was alone that night. My wife Sofia was on a business trip. The next thing I knew, I was at the execution chambers and pulling a knife out of some dead woman's neck. The absence of blood on me, the walls and the floor made little sense. There were only a few droplets of blood here and there. Yet the bodies all looked pale."

Zendaya squinted her eyes. "Have you upset any powerful vampires lately?" she asked.

"See what I mean? Already you are asking the right questions. I've had no dealings with vampires. However, I need you to get me answers before my bail hearing. My attorney delayed it until Wednesday. That means you have twenty-four hours to get me information that will ensure I make bail. Once I am free, I will be in a better position to clear my name?"

"And why should I help you?"

The commissioner lets out a deep sigh. "A secretive meeting of highly respected individuals who are part of an exclusive club is scheduled for tomorrow evening. They will gather for some very questionable sports and recreational activities. Sort of like their own sick, twisted version of the hunger games." Grimshaws voice is hushed and unsettling. "They find civilians that are desperate for fast money as well as prisoners that have been sentenced to life and lure them into becoming participants. I am sorry to say this, but your brother took part in one of these activities and it led to him losing his life."

Shock and disbelief flooded Zendaya's mind, leaving her in a whirlwind of emotions. A wave of rage threatened to overtake her, but she steeled herself and demanded answers. "My brother was smarter than that. Zane knows he has a family he can rely on and knows how much we love him. He would never resort to something like that, no matter how desperate he is. How did he end up getting involved in this?"

"Get me what I need within the next 24 hours, and I will give you the coordinates for the meeting. You can find these people and ask them yourself."

Zendaya closes her eyes for a moment and inhales deeply, trying to steady her pounding heart. She blinks furiously, trying to hold back the tears and steady her resolve. "Twenty-four hours is not enough time?"

"It should be for a witch and detective of your caliber. I am sure you will conjure up something."

A tense stare down ensued before Zendaya broke the brief silence. "What part did you play in my brother's death?"

A puzzled expression crossed Grimshaw's face. "Excuse me?"

"You fired me just as I was about to make a breakthrough about the dodgy activities at the prison where my brother was working. Why did you stop me?"

"I was just following orders?"

"Whose orders?"

"Get me what I need, Zendaya. I've already given you a lot," Grimshaw retorted impatiently.

"All this time, you knew what happened to my brother, yet you kept silent and watched me run around like a headless chicken trying to make sense of everything."

"Well, the headless chicken grew a head and started pecking at the wrong people. You are lucky they just plucked your feathers. They wanted to kill you, but I asked for leniency. So I was pulling favors for you long before you knew you needed them," he raises his voice. "Now it's your turn to return the favor."

"You called me here because you are desperate and have no other options." Zendaya leaned in closer, her voice dripping with resentment. "I will get the information you need. And when all of this is done, depending on what I find out about my brother's murder, maybe you will never see me again, or maybe I will pay you another visit."

Grimshaw leaned in and reciprocated her intensity. A smirk played on his lips. "That's my girl."

When Zendaya walks out of the room, Special Agent Folly is waiting outside. "What did he tell you?" he asks.

"Nothing I want to be a part of. He said I should tell you he would like to have those tacos now." Zendaya walks away.

Folly furrowed his brow, frustration etching across his features. "Stay out of this, Zabalaza," he yelled, his voice echoing with a mix of warning and frustration. "This is a federal investigation. You're no longer a cop."

Zendaya ignored him as she disappeared around the corner and left the building.

PART TWO

INITIATION

CHAPTER EIGHT

INITIATION

Mariah is curled up in a fetal position on the sofa, her arms wrapped tightly around her knees. Her eyes are fixated on the window, blinking only once every three minutes or so, betraying her inhuman nature. She hears the faint echo of Gundo's footsteps as he descends the stairs. With each step he took, the sound grew louder and more distinct until she could hear his breathing. As she lies on the sofa, she can feel his presence behind her. With a steely resolve, she refused to acknowledge him and remained stoic.

"You alright?" Gundo's voice pierced the air, breaking through Mariah's detached reverie.

Mariah stirred from her position, her body unwinding as she sat up. "I don't know if I am alright. I don't even know what I am."

With a gentle touch, Gundo soothed her tense shoulders, his fingers kneading away the knots of anxiety. Mariah, succumbing to the comfort of his touch, closed her eyes and nestled her head into the curve of her neck. "You are overthinking everything. For a person who has just gained eternity, you need to learn to take it one day at a time. You are a newborn vampire. Baby steps are important."

"It's hard not to overthink when I am stuck in this place. There is nothing else to do. You say I have eternal life, but do I even have a life?"

"Alright. When was the last time you went out? Like clubbing?"

She scoffs. "Must have been ages ago."

"Well, I think a night out is just what you need. Why don't you slip into something more comfortable? I've been booked to provide catering services tonight at one of the top clubs in New York."

Mariah tilts her head backwards and looks up at Gundo "You're into catering?"

"Sort of. You will understand when you see it," Gundo replies. There is a mysterious glimmer in his eyes.

"I don't think I will survive a night of clubbing. It has never really been my cup of tea."

"Cups of tea are for old people. You are not old anymore. You are immortal. Clubbing with vampires is exactly the kind of scene you need now. The sooner you mingle with more of your own kind, the faster you will learn and embrace what and who you have become. If you want to get a life, it's best to start with a social life. That is what will make you feel human again."

After a thoughtful pause, Mariah surrenders. "Alright Gundo. I'm in."

"Not while you are still wearing those prison clothes and adult diapers they gave you for the execution."

"My goodness. I even forgot I was wearing a nappy. Boy, Im glad I didn't get to use it. But I must admit, when I felt that lethal injection running into my veins, I almost shat myself before I was even dead."

"Fortunately, my venom was already in those vials."

Mariah raises an eyebrow. "Wait. I thought you said you needed my permission before you could turn me."

"Yes. But I was also pretty sure you did not want to die."

"What if I had said no?"

"You did say no. But then you changed your mind."

"But…"

"Mariah. I knew what I was doing. Now, focus. We need to get you an outfit for tonight." Gundo grabs his laptop from a nearby study desk and opens it. He logs into an online store and starts browsing through the women's section. It doesn't take long before he clicks the add to cart button on a small, black dress that oozes with an undeniable sensuality.

Mariah raises her eyebrows "You're not even gonna ask me what I like?"

"You said it yourself. You know nothing about the clubbing scene. How could you possibly know how to dress for it?"

A flicker of defiance flashed in Mariah's eyes. "What's wrong with dressing for myself?"

"You mean like a fifty-year-old?"

"And what's wrong with that?"

"When was the last time you looked at yourself in the mirror? Your wrinkles are gone. Not a gray hair on your head. Turning into a vampire was literally the same as taking a dip in the fountain of youth."

"Well, where is your mirror?"

"You can play mirror, mirror on the wall with the tall mirror in the bathroom upstairs. While you are at it, feel free to take a nice long bath. In the meantime, I'm sure I can find you a few more fashion items and have them delivered today."

"That fast?"

"Depends who you know. Now, off with you." Mariah stands up

reluctantly and runs her hands on her bloodstained trousers.

"Go on, bloody Mariah. Or would you like some help with taking a bath as well?"

"In your dreams." Mariah scurries upstairs. Gundo watches her until she disappears.

"Right." His attention shifts back to the computer screen. "Now for a nice handbag and matching shoes." Gundo continues shopping with a sly grin on his face. He tries his best to purchase items based on a look he has imagined in his head for Mariah.

Upstairs, the bathroom fills with the tantalizing aroma of fragrant steam as the bathtub brimmed with hot water. Mariah indulged in a lavish ritual, meticulously pouring a plethora of bath lotions and essential oils into the water, creating a captivating blend of flowery scents that intertwined with the rising steam. After testing the water's temperature with her delicate hand, she concludes she does not need to open the cold water. Of Course it is piping hot but her skin can withstand much higher temperatures of heat. As long as it is not the sun. She takes off the bloody prison regalia, chugs it into a refuse bag and steps into the bathtub. She buries her body under the snow white bubbles.

After spending most of the morning thinking about her situation and her family, a nap would do her good right now. Her heart is still too painful to listen to, but she still manages to slow down her pulse and soon she falls asleep.

It was during this slumber that Mariah stumbled upon another facet of her vampiric existence—a unique twist on dreaming. The dreams that unfolded before her were not always her own; instead, they belonged to the very individuals whose blood she had consumed from the blood bags. Within these vivid dreams, she encountered the people themselves, their memories acting as a portal into their lives. Their stories of family, secrets, heartbreaks, and experiences melded together, forming a kaleidoscope of overwhelming memories that jolted her body, triggering a rapid increase in her heart rate. The bath water gushes up and spills to the floor as she bursts out of her sleep. When she has gathered herself, she realizes that the water has turned cold and all the bubbles that were covering her have disappeared.

She steps out of the water and notices a black suit cover hanging behind the door. A blue towel is within her reach. After stepping out of the tub, she wraps herself with it and unzips the suit cover, revealing a black dress. She takes out the dress and holds it in front of her. A tingle runs up her spine, triggering an involuntary smile. Her skin is not the only thing that regained its youthfulness. She feels a sense of excitement and willingness to take risks she last experienced in her prime. When she has adored the dress enough, she walks up to the tall mirror. The person in the reflection is not who she was yesterday, nor a stranger. She recognizes her thirty-year-old self. After endless minutes of playing mirror, mirror on the wall, who is the fairest of them all, she makes her way to one of the bedrooms to finish getting ready.

***

Gundo paced back and forth in the narrow space between the elegant kitchen island and the cozy sitting room, his steps filled with restless energy. Suddenly, the distinct click-clack of stilettos echoed from the staircase, causing him to pause abruptly. He lifted his gaze, captivated by the enchanting sound. Mariah's graceful descent was accompanied by the gentle flicker of her lush black afro. Her eyes met Gundo's, and she couldn't help but notice the way his gaze traveled up and down her figure, a subtle smile playing on his lips. He tries to hide his blush by tugging at the bottom end of his goatee styled beard. She also noticed the nervous gulp in his throat as he swallowed saliva and held out his hand, beckoning her to come to him. Even as Mariah focused on maintaining her balance and descending the remaining steps with utmost care, she was keenly aware of Gundo's racing heartbeat, its rhythm accelerating as she closed the distance between them. Gundo couldn't help but notice how, with each stride of her left leg, a glimpse of Mariah's slender thigh and velvety caramel skin peeked through a daring slit in her dress. He does his best to keep his eyes focused on her eyes instead. With a few more steps, Mariah's delicate hand found Gundo's, and he lifted it gallantly, tenderly pressing a kiss to her fingertips.

"You look ravishing."

"Thank you for the compliment. But your racing heart beat- beat you to it."

A warm flush colored Gundo's cheeks. "Go easy on me, young

lady."

"You seem stricken, young man."

Gundo smiles. "As any man would be if he laid his eyes on such a beautiful sight."

Mariah smiles back and strikes a pose. "So, am I appropriate for the scene?"

"You are the scene itself, and you are flawless," Gundo responded, handing her a stylish handbag, which she gracefully draped over her shoulder. He went with a semi formal look, choosing to wear jeans and sneakers with a black shirt and formal jacket. Of course, he never goes anywhere without his panama hat. "Come, my lady, our chariot awaits." Gundo raised his elbow, gesturing toward the door with a touch of old-world charm. Mariah giggled with delight as she took hold of Gundo's arm, and together, they stepped out into the cool evening air, making their way toward a sleek black Mercedes parked gracefully in the driveway.

"You even arranged to have a chauffeur?"

"Nope. Uber black." Gundo clarifies as he opens the door for her. As soon as she is comfortable, he closes the door with a satisfying thud and walks around the car to hop in. The sound of the engine hummed softly as the sleek car glided away from the curb.

"Is he under your...?"

"Yes. But I will pay him handsomely. He is a good man. I just want us to be able to speak freely."

"Alright, but why the distance?" Mariah gently taps the space between them in the backseat with her hand. "Come closer. I promise I don't bite."

"Yes, you do. You're a vampire, remember?"

"But you are a more powerful vampire. Oh, hang on. I see. Deep down, you are still a man." Gundo smiles and keeps looking forward and out the window. "I see you working hard to avoid looking at me."

"It's called being respectful."

"Respectful? Ironic coming from the man who chose my outfit."

"You look gorgeous. But they say it's rude to stare."

"What if I gave you permission?" Gundo smiles and runs his fingers over his beard. "Go on now. Before I change my mind." After a brief reluctance, he relented and allowed his eyes to take a journey on her. Starting with her captivating face, his eyes traveled downward, taking in her chest, waist, crossed legs, the brown, velvety skin on her thighs, and ultimately settling on her toes peeking out from her light brown stilettos. "Your heart is racing again," Mariah playfully taunted.

"So is yours." The grin on her face vanishes at his quick response. Her chest rose as she took a quivering breath. Gundo switches to a serious expression. "Mariah. When you turn into a vampire, for the first few days, all your senses can be so... extra. Including your mood and emotions. You must have noticed it. That is why you and I cannot trust anything you are feeling right now. And I don't want to take advantage of you."

"Damn boy. You sure know how to douse a fire." Mariah scoffs. "But since you are a seasoned vampire veteran, and totally in control, can we trust your emotions, right?" Gundo wrings his hands, his eyes darting around nervously as he struggles to find the right words.

Mariah, sensing his discomfort, spared him further torment. Even though she was enjoying every moment. "You're a good man, Gundo. A truly good man," she whispered, turning away to gaze out the window. Gundo breathes a sigh of relief which Mariah notices as well and smiles with her head turned the other way. Minutes passed in silence before she turned back to him, stretching out her hand and placing it delicately on the seat between them. "Gundo, I've said a lot of things to you since you saved my life, but I haven't said thank you."

"Don't thank me yet. You still don't know if you will like being a vampire. Maybe you just may decide it sucks and walk out into the sun to end it."

Mariah's expression softened. "No, seriously Gundo. Thank you. You gave me a shot at justice when I had given up all hope."

Gundo took her hand, cradling it in his own. "You are a good woman. And you deserve much more than what I have given you. I thrust you into this world, and I promise I will be holding your hand through it all, until you have your eternal life all figured out."

Mariah narrowed her eyes. "What about you? Have you figured out your eternal life?"

Gundo pauses for a moment. "Not yet. But I will."

Mariah nods and chooses not to probe further. After a minute, she pursues another subject. "You said you will be providing a catering service tonight?"

"That's right. As I mentioned earlier, vampires need to feed so we can experience life. So we can have a good time. Blood bags are great as a portable source of blood, but the best quality blood that offers the best feeling is when we drink it directly from a human. That's what makes my powers perfect for catering. I use my psycho telepathy to attract humans to the club so there can be enough supply of warm blood directly from the source."

"You mean you compel them to give blood? That doesn't sound right," Mariah contorts her face.

"Look at the bigger picture. The catering helps prevent situations where vampires attack humans for warm blood and may end up killing them so they don't tell anyone about it. We don't see it as an ethical issue because nature works out better for everyone if the food chain is respected and maintained."

"I hear you preaching, but it still doesn't sound right. It would be better if they volunteered. Maybe many people would be happy to if they got paid for it."

"It's not that simple. Allow yourself more time as a vampire. I promise, you will eventually understand our ways and see how we maintain a balance for the good of everyone."

"I dont know..."

"Mariah. Remember, I need you to trust me."

"Alright master Yoda. Trust you I will," Mariah sneers.

"Star Trek? Really? You just gave up your age there granny," Gundo teases.

Mariah laughs. "For your information, I am proud to be a grandmother. Don't let these new found youthful looks fool you. Besides, you already knew my age." The two engaged in light banter, their conversation eventually fading into silence as they admired the passing cityscape through the window. The shimmering lights of New York City reflected upon the car and its windows, while nocturnal souls flooded the streets, ready to embrace the vibrant nightlife.

Forty minutes later, they finally arrive at the club. Gundo lets himself out, walks to the other side of the car and opens the door for Mariah. She steps out like a star arriving on the red carpet at an awards ceremony. There are no flashing lights from the paparazzi, but the New York city street lights could convince her otherwise, making her feel as though she was the center of attention. She hooks her hand under Gundo's elbow. They walk past the bouncers and into the club.

"The bouncers are vampires," Mariah notes.

"Yes. This is a popular spot for vampires. The owner is also a vampire. We are his special guests tonight in the VIP section."

"Can we grab something to drink first? I feel like I might sink my teeth into someone."

"You won't hurt anyone. Trust me. Be patient." Gundo says. They make their way through the club. Mariah has not had any blood in a while now. She is not comfortable having to beg for it, so she tries to restrain herself. Ascending a flight of stairs, they passed yet more imposing bouncers and emerged through a glistening glass door that unveiled the club's second partition. The room welcomed them with a multitude of plush, circular sofas lining the walls, while an expansive dance floor lay exposed in the center, already claimed by the rhythmic movements of other vampires. Anxious and intimidated by the sheer presence of her own kind, Mariah clung tightly to Gundo's arm, her delicate fingertips barely grazing his skin. Despite her shared vampiric nature, the unabashed stares and predatory gazes directed towards her unsettled Mariah, as if she were still a vulnerable human amidst a den of predators, forever caught between fear and fascination.

"Ah yes. Finally, Catering has arrived." A tall caucasian man in a red suit that shines as if it was dipped in glitter approaches them. With his blond hair slicked back into a short ponytail, he has a typical dracula look and is clad in impeccable black trousers. "I was starting to think you had rejected my invitation," he said in a Russian accent.

"Victor. Have I ever disappointed you?"

"Not even once. And who is this gorgeous trophy by your side?"

"Trophy?" Mariah objects.

"This is Mariah. She is not a trophy. She is my plus one."

"No, I would say she is a ten out of ten, five stars and a cherry on top." The compliment quenches Mariah's wrath as Victor takes her hand and kisses it. Mariah leans back as he sniffs her neck area. "You are a newborn. Mmm, fascinating. Will you be initiating her tonight?"

"Initiating? What initiation?" Mariah asks.

"Darling. You are in the VIP section. But the VIP does not stand for very important people. It stands for Vampire Initiation Party."

"Gundo. What is he on about?"

"Don't worry about it. I will explain later. You will be fine."

"No, tell me now. I don't like surprises."

Gundo takes both her hands. "Have I given you any reason not to trust me so far?" Mariah shakes her head. "Then please. Trust me."

Victor leads them to the sofa and introduces them to his entourage. A waiter gives them glasses. Mariah struggles to hide the signs of her hunger as ripples in her glass expose her trembling hands. Unbeknownst to her, ominous black veins have stealthily emerged around her eyes and are visible even through her makeup. When she takes a sip, there is no taste. Not even the feeling of the moisture from the wine in her mouth. Only the weight of it.

"Gundo. I am starving," she says, her voice barely above a whisper.

"I know."

"So feed me."

"Not yet."

"Why not?" she growls.

"A newborn vampire can take weeks and sometimes months before they learn to control their hunger." Gundo speaks softly. "The longer it takes, the more likely they will end up killing innocent people while trying to satisfy their hunger instead of learning to control it."

"But I have you to teach me that."

"And that is what I am doing. It's precisely why I brought you here. You are not the only newborn here. The Vampire initiation party is the best and fastest way to teach a new vampire to control their thirst. I promise, when we leave this place, you will be fully in control of your hunger and should even be able to last longer without feeding. You must acclimate yourself to consuming more than just blood, even when hunger gnaws at your very core."

"It feels like I am drinking a glass of air." She sips anyway and holds it in her mouth before struggling to swallow as if it's a large bite of an apple that has not been chewed.

"Take another sip," Gundo instructs. Mariah complies, but this time her trembling hands reach for the entire wine bottle and she starts drinking directly from it. Some of the wine runs down the side of her lip and on to her dress. Victor and the others are entertained by the spectacle, their amusement evident in their smiles and chuckles.

Gundo waits till she reaches the bottom of the bottle before he breaks the news to her. "Did I mention that vampires are not capable of getting drunk?"

Mariah's face frowns and twists as she lets out an uncouth burp. "You know that trust thing we have been discussing?"

"Yes?"

"I've decided I don't trust. In fact, I can never trust you."

Gundo chuckles at her. Mariah labors for deep breaths as she fights to prevent herself from going into what feels like a panic attack. It feels as if she is about to black out. As if something inside her wants her to step back and let it take control.

"Looks like she is on the brink. I say we get started." Victor stands and walks to the middle of the dance floor. Everyone recognizes it as a signal as they move to occupy the chairs and sofas that are at the edges of the hall. They also pushed the chairs and tables that were in the middle of the hall to the walls on all sides. Those that cannot find seats stand and lean against the walls. "Ladies and gentlemen. It is my pleasure to host you on this special evening. Tonight, we have five newborns that will take part in a good old-fashioned initiation." Applause rippled through the crowd. Victor points to the entrance. "Please welcome our in-house mistress of enchantment, Lady Celeste

Mayhem."

A woman emerged from the shadows, draped in a flowing crimson gown that cascaded like liquid silk. Lady Celeste held a delicate purple vessel, its contents a mysterious blend of ashes. With a deft hand, she gracefully traced a grand circle on the floor, the ashes leaving a smoky trail behind. Her gaze swept the room until it rested upon Mariah, whose heart skips a beat when their eyes connect. She walks over to her and takes her by the hand. Gundo gives Mariah an assuring nod. Celeste leads her until they are both standing in the middle of the circle with Mariah facing Gundo's direction. Celeste takes a few steps back. Once she is outside the circle, she closes her eyes, locks her hands together as she murmurs an incantation too soft to be heard. The room was enveloped in a swirl of smoke tendrils as the ashes crackled and burned, casting an otherworldly orange glow upon the mystical proceedings.

Mariah can feel her heart drumming in her chest as she wonders what will happen next. She notices that the collective gaze of the onlookers has shifted to the entrance. With a glance towards the same entrance, Mariah's eyes alight with horror. She sees a face she knows all too well—her own daughter. She approaches and enters the circle with her. "Gwen, what are you doing here? You can't be here." She says. Gwen is unresponsive and has a vacant look on her face. Mariah grabs her by the shoulders and shakes her. "Gwen, what's wrong?" She turns and looks at Gundo. "What did you do to her?" Gundo squints his eyes but does not answer.

"The rules are simple." Victor proceeds. "The newborn is placed in the circle with a loved one. The only way for the newborn to save their loved one is to fight the edge to feed and master control over it. Nothing tames a vampire better than the blood of a loved one. Should they fail, we will all watch as they drain their loved one to death. If the blood of a loved one does not tame the newborn, the vampire that brought them to the initiation must take responsibility and kill their newborn." Mariah looks at Gundo with horror and disbelief. "They say blood is thicker than water. Is Mariah's bond with her daughter strong enough to tame her? Is it blood, or is it water?"

An undercurrent of fury electrifies Mariah's voice, "Gundo, now you listen to me. You can play as many games as you want with me, but not with my daughter. You have crossed the line. Get her out of here before I…" Mariah pauses as a sharp tang of fresh blood runs up her nostrils. Her pupils enlarge and turn into a bright blue color. Black veins protrude from the flesh surrounding her eyes. "Please, no," she whispers as she turns and sees that Gwen has made a cut in her palm. Blood is dripping to her feet. Mariah's voice erupts in a primal scream as she attempts to escape the circle, but an invisible barrier blocks her. She hammers it with her fist, each strike harder than the last, until she falls to her knees. "Son of a bitch," she unleashes a wrathful cry, her voice piercing the air and directed fiercely at Gundo.

"FEED, FEED, FEED," a maddening chorus rises from the crowd.

"Control it Mariah." Those are the last words she hears before she loses the battle for control and her humanity blacks out. The monster takes over. She hissed with feral intensity, her instincts overriding reason as she lunged towards her own flesh and blood. The force propels Gwen to collide back first into the invisible barrier as her mother sinks her teeth into her neck. Gwen remains under Gundo's spell and is oblivious to it all.

Mariah sucks the blood from her daughter's veins. The blood does not come empty, it comes with memories of the greatest bond known to men. The bond between mother and child. A memory of the first time she held her in the delivery room. The pain she felt from the first time Gwen latched onto her nipple and suckled milk from her breasts. Memories from when she learned how to walk and took her first step. It all runs like a time lapse in Mariah's mind, from when Gwen was in her teenage years until she became a grown woman and a mother herself. Even the moment when Gwen gave Mariah the privilege of naming her granddaughter and she chose the name Evelyn, after her own mother. In the memories, she does not only see the past, she feels every emotion that she had experienced. It was as if she is reliving each moment, the sensations raw and vivid, transcending the boundaries of time.

It is the power of these memories that Gundo hopes will help tame Mariah. He has been seated and calm since the proceedings began. Now he feels his heart racing in his chest and stands on his feet. The last time he saw anyone as pale as Gwen was when she rescued Mariah from the execution chambers and she had fed on the jury. "Open the barrier. He commands." His voice cut through the noise. His command directed at Celeste.

"The process is not done."

"It's been too long. Open the barrier now," he shouts. Everyone goes silent.

Victor approaches Gundo. A look of concern etched across his face. "My friend. I have never seen you panic like this for a newborn. Surely, you understand the importance of adhering to the rules. We must allow events to unfold naturally. Nobody gets special treatment. My clients hate interference, and it is bad for business."

Just as Gundo grabs Victor by the collar, Mariah pulls her fangs out of Gwen's neck and releases her. With a deep gasp for air, she regains control of her will. She stands and takes three steps back, horrified by the motionless and unconscious body of her daughter lying in front of her. Murmurs swept through the audience, their collective thoughts lingering on whether she pulled out in time.

Mariah gasps and holds her hands out, feeling out her surroundings like a person trying to feel their way through peach blackness. The room vanishes as her mind pulls her consciousness into another memory. After a few seconds, which to her felt like much longer, she fell to her knees. Her eyes return to normal and her fangs retract. A few feet from her, Celeste's hand moves in a circular motion, delicately applying a peculiar ointment to Gwen's chest. A radiant circle of runes appears on the surrounding floor, emanating a soft, green glow. Relief washed over Mariah as she witnessed Gwen's chest rising and contracting more confidently with each breath she takes. Gradually, her pallid complexion regained its natural hue, and the bite marks on her neck faded, almost entirely healed. Still uncertain that she has full control of herself, Mariah remained in the background, allowing Celeste to complete her work.

Gundo approached and knelt beside Mariah, his hand gently resting on her shoulder. "Are you alright?" he inquired, his voice filled with a mixture of worry and relief.

Mariah takes a moment before turning to face Gundo as they rise to their feet. She slaps his hand away. "I remember you." Mariah whispers. Gundo arched his brow. "I remember you," she repeated, this time allowing the words to slowly roll off her tongue.

A tightness gripped Gundo's throat. He folds his brow and clears his throat. "It can't be. Gwen's blood broke the spell. But how?" Gundo takes a step closer to Mariah. She matches it with a step back.

"She is fine." Celeste breaks the standoff and recalls their attention back to Gwen. "She just needs rest and a lot of iron, just to make sure she does not end up anaemic. Her mother took a lot more blood from her than expected," Celeste advises.

"We will get her home immediately," says Gundo. A man in a black suit approaches and lifts Gwen into his arms.

"Wait, where are you taking her?" Mariah stops him before he walks away.

Gundo steps forward. "He is under my spell. He will take her straight home. She will not remember this place and everything that transpired here."

Mariah turns to Celeste. "That ointment you applied to her chest. What was that? Will it have any side effects?"

"It's called the potter's clay. A special ointment that can only be found in a place known as the cradle of all kind. There is no better balm. And no, there will be no side effects. In fact, she will feel better than ever. It heals everything." And on that reassuring note, Mariah allows them to walk away. She watches until they disappear out the door.

Gundo approaches her again. "Mariah…I."

She turns to face him once more, a mix of emotions played across her face. "I remember you. Like a memory or part of my life that was erased from my mind and has now resurfaced. Gundo Napoleon Mbevana. I remember everything. I remember us. Even the one and only night you and I ever made love. For many years I have struggled to explain to Gwen who his Father is because I just couldn't figure it out. The explanation I settled for is that perhaps I was drugged and raped at some point, but it never felt true. Heck, at some point I even thought maybe I was another Mary from the bible. But I remember when we made love." She points to the door where Gwen had just been carried away. "And that's how she was conceived."

Gundo removes his Panama hat and clutches it with both hands. "Wait. Mariah. What are you saying? Is she?"

"Gwen is your daughter, you imbecile. You almost got your own child killed at the hands of her mother, whom you have turned into a monster. And tonight you showed me it was all for sport. For your amusement and that of your friends."

"Mariah. If I knew, I wouldn't have…"

"You wouldn't have what? So you think this madness is fine as long as it's not your own child's life that is on the line? You are all sick and twisted for this," she gestures to everyone around her.

"That is not what I am saying. I was just trying to help."

"You erased yourself from my memory and my life. Why have you walked back into my life?"

"To save you."

"You didn't save me. You cursed me and almost cost me my daughter."

"Mariah. If you can just give me a chance, I can explain. I can make things right."

Victor steps between them. "Forgive me for interrupting what has turned out to be a heartwarming family reunion. However, time is not on our side and we need to move on to the next newborn. I have to kindly ask you to continue this conversation elsewhere."

"I am not going anywhere until Gundo answers my questions," Mariah insists. "Besides, why would I want to let you continue with this sick, twisted game?"

"Darling, this sick, twisted game worked out in your favor. Look at you, completely in control of the demon within you."

"You say that as if you are in control of the monster inside you." She turns and starts addressing everyone. Her voice reverberates across the room. "You say you are taming newborns, yet your methods tell me you yourselves are monsters. You have lost your humanity completely. Who will tame you?"

"Young Lady. I am trying my best to be nice, yet you insist on embarrassing me in front of my guests and being disrespectful. I suggest you reconsider your attitude and choose your next words carefully," Victor's nostrils flair.

"Everyone get out. Now." Gundo commands with an authority that captivates every person in the vip section.

Victor's jaw line tightens, and a vein protrudes from his forehead. "Gundo. What do you think you're doing?"

Gundo's voice dropped to a low, menacing tone as his eyes transformed into a fierce icy glow. "I won't ask again." He growls. The room erupted into a frenzied rush as the crowd stampedes towards the door and into the first section of the club where mostly humans enjoy the party.

Despite the chaos, Victor and Gundo remained locked in a tense stare down, their unyielding gazes holding the weight of unspoken confrontation. As the last of the patrons fled, the room fell into an eerie silence, except for the distant hum of music emanating from the first section of the club where humans party on, oblivious to the vampire activities unfolding in the VIP area. Gundo's voice slices through the tension. "Lock the door behind you." His arm is stretched out over Victor's shoulder as he points to the door behind him. With a deep exhale, releasing the pent-up breath he had been holding since Gundo's initial threat, Victor finally yields and makes his way out. Gundo wipes the sweat from his brow and retreats behind the bar, leaving Mariah standing alone in the center of the room. He fills two glasses with wine and walks back to Mariah, extending his hand to give it to her. She ignores him and continues staring intently into his eyes. "You can drink now. It will have a flavor." She squints her eyes and continues staring at him. "If you don't drink, I won't say a word."

Mariah finally snatches the glass from his hand, causing a few drops to spill. She gulps it all down in one go before smashing the glass against the wall. "Talk."

CHAPTER NINE

A MOTHER'S LOVE

"I loved you," says Gundo. Mariah subtly shifted her stance, drawing one leg back and shifting her weight onto it. She folds her arms and scoffs. "When we last saw each other, I made you a promise that I would go back home to South Africa. I needed to talk to my family and tie up a few loose ends, so I could come back and make you my wife. Every fibre in my body was looking forward to spending the rest of my life loving you. Little did I know that the same body was failing me. I was dying." Desperate for a flicker of emotion in Mariah's expression, Gundo strained to read her face, hoping for a glimmer of understanding or compassion. However, her reaction remained guarded, her response marked by a slight upward lift of her chin, a raised brow, and a subtle tilt of her head. "When I arrived back in South Africa, I felt sick. The doctor ran some tests and discovered I had cancer. He said it was already at an advanced stage. He said chemotherapy would buy me time, but it would not save me. Maybe I had six months left to live. When I remembered the promises I made to you and the plans we had, I could not bear the thought of letting you go through all that pain. Not for me. I had promised to come back so I can make you my wife. I would have made you a widow instead, and I could not bring myself to do it."

Mariah looks away, looks at Gundo again and blinks, releasing a tear. She speaks slowly. "I am sorry for what you went through. But you had no right. I was a fully grown woman and capable of making my own choices. When I chose to love you, it was not conditional and I was not expecting life to be a bed of roses. I was not a child, and I would have stood by you and supported you. My mind was made up about you, and I was ready to become your wife. If that meant I would have become a widow a few months down the line, so be it. What matters is that I would have kept my vow and loved you till death do us part. I'm not saying it wouldn't have hurt. It would have hurt like hell, and eventually I would have healed or learned to live with it. It would have been better than giving birth to a child and not understanding when and how I fell pregnant and by whom? I would have been woman enough to love you, even with your cancer. You should have been man enough to be honest with me." Mariah places her hand on her chest. "You're a coward, boy," her voice quivers.

"I see that now. But it was not as simple as that. There is more." Gundo clears his throat. "When I could not find a solution for my illness in western medicine, I turned to African medicine. The healer I consulted was a Zulu Sangoma."

"A Sama what?"

"Sangoma. Powerful African traditional healers with a powerful connection to the spiritual and supernatural realm."

Gundo starts recalling the events that led to him becoming a vampire. In exchange for a large sum of money, the Sangoma had introduced him to Shaka. He claimed he could cure him. When Gundo asked how much it would cost, Shaka said everything. But he encouraged him not to worry about that yet. Shaka said there was a ritual that could cure Gundo, however, it required his family to take part in order for it to work. No additional information was provided.

Shaka demanded faith if Gundo required his help.

He booked a flight from Johannesburg to Lagos for Gundo and his family, including himself and two of his subordinates. Gundo's mother, father, brother and sister were seated in the last row of the economy section just before the partition where the business class begins. Gundo sat in the business class section next to Shaka. During the flight, Gundo was not able to sleep as he had grown more anxious than ever and decided to find out more about the ritual. He had not slept for days.

"Forgive me, Mr. Shaka, but I cannot stand this any longer. I am running out of time and cannot afford to waste time and money on remedies that I have no guarantee will heal me. Please, tell me how exactly you intend to cure my sickness. How does the ritual work? How long will it take for me to heal? Especially since my family is involved. I do not want their lives to come to a standstill on account of me."

"Before the plane reaches its destination, you will already be cured," Shaka responded.

Gundo was left bewildered by his words. "What do you mean?" he stammered, his heart pounding in his chest.

At that moment, thirty-eight thousand feet in the air, was when Shaka revealed what he truly was. His eyes changed and glowed in an icy blue color. "The ultimate cure for terminal illness is not western medicine, African herbs or sacred rituals. The cure for your illness is immortality," Shaka declared, his voice infused with an unsettling and sinister tone. "And it is a privilege I have chosen to bestow upon you."

Gundo turns around and sees that Shaka's subordinates have also revealed their true nature, their eyes now ablaze with the same eerie glow and dark veins encircling them. He recognizes the creatures before him from the many tales his parents and grandparents used to tell them when they were growing up. Still, he hopes it is not true. "No. This is not what I want."

"My boy. Gifts are not always what we want. Sometimes they are what we need. They are to be appreciated nonetheless."

"My family. Why did you bring them into this?" Gundo asked.

"Once you turn, you will be a monster. A newborn vampire with an unquenchable thirst for human blood. This plane is the best place because you will feed on a controlled number of people. Not one soul more than necessary will be harmed. More importantly, the best way to tame a newborn is with the blood of a loved one. One should be enough, but I thought it's better to be safe than sorry. So I made sure they all came along for the ride."

"No!" Gundo's voice erupted as he made a desperate attempt to leap out of his seat. But Shaka seized him by the elbow, halting his escape. He yanked him back, forcing him to sit on his lap as he sank his teeth into Gundo's neck. An overwhelming surge of terror washed over Gundo as he felt his blood escaping his veins. The passengers around them start screaming as Shaka's subordinates also start feeding. They however grant the none of the passengers the privilege of immortal life. Only death. Some passengers manage to escape to the economy class.

Once Shaka has drank enough of Gundo's blood, he releases his venom into his veins. The young man feels a fiery sensation spreading through his bloodstream, intensifying his struggle to break free from

Shaka's iron grasp, but his efforts prove futile. When Shaka is done, he finally releases Gundo, flinging him callously to the floor.

Shaka rises to his feet. Blood dripping from his mouth. "I drank most of your blood before depositing my venom into your bloodstream. This should speed up the transformation and ensure you have quite the appetite. Enjoy the ride, my boy."

Crawling on all fours, Gundo escaped the chaos unfolding in the business class section, his singular focus fixed on reuniting with his family. They are seated just beyond the partition that separates the economy and business class sections. His father's worried voice reached his ears amidst a haze of horror. Gasping for breath and plagued by a burning sensation in his veins, Gundo attempted to convey the unfathomable terror he had just experienced, yet his parched throat and searing bite marks rendered him speechless.

"Gundo. What is it?" His father asks. All he gets in response is a look of horror, coughs, and gasping for air. The venom feels like lava running through Gundo's veins. His neck and throat are inflamed and the bite marks feel like red hot needles have been pressed into his flesh.

Gundo's mother, Londeka, bends down, supports his son's head and inspects his neck. When she sees the bites, she knows. "Vampires," she exclaims. Panic has already spread throughout the plane. Screams can be heard coming from the business class. All the passengers are on their feet and murmuring amongst one another, trying to make sense of the situation. The air hostesses' pleas for people to remain calm are in vain.

Gundo is desperate to tell his family to run, but he cannot. He breaks away from his mother's arms and starts crawling towards the cockpit door, hoping his family will follow.

"Did you say vampire?" Gundo's father Abel asks.

"Vampires do not exist," Gundo's elder brother, Dembe, remarks.

Londeka takes her daughter Lupita by the hand, slowly walking backwards with her. "I wish that were true. For the sake of every man, woman and children on this plane. Oh, how I wish that were true," Londeka replies with a trembling voice and teary eyes. "Come," she roars with a commanding voice.

Abel and Dembe do not believe in vampires, but the horrific screams and river of blood that flows from the business section are motivation enough to listen to the woman's instruction. Abel helps his son Dembe up from the bulkhead sitting area and hands him his crutches. There is no time for Dembe to put on his prosthetic leg as they scurry to the cockpit end of the cabin and make their stand with their backs against the cockpit door. One by one, the other passengers follow their lead. Londeka's eyes search for her son, but she cannot see him. Gundo has vanished somewhere under the seats. *Is he even still human?* She thinks to herself.

There is now a tenuous silence in the business class and the entire plane. A crackle from the intercom slices through it. "Ladies and gentlemen, this is your pilot speaking. Please remain calm and seated." The Captain blurts out, but nobody pays attention.

Londeka is a thick, rounded woman with a black and grey afro that is well kept. She is big enough for her entire family to tuck in behind her and feel like they are well shielded. Their eyes, just like every other passenger, are fixed on the partition that separates the business and economy class. The white curtain is now red and white with bloodstains all over it. She has dealt with vampires before, but never in such a hopeless situation. Knowing the type of evils that exist in the supernatural world, she had done everything in her power to shield her family from being exposed to it. Even when she told them stories about these supernatural creatures, she always maintained that it was all fiction. A normal, healthy life is what she wanted for them, especially her children. Now she finds herself thirty-three thousand feet in the air. His son is turning into a vampire and her daughter, husband and eldest son are about to be devoured along with everyone on the plane. Her husband, Abel, is old and frail. He uses his walking stick to support himself as he stands behind his wife. His eldest son Dembe is in his late 30's but on crutches. The reason he is standing behind his mother is so that once he knows what they are dealing with, he can be in a position to try to infiltrate the cockpit. Perhaps they can seal themselves in there with the pilots until the plane lands. It's also because he knows his mother is powerful.

Londeka crosses her arms over her chest. And closes her eyes for a few seconds before she opens them again. *I cannot connect to the pilots. Of course, they are also vampires. This was all planned out.* She thinks to herself. She had hoped to control the pilots and cause them to crash the plane in the mountains, granting all passengers the mercy of a quick death, along with the vampires.

While she still thinks of Plan B, the passengers scream as the blood stained vampires appear from the other side of the partitioning curtain.

There are three hundred and forty passengers in the economy section and all of them are pushing towards the cockpit. Londeka realizes she and her family will be crushed by the passengers in front of them. She spreads her arms to her sides. The mother opens her palms and slowly clenches them into a fist as she telepathically takes control of the minds of half the passengers that are in front of them. Her mastery of her power allows her to filter through the vast collection of minds, making sure she moves the weakest to the front and the strongest to the back. This results in most of the female passengers ending up in the front line.

As for the children, she places all of them in a deep sleep. She brings her open hands together in front of her as if she is crushing a large invisible ball and unifies the minds of all the passengers into one mind. "Forgive me," her voice quivers with tears running down her chicks. The old witch manages to halt the stampede towards the cockpit section as she commands the passengers who are under her control to turn and hold back the rest of the passengers that are pushing towards them. Her own horde to command in a battle she never imagined she would find herself fighting, thirty-three thousand feet above the ground.

The vampires have already had their fill of blood from the passengers in the business class section. This will just be a massacre for fun. They begin punching through the chests of passengers and pulling out their hearts. Some they decapitate. They throw some of the hearts and heads towards those who are attempting to flee. Some of the decapitated heads and hearts land next to Londeka's feet. She almost loses control when she feels a dead man's heart striking the right side of her face and staining her cheek with warm blood. She manages to steel herself and maintain control.

Lupita is hiding under the seat just behind her. She is in a pupal position and covers her ears with her hands. When a decapitated head rolls towards the little girl, Londeka kicks it away. She checks behind her and sees her son Dembe. He is so frozen in horror; he may as well be dead. She searches again for her husband and finds him on the floor. The old man's heart could not take it. He is gone. There is no time to process it and mourn.

She faces forward and uses her rage to focus as tears run down her eyes. The screaming slowly subsides as the vampires deal with the last of the passengers that are not under Londeka's control. She had grown weary during the attack and had to keep releasing the passengers he was controlling, a few at a time, to maintain control. Only twenty-five remain.

The vampires eventually notice the unusual composure and vacant demeanor of the passengers that remain and decide to stop and investigate. The stench of blood, bile, human excrement and intestines fills the air with only twenty-five passengers remaining between Londeka and the vampires. She is spent. Sweat covered every inch of her body like dew on a dying flower in the early morning. The cabin that used to be mostly white and gray inside is now painted red with bood. The remaining white spots look like stains on a crimson surface.

"Hello back there?" Shaka calls out. "Whoever you are, it seems you are hell bent on spoiling our fun. Nobody likes party poppers.

Victims that do not scream are no fun." The other vampires chuckle behind Shaka.

"There will be no more screaming," Londeka growls. "I cannot save these people. But I can spare them the horror that comes with this evil thing you have done to them."

"A telepath. A powerful one at that. I must admit, I never considered the possibility of a witch among the passengers. This could have gone south if there were more of you here. But you, my dear, are a hypocrite. Condemning us for killing these people, yet you use them as a shield to save your own skin and your kin."

"We are not the same. I made sure they were not conscious of the pain that you inflict on them. You are cowards. Attacking innocent people, even women and children. Spare the ones that remain, and I will wipe this nightmare from their memories. Your existence will remain a secret."

Shaka chuckles. "Unfortunately, that will not work for us. I am so sorry, big mama, but you know what they say. It's not over till the fat lady sings. And in this case, that's you." The vampire's laugh.

"Have you not had your fill? Is the blood you have shed not enough?"

"Correct. We have had our fill. And I promise you, we will not be killing anyone else. Unfortunately, I cannot say the same for your son, who should almost be done turning into a vampire."

Londeka's heart skips a few beats, sending her into a brief dizziness. She closes her eyes and searches for her son's mind to determine his location. The little humanity that is left in him allows her

119

access. Even that is quickly fading away, like spilled water being absorbed into parched ground. She weeps. Her tears land on the forehead of her daughter Lupita, who is now kneeling at her feet with her arms wrapped around her leg.

Just before he passed out, Gundo had crawled under some seats close to where Londeka and the rest of her family were standing. She realizes that once he turns, they will be in danger. She uses the last of her connection to her son to launch an attack using her own son and move him away from them. Gundo appears from under the seats and leaps towards Shaka. The old vampire easily catches him by the neck and slams him to the floor. Gundo struggles for a few more seconds before his body stiffens as he enters the final step of the transformation. Death.

Londeka can feel that little tether that she used to control her son has been severed. After a minute of silence, Gundo's eyes snap open. Dark gray veins run all over his body. Londeka's heart races as she sees his son turning around and his eyes locking onto the twenty-five remaining passengers. An evil laugh from Shaka. And then a command. "Feed boy."

One by one, Gundo rips through the passengers. Sucking the blood from them quickly and biting chunks of flesh from their necks when he pulls his teeth out.

Just as Londeka promised, there was no screaming. The passengers are under her spell and oblivious to what is happening. The loving mother had placed her daughter in a trance to shield her from the horror that was unfolding. She compelled her to hide under the chairs when it all began. To block her ears. And to crawl out and wrap her arms around her leg so she could feel her presence and know where she was when her own eyes and mind needed to focus on controlling the passengers.

Now she casts the spell on herself and her daughter. Relocating their minds back home in South Africa, where they are seated around a barn fire and singing their traditional family songs. Gundo is there. Her husband and eldest son Dembe are also there. Lupita is playing the drum while Londeka plays the tambourine. Everyone is happy and well. Yet in the same illusion, and in reality, tears flowed from Londeka's eyes. Tears of joy in the illusion, and tears of pain in the horrific reality where she makes her brave stand. All the passengers have now fallen and Gundo has finally reached her mother. When he sinks his teeth into her jugular and starts sucking in her blood, the spell is broken. Lupita, who is still holding on to her mother's leg, looks up and witnesses the horrific scene her mother had hoped to spare her. An experience she managed to shield all the passengers from, but not her own daughter.

"Gundo. Gundo." Lupita taps his big brother's leg as he calls to him. "What are you doing?" She notices how her mother is covered with blood and notices her dead father at her feet. Her brother, who has made his way into a space between the sealed exit door and cockpit, curled into a pupal position and hid himself. "Gundo, stop, you are hurting her." She yanks her brother's trousers, but there is no response.

After almost a minute, Londeka's blood finally tames her son. His eyes return to normal. He gently retracts his fangs from her neck. There is no bleeding. He has bled her dry. "Mama. Mama. What have I done? Mama, wake up," Gundo screams as he sinks to the floor with his mother's corpse in his arms. He is on his knees with his arms supporting his mother's head. "Lupita. What have I done? Look what I have done to our mother? Look at Papa. I killed them. I killed them." Gundo's screams reverberate throughout the plane like a violent wind passing through a dark, cold valley.

Lupita watches on in silence with tears running down her eyes. Every part of her body trembles with fear, shock, and sadness.

"How old are you, little girl?" Shaka steps forward and questions her.

"Eight years old."

"Such a beautiful young lady. You are mine now." Are the last words Lupita heard before she passed out.

The vampires would evacuate the plane along with Gundo and Lupita. Dembe was left behind to die when the plane was deliberately crashed into sea. Never to be found again.

CHAPTER TEN

JUDGEMENT

By the time Gundo finishes his story, he and Mariah are both sitting on the floor in the circle of ashes Celeste had used to create a magical barrier.

"Before I lost my humanity completely, my mother connected with me and told me she loved me. She was a powerful witch. But her greatest power was being a loving mother. When a vampire drinks the blood of a witch and kills them, he inherits their power. My telepathic abilities are the only legacy from my mother I have left. Also, a witches' power is amplified when a vampire wields it. It is further amplified if the vampire gained the power from drinking their own kin to death. That is why Shaka saw me as an important asset he could use for his purposes. He made me second only to him. My power makes it easy for him to manage public spaces that are full of people, security and surveillance. It makes it possible for us to exist without being seen and without leaving any trace that we were ever at any place at any given time. People will always see and remember only what I allow. And that is the power Shaka values me for."

"What about your sister, Lupita?" Mariah groans. She blinks back tears.

"Shaka took Lupita and raised her as her own daughter. She is the last person I had in all the world besides you. He uses her as leverage to make sure I submit to him. The only thing she remembers about that night on the plane is the moment I killed our mother. She also says I killed our father and brother. I do not know. I do not remember.

Lupita hates me with all her heart and has vowed to kill me one day. The only reason she has not done it already is because her lover is sired to me. If I die. He dies."

"Hang on a minute. So if your ass dies, I die?" Mariah gestures toward herself in disbelief, her eyebrows raised.

"Yes, mam."

"Oh, my goodness. I guess that's one way to make sure I can't kill you for messing with my daughter… and my heart."

"But you see, when I erased myself from your memory, I was erasing a monster. How would I have been able to live with you, and build a life with you when I was struggling to live with myself? If Shaka found out about you and our connection, he would have exploited it to control me. I had to protect you, because I love you."

"Gundo, you do not walk away from a person you love, no matter what. You fight alongside them to the end, just like your mother did." Mariah's eyes glitter. "You and I have a child together, and I had to raise her on my own. She wanted answers I could not provide because you erased them from my head."

"I didn't know you were pregnant until now."

"That's because you left us and never looked back."

With a smooth motion, Gundo transitioned from a seated position to kneeling before Mariah. With a gentle touch, he clasps her hands in his. "I am here now."

Mariah yanks her hands free from Gundo and rises to her feet. "Why now? What do you want, Gundo?"

"I never stopped loving you, Mariah Pepper Jenkins. I used my powers to rescue so many people from being executed unjustly. How could I not save the only woman I have ever loved?"

"You don't erase people you love from your life," Mariah shouts.

"Not unless it is the only way to protect them."

"I don't..."

"Shhhh," Gundo interjects and places his finger on Mariah's lip as he rises to his feet.

Mariah swatted his hand away. "Don't shush me," she snapped.

"Shhh, listen." Mariah turns to face the door. "The main section of the club is silent. Where did everyone go?"

The doors swing open as Dabula, Yaya and Ramsey storm in. Lupita, wearing blue jeans and a long hooded black jacket, walks between them. The vibrant colors from the disco lights were mirrored on her dark skin, which was covered in delicate flecks of glitter, her favorite touch up. Her dark, velvety skin resembled the richest cocoa. High cheekbones graced her face. Her eyes, large and expressive, shone like polished onyx, framed by lashes that cast gentle shadows on her skin. From beneath the protective folds of her hoodie, her radiant afro peeked out. It also had traces of glitter on it.

Her compatriots share her equatorial skin complexion, but hers is smooth. Dabula's head is bold, while Yaya and Ramsey have long, rich, well-maintained dreadlocks. It's easy to mistake them for twins. A brown coffin levitates two meters above their heads and follows behind them. It stops and remains suspended in the air when they come to a halt.

"Lupita," Gundo remarks.

"That's your sister?" Mariah asks.

"What are you all doing here?" Gundo asks.

"Brother, this is no way to greet family. Or are we no longer family?" Dabula replies.

"I am not your brother, Dabula. I made it clear to Lord Shaka that I no longer wish to be part of your guild."

"Foolish words coming from you, Gundo. Nobody simply leaves the guild. Lord Shaka releases you at his pleasure."

"I have never been one to follow foolish rules."

"Then you will face the consequences of your decision. You have proven time and again that you despise the blessing of immortality— the very gift you bestowed upon us. You subject us to a life of constant anxiety, never knowing when you might reach your breaking point, and dragging us down with you into eternal death."

"I see immortality as a gift, but only if we share it with those we hold dear," Gundo retorted, his voice filled with anguish. "All of you still have the people you love. Lord Shaka made sure that he gave me eternity at the expense of my family and killed them all," Gundo shouts. "He turned the only person I had left against me." He points to Lupita. "I refuse to spend my life surrounded by my enemies."

"You sired too many important vampires that are loyal to the guild, including us. If you die, we also die. Unlike you, we still appreciate the privilege of eternal life. For one vampire to decide the fate of so many would be an injustice and an act of selfishness. The guild has therefore passed judgment. Gundo, you must be put to sleep, so the rest of us can live." Dabula shouts. His friends echo murmurs of agreement.

"Wait, you are suicidal?" Mariah asks Gundo. He looks at her and looks away, but does not respond.

"He is foolish," Dabula responds on his behalf. "Even though there are many vampires that are older than you, more worthy than you, Lord Shaka loved you and made you second to him only. He loves you like a son."

"He loves my power. A power I inherited when he made me kill my family. My father, my mother and my brother. The smell of their blood has never left my nostrils. Nobody should have to live like this forever."

"Then you will find solace in a thousand year slumber."

Gundo turns his attention to his sister. "Lupita. I know you still hate me for what I did to our parents. But please believe me, I was powerless to stop it."

"You should have killed me along with Mama, Papa, and our brother. When you killed them, you also killed all the love and respect I ever had for you. I hope the smell of their blood never leaves your nostrils. It is a punishment you have earned. Their way of reminding you of your guilt from beyond the grave."

"It was Lord Shaka who did this."

"If they meant anything to you, the same way you resisted killing me, you should have resisted killing them."

"It's not that easy." Mariah steps forward from behind Gundo to interject. "I just experienced the same ordeal with my daughter just minutes ago. Resistance is not easy."

"How many family members did you mall down before resisting and sparring your daughter's life?"

"I only had my daughter."

"Then you know nothing of what you speak," Lupita retorted sharply, her words laced with disdain. "I suggest you shut up and mind your own business, before you end up dead for entangling yourself in matters that are of no concern to you."

"Lupita. You are my baby sister. You know how much I loved our mother," Gundo's voice trembles.

"And yet, you slaughtered her." Lupita's voice dripped with venom, her words lashing out like sharp fangs. "I am no longer your sister. I have become the monster you birthed, nothing more. My humanity will be restored only by your death." With a solemn gesture, she raised her right hand, as though carrying the weight of the heavens. The levitating coffin obediently shifted, positioning itself directly above her head.

"What is the coffin for?" Mariah asks.

"This is a special coffin I made especially for you, brother. Once we have put you inside this coffin, it will drain all the oxygen from your body and keep it out, placing you in a deathlike sleep while preserving you for eternity, or until Lord Shaka decides to wake you. It's the closest thing to death I could come up with."

"Can't you see Gundo. This is what is best for everyone. All vampires that were sired by you will continue to live without having to worry about your suicidal tendencies. And you will get to rest in a sleep that is similar to the death you desire so much," Ramsey adds.

"This is unnecessary. I have just found out that I am a father. I have every reason to live. Lupita, I have a daughter. Your niece."

"We don't care," Dabula responds.

In a sudden surge of rage, Gundo seizes Dabula by the neck, hoisting him effortlessly into the air. His eyes ignite with an intense, scorching blue glow as he growls through gritted teeth. "I am the one who sired all of you. I gave you eternal life. Yet today, you deem yourselves better than me, more deserving of life and love than me?"

"Enough," Lupita shouts. "Let's put this dog on a leash." She holds out her left hand, opens her palm, and when she closes it, the entire room is drained of oxygen. The atmosphere grew suffocating, causing everyone to collapse to the floor, gasping desperately for breath.

Dabula and his compatriots swiftly react, reaching into the hidden pockets of their leather jackets to retrieve small, portable oxygen masks. As the oxygen filled their lungs, they regained their footing. Dabula strides purposefully towards Gundo, a hint of menace in his gaze. Without hesitation, he aimed a forceful kick at Gundo's sternum, propelling him to roll until he lay alongside Mariah, who struggled for breath, teetering on the edge of unconsciousness.

Gundo, though on the verge of blacking out himself, summoned every ounce of strength to maintain consciousness. As Dabula approaches again, Gundo seizes Mariah, his fingers grasping desperately for her. Summoning his final reserves of energy, he hurls her out of the nearest window. The resounding crash of shattered glass follows her descent, mingling with the relief of fresh air that filled her lungs as she landed in a dumpster. Shards of glass rained down on her. As soon as there is enough breath in her lungs, she jumps out of the dumpster and starts running, trying to make her way around the building so she can reach the main entrance. "I have to hurry," she blurts as she tries to tap into her vampire speed, but her mind is still too fuzzy and her body still recovering from being starved of oxygen.

Meanwhile, Dabula, his grip firm around Gundo's throat, lifts him effortlessly, the man still gasping for air, his strength waning. A hint of sadistic satisfaction gleams in Dabula's eyes as he taunts his weakened adversary. He takes a deep breath before removing his oxygen mask to speak. "You once believed yourself more important than you truly were. Look at you now," he sneers, sensing Gundo's diminishing resistance. "He's almost finished," he proclaims, a cruel grin playing on his lips.

Lupita drops her right hand forward, lowering the coffin and positioning it waist high next to Dabula. The lid ominously creaks open. "The coffin will do the rest," she advises. Dabula choke slams Gundo into the coffin causing it to bounce mid air. Lupita closes her fist and the lid of the coffin falls. It is sealed shut with a hiss as oxygen escapes from inside. "Piece of cake." she smiles.

Dabula moves towards Lupita, his hands finding her waist as they celebrate with a kiss. "Time to deliver to Lord Shaka. He will be pleased." They make their way out, with the levitating coffin following behind them.

Meanwhile, Mariah has reached the club entrance. Victor and twelve of his bouncers stand guard at the door. "Victor, Gundo needs our help."

"A moment ago, you and your boyfriend kicked me out of my club." His tone is tinged with lingering resentment. Then came along his sister and her cronies. She takes my patrons' breath away, and not in a good way, so they all vamoosed. They literally shut down my business on a special night that took weeks to plan. Now you want me to go back inside and save him from the same crazy witch and her friends? Sweetheart, you are more trouble than you are worth."

"Victor, he is your friend."

"Not anymore, sweetheart. Not after the stunts you pulled off tonight. If anything, he is my investment, and that is the only reason I will save him."

Lupita and the vampires appear at the entrance as they walk out. They halt when they see Victor and his vampire bouncers. Victor steps forward to meet them. "Let me ask you something baby girl, can you empty the entire city of oxygen or is your oxygen trick limited to enclosed spaces?"

Lupita giggles, a mischievous glimmer in her eyes. "Oh, darling, I'm afraid the entire city would be a tad excessive, even for me," she replied, her voice laced with playful confidence. "But within a certain radius, you and your minions are firmly within my range. Perhaps you'd like a demonstration?"

Multiple small laser lights, vibrant and crimson, materialized on Lupita's chest, like fiery orbs of warning. "You are also within my sniper's radius, sweetheart. I know your vampire friends will survive the shots, but you won't. Bullets don't need oxygen to pierce your chest.

Now drop that coffin and release my Gundo before I drop you."

Lupita steps forward to retaliate, but Dabula grabs her by the elbow and restrains her with a firm but gentle grip. "No babe. It's not worth the risk."

"We may never get another opportunity to capture him," Lupita points out.

"A slight inconvenience compared to losing you forever. Please, my love." Dabula pleads. After a momentary pause and a final defiant glare at Victor, Lupita reluctantly obeyed and lowered the coffin. The lid creaked opened, and Mariah hurried to pull Gundo out, carefully placing him on the floor.

"Thank you for your cooperation. Now, if you don't mind, please leave my premises before I decide to decorate my walls with your blood." Victor's eyes glow like a blue flame. Lupita and the vampires get into a black van. The coffin levitates into the back. They shut the doors. The wheels screeched against the tarmac as the van sped away.

Mariah kneels on the ground, her thighs supporting Gundo's head, while her hands gently rested on his cheeks. "He's not waking up," she mutters, her voice laced with concern. Just as the words escaped her lips, Gundo gasps for air, his eyes open in a jolt. He leans to the side, coughing uncontrollably, as Mariah soothingly rubs his back. "Are you alright?" she asks, worry etched across her face. Gundo manages a thumbs-up. With Mariah's support, he struggles to his feet.

Victor approaches them. "Right. Now that I have saved your life, the magnitude of your debt to me is beyond measure. Especially after the disrespectful manner in which you broke the professional trust between us."

"Victor, I am so sorry." Gundo croaks. "I will make up for all of this."

"Damn straight you will. I just need time to think of an appropriate way for you to pay." A black suburban pulls up on the sidewalk. "Dorian will take you wherever you feel is safe for the rest of the evening. I will be in touch soon enough. Now get out of my sight. I have a lot of damage control to do." Victor briskly dismisses them. He retreats into the club.

Mariah helps Gundo into the car. For the first time in ages, Gundo has to tell the driver the address of their destination. He cannot compel him because he is too weak. Also, because the driver is a vampire. Gundo's home is no longer an option. He knows they need to find a new safe house where they can regroup and come up with a way forward.

CHAPTER ELEVEN

STEALTH

Just like the city that never sleeps, the Police station in New York operates around the clock. Day and night, officers and detectives are tirelessly on duty, rotating shifts to ensure public safety and protect the city. In the dimly lit public parking lot across the street from the police station, Zendaya and Jabu sat in their car. Now and then they can hear the occasional siren in the distance. Despite the late hour, the parking lot was bustling with activity, including police vehicles with their flashing lights.

"What time is it?" Zendaya asks.

Jabu shoots her an impatient glance. "About time you stop dilly dallying and get it done. We've been here for two hours already."

"I am not dilly dallying, I am thinking. The station is way busier than I expected."

"Well, busy places are the easiest to sneak around in without being noticed and perfect for blending in. Couple that with your power, and I'd say you have nothing to worry about."

"Okay, you're right," Zendaya replies, taking a deep breath to steady herself. "I'm panicking for nothing."

Just then, Jabu's eyes widen, and he leans forward. "Look, over there, an officer is walking this way. You won't get a better chance than this."

"There's too many other people sitting in their cars. There is no way they won't notice," Zendaya points out. They observe intently as the officer strolls past their car. He crosses the road behind them, disappearing into a fast-food outlet on the other side of the street behind the parking lot. After placing an order, the officer heads toward the men's restrooms within the diner. Zendaya's face lights up. They can see his every move through the glass windows of the establishment. "Looks like we're in luck. I'm gonna have to borrow your body."

"What?" Zendaya touches Jabu's shoulder before he can protest.

One slow blink and when Jabu opens his eyes, he is in the passenger seat and in Zendaya's body. Zendaya is now in his body. "I hate it when you do that without warning me." Annoyance flickers across his face.

"I did. I have to hurry." Zendaya dashes off. She had become adept at maneuvering Jabu's body, having commandeered it on many occasions in the past. With a surge of agility, she darted through the bustling parking lot, skillfully evading the passing cars as she swiftly crossed the road. With a flicker of determination, she pushed her way through the heavy diner door, causing it to swing wildly as she enters the establishment and makes her way to the men's restrooms. Once she is inside, she feels something hard in Jabu's jacket poking her side and puts her hands in the concealed pocket to inspect. Her fingers brush against a solid, rectangular object, compelling her to withdraw it and examine its contents. As the door to the bathroom creaked shut behind her, she stood there, her mouth agape, as the realization struck her like a bolt of lightning.

The police officer at the basin glanced up as he was washing his hands. His curiosity piqued. "Wow, dude, are you planning to propose? Who's the lucky girl?" he inquired, a bemused expression etched on his face.

"I think it's me," Zendaya responds, her voice tinged with a mix of surprise and uncertainty. The officer's perplexed gaze lingered on her, prompting her to regain her focus on the mission at hand. "Thank goodness you were not doing a number two. I don't cope well in those situations." She quickly puts the box back in the pocket.

"Hey Pal, there is no need to ruin a perfectly good moment like this by being rude. How about...HEY," Zendaya lunges towards the unsuspecting officer who thinks he is about to be attacked and swaps bodies with him. Jabu's body, now containing the officer's soul, collapses to the floor.

"Oooh, so tight," Zendaya whispers as she kneels and touches Jabu's body, causing his soul to return to his body. She takes Jabu by the arm and yanks him up like a rag doll.

"Whoa, hang on dude, don't touch me," Jabu protests and pushes Zendaya back.

"Relax babe, it's me." Zendaya responds from within the officer's body. The deep voice freaks her out as well. Even though she has taken over many bodies in the past, she can never get used to speaking with a male voice. Especially deep ones.

"Damn babe, that dude is ripped!"

"Yeah, he is pumped full of steroids. I could totally kick your ass right now," Zendaya taunts.

"Whatever babe. Wait. If I am back in my body, where is the officer?"

"He's in my body, back in the parking lot,"

"In the car?" Jabu points back over his shoulder with his thumb.

"Yeah, but don't worry. I made sure he would stay unconscious. He should stay that way for at least 15 minutes."

"Well then, you better hurry, babe."

"Oh yes, right?" Zendaya puts her hands on Jabu's cheeks and tries to pull him in for a kiss. He is quick to wiggle out of the hold and push her face back.

"Hell no babe. Not in that body."

"Sorry, I forgot," she giggles awkwardly in a deep voice as she dashes out of the bathroom.

"Officer, you forgot your food." A waiter stops her just as she is about to walk out of the diner.

"Give it to that guy," she points to Jabu and runs out. Jabu accepts the food, his hurried strides leading him back to the car just in time to witness Zendaya's graceful entrance into the police station. Amused, he can't help but chuckle at her exaggerated sway, her movements accentuating her newly acquired muscular physique.

"She is doing too much," Jabu says to himself with a smile. He watches as she frequently adjusts the tight police shorts, seeking relief from the discomfort they cause. She constantly grabs the crotch to adjust the crown jewels into a more comfortable position.

Once Zendaya is inside, she makes her way to the evidence storage room. When she gets there, the steel door is locked and can only be opened using an access card. The officer that is on night shift has left a sign that says be back soon. There is a paper on the wall with a rooster for the different shifts. Zendaya sees the name of the officer that is on duty. Conscious of the little time she has left, she looks at the clock on the wall before she quickly walks back towards the main offices. When she reaches a large office space that has many desks occupied by officers, she asks, "Hey, has anyone seen Walker from the evidence section?"

"Check him in the restroom. That's his favorite place," an officer shouts.

Zendaya makes her way towards the male restroom, located conveniently on the same floor. As she approaches, an officer emerges from behind the door, crossing paths with her. Exercising caution, she discreetly inspects his badge, ensuring he is not Officer Walker. With a slight nod of reassurance towards the officer and a smile, she entered the restroom. As soon as she was within, a putrid odor seeped into her nostrils. "Oh, my goodness. Please don't let it be him," she prayed, her face contorting in disgust. Desperate to alleviate the assault on her senses, she pinched her nose and attempted to breathe through her mouth. The respite was minimal. Summoning her determination, she called out, "Walker?" she raised her tone. "Walker?"

From one of the cubicles, a voice responded with clear annoyance. "Yeah, what is it?"

"Damnit," Zendaya muttered under her breath. She walks to the cubicle where the response came from. "You need to come out right now. We have a serious problem."

"I'm trying to take a shit here. What the hell do you want?"

Zendaya grimaced and tried her best to suppress her revulsion. "You better get off your stinking ass man. There is an emergency in the evidence room."

"Oh, for Pete's sake," the officer grumbled, his words mingling with the sound of the toilet flushing. When he opens the door, Zendaya pushes him back onto the toilet seat.

"What the hell?" He moans, but the body switch is made. Zendaya places the buff officer now containing Walker's soul on the toilet seat and leaves him there unconscious. Unlike her previous vessel, officer Walker's clothes are tight and uncomfortable for a different reason. He is obese. Zendaya can't even reach the crotch area to make adjustments.

"Oh my goodness, I hate this so much," she complains to herself. "Alright girl. Focus and get this over with." Zendaya makes her way back to the evidence room as fast as she can. When she arrives at the corridors that lead to the evidence room, she is heaving and sweating. She stops a few seconds to catch her breath. "My goodness, this man will have a heart attack if he doesn't watch it." As she approaches the office, she finds a queue of six officers waiting to submit evidence. She knows she has less than five minutes left before the buff officer wakes up in her body.

"Walker, you really are a piece of work, you know that? All these people waiting here trying to get some real Police work done while you take your sweet time in the restroom as if you are on a vacation," the officers chastise her.

"I am so sorry, officers. Please, just give me a moment." She swipes the access card, hurries into the evidence room and closes the door behind her. She can hear the officers becoming more agitated and complaining on the other side. A file lies atop the desk, revealing a comprehensive list of submitted evidence. It takes her little time to locate the case number assigned to the commissioner's file and the corresponding section on the storage shelf. Darting across the room, she deftly pulls out a sizable drawer from the shelf, carefully flipping through the tangible paper files using her fingers.

And there it is — the file she is looking for, adorned with a prominent sticker that reads "Reserved for the FBI." She extracts it from the drawer, opens it with urgency and begins to scrutinize its contents. The officers outside pound on the door, their impatience reaching a crescendo. Yet she remains undeterred, her focus unwavering. Her hands delve into the officer's pockets, where she discovers a phone. It is locked, but a stroke of luck allows her to unlock it with the officer's fingerprint. She uses the camera to scan as much information as possible.

Back in the car, Jabu notices Zendaya's phone blowing up with notifications as she sends the evidence to her device.

"She got in. Good girl," he snickers. His celebration is short-lived as Zendaya's body starts moving. "No...Oh no. Sleep, go back to sleep," Jabu gently pats him on the shoulder as if he is trying to put a baby to sleep.

The officer groans as he regains consciousness within Zendaya's body. "What the hell is going on? Where am I? Who the hell are you?" the officer asks. He gasps, and his hand flies to his mouth in disbelief. "What the hell is happening with my voice?"

"Dude, listen. Just relax."

His hands instinctively reached for his head, fingers entangling in Zendaya's hair, his eyes rolling upwards to inspect the unfamiliar mass. He tentatively explored his chest, finding an unfamiliar presence. "Are these... boobs?" he blurted out.

"Please don't touch those."

"Why the hell do I have boobs? Why am I wearing a skirt?" He starts panting uncontrollably.

"Man, please just...here. Have some fries and soda. This will help you calm down." Jabu offers as the officer frantically explores the rest of what he thinks is his transformed body, tugging at the unfamiliar clothes. "Alright, see now you are doing too much. Don't touch those." Just as the officer is about to scream, his head tilts back and his eyes roll toward the back of his head.

A few blinks of her eyes as she settles back into her body and Zendaya lets out a breath of relief. "I did it," she remarked.

"Babe, is that you? Oh, thank goodness. I was about to knock that guy out?"

"You were about to punch me?"

"I mean. Of Course not. But you took too long, and he was doing too much."

"We will talk about that later. Right now, I need you to drive to the alley behind the police station."

"Why?"

"There was no time to erase the messages I sent to myself. So I threw the officer's phone out the window." Jabu starts the car and they pull out of the parking lot.

When they arrive at the alley, she scours the ground using the torch on her phone and soon finds officer Walker's phone. Fortunately, homeless people avoid sleeping in the alley because the Police always chase them away. The officers can still be heard shouting and arguing with officer Walker on the second floor as they try to make sense of everything. Zendaya jumps back into the car and they drive away. As soon as she settles into her seat, she studies the evidence on her phone.

After driving for a while, they spot some homeless people standing around a fire under a bridge. "Pull over." She takes the phone and wraps it with the paper bag from the fast food diner, along with other rubbish in the car. When the car stops, she walks to the homeless people and throws the bag into the fire. She also gives them fifty dollars, which is enough for them to ignore her and whatever she threw into their fire. The homeless people watch as she jumps back into the car. She and Jabu drive away into the night.

CHAPTER
TWELVE

THE CURE

"You haven't said a word since we left the club," Gundo tries to reach out to Mariah, but she has erected an invisible emotional barrier between them. So far, it has been enough to keep Gundo silent. Before the first rays of dawn can creep over the horizon, they pull into the driveway of a residence in Long Beach Island, twenty-eight miles from New York City. Gundo hopes he has given her enough time to process everything and tries to start a conversation. "Thank you … for saving my life." He hangs his head low as he waits for an answer that only comes after a prolonged silence.

"Victor saved your life," Mariah retorted, the timing of her response matching the car's abrupt halt as it came to a complete stop.

"Look. I know you still have a lot of questions, I promise…"

"No. I don't have questions. And I don't want any promises. Not from you." Her voice is resolute and devoid of any hint of compromise.

"Please don't shut me out."

"You were never in to begin with. How about we keep it that way?" Mariah opens the door, steps out into the brisk air and slams it shut. Gundo thanks the driver and gingerly steps out of the car. He watches as it speeds off. "Where are we?" Mariah asks.

"A friend's house. She is expecting us. I called in a favor so we can have a safe place until I can figure out our next move."

"Not our move. Your next move. I will think about my own."

"Mariah. Please don't do this."

Mariah's gaze hardened, her eyes piercing with resentment. "You did this. All of it. Not me."

"Alright. I think we need to get inside. It's chilly out here." Gundo takes off his jacket and tries to put it on Mariah's shoulder. She swiftly moved away before it could even touch her as she strode towards the door with determined steps.

"Come on Mariah," Gundo pleads.

Mariah turns and looks him daggers in the eye. "Save it Gundo. I've had enough of your toxic chivalry. Besides, you know damn well the cold doesn't faze me."

The front door creaked open, revealing a woman adorned in a flowing nightgown. Her gaze scrutinized the pair before her. "Well? Are you two just gonna stand outside my house?"

"Hello Tasneem."

"Hello Gundo. It's been a while. Come in," Tasneem invites them. As they entered the house, a divine fragrance permeated the air. The illumination in the room provided solely by the flickering glow of scented candles. Gundo and Tasneem share a hug before he introduces the two women to each other. They all make themselves comfortable on the sofa. Mariah rushes to sit on the single sofa before Tasneem can reach it just so she can avoid having to sit next to Gundo. Tasneem gives Gundo a perplexed look. They end up sharing the two-seater sofa.

Mariah's eyes scan the room, trying to collect information that can tell her more about their host. Tasneem, a woman of Arabic descent with beautifully bronzed skin, possessed luscious black hair elegantly braided into a ponytail cascading down to her waist. Her alluring

Middle Eastern accent spoke volumes about her heritage. That, along with the decorations and finishings in her home, makes for an open book of her origins.

"Is that your husband?" Mariah asks when she spots a picture of Tasneem with a man that looks much older than she is on the wall.

"He was. Passed away five years ago. Car accident."

"I'm sorry to hear that."

"Don't be. He lived a full life," Tasneem replied with a touch of strength in her tone.

Mariah looks behind her and sees a wedding photo of Tasneem with a noticeably younger man. "Did you marry again?"

"No. Look closely. That is the same man. My husband."

"Do you mind?" Mariah waits for a nod from Tasneem before she picks up the framed photo and reads the date on the bottom. "Girl, you haven't aged a day since 1995. Your husband, on the other hand, aged like parched spinach." A weighty silence hung in the air. "You're a vampire?"

Tasneem's lips curved into a weary smile. "Not anymore." Gundo leans back, covers his face with his hands and shakes his head.

Mariah's eyes widen. "Wait, there is a cure?" she asks.

"You didn't tell her?" Tasneem looks at Gundo.

He lets out a deep breath and shrugs his shoulders. "Even if I had told her, there is no way to get it. I didn't want to give her false hope. Besides, she is safer living as a vampire. For now."

"You have no right to dictate how I should live. You have crossed that boundary far enough as it is." Mariah rises to her feet.

"Mariah, please."

"Tell me what is the cure. Where do I get it?" Mariah interrogates Tasneem.

"I don't know what is happening between the two of you, but I do not appreciate you taking that tone with me," Tas asserted.

"Tas, I am so sorry about this. You know how newborns can get with their temper." Gundo intervenes.

"Alright. I see asking nicely won't get me anywhere." Mariah hisses before lunging towards Tas, causing the sofa to fall back with all three of them. She pins Tasneem down by her shoulders and plants her fangs into her neck, delivering her venom before extracting them.

Gundo springs to his feet. "Mariah, are you crazy."

Mariah grins, with Tas still firmly pinned under her. "So sorry Tas. But maybe now that you also need it, you can tell me where the cure is. We could team up and get it."

Tas giggles before she pushes Mariah with her feet and sends her flying to the other side of the room. She lands on the coffee table, breaking it, and watches with a stunned look on her face as Tasneem gracefully rises to her feet. "First of all; It will take a few weeks before your poison is potent enough to turn anyone into a vampire. Second, when a person is cured with Angel blood, it cures the vampirism, but you get to keep your strength and stamina. Unfortunately, you don't keep your immortality, but you age much slower and can live up to three hundred years or so. That is why my husband aged like parched spinach, as you rudely put it. It's also why I have not aged a day." Gundo helps Tas reset the sofa back to its position as she reclaims her seat. "So, for now, I am much stronger than you because I was a vampire for much longer than you have been. And if you don't start showing some respect. I will kick your newborn ass and throw you out of my house." Tas uses her hand to apply pressure to the bite marks on her neck and within seconds, the bleeding stops.

"Are you alright?" Gundo asks Tas.

"Don't worry. I heal real fast." She assures him. They watch as Mariah lays face down on the floor. Her body curled inward, head buried in her trembling wrists as she sobs uncontrollably. Each sniffle and gasp punctuates her raw emotions. Gundo and Tas look at each other and decide to allow her the time she needs. It is a much needed catharsis for her. After ten minutes, Mariah stops and recollects herself. When she finally lifts her head, Gundo is not there. Only Tas, who tosses a large pack of blood that lands next to her head.

"I'm not hungry." She groans.

"Yes, you are," Taz counters gently. "I saw your story on the news. Hectic stuff. If you take a seat and drink, I will tell you my story and how I got the Angel blood. The blood will also help with your emotions." Tas advises as rays of the rising sun break through the curtain and rest on her face and hair, making her seem like an angel herself.

Mariah pulls herself together, takes the blood pack and settles into a curled position on the sofa. She watches as Tasmeen wipes a few droplets of blood from her neck. "I am sorry about that."

"It's ok. A clever plan. It would have worked under different circumstances."

Mariah sniffs. "You said Angel blood is the cure?"

"Before I can tell you about the cure. Let me tell you how I came to be a vampire. The information will help you. I was born and raised in Afghanistan. My parents were farmers, and like most families where we lived, we survived on the land. Most of the educational facilities in Afghanistan had been destroyed because of the war. Even so, I managed to get an education by reading books and working under the tutelage of a journalist I respected and looked up to. As I grew older, wiser and braver, I started writing articles about the struggles of women under the tyranny of the Taliban. This was very risky. My mentor advised me to stop writing the articles as it was too dangerous.

"The BBC got hold of some of my articles and arranged for me to write for them. When my life was in danger, they arranged for me to be safely removed from Afghanistan. I stayed and worked in England for two years. Life in England was great, but it was not home. Eventually, I missed my family. And so I made secret arrangements to visit them. They did not know I was coming to visit. They were so surprised and delighted."

The two women exchange smiles that quickly fade as Tasneem continues. "Somehow, the Taliban found out that I was around. They came in the middle of the night and kidnapped me from my home. They kept me prisoner for a few days. I even made the news when they released a video where they forced me to read a statement and made me retract everything I wrote about them. They said they would release me if I cooperated, which I did. But the next day, as the sun was setting, they dug a deep hole in the ground and put me in it, leaving only my head exposed. They collected stones and placed them close by as they prepared to execute me.

"I remember when the first stone struck my forehead, my eyesight became blurry. I was crying and screaming, but they continued to stone me. I remember becoming frustrated, feeling like it was taking too long for me to die. I kept thinking to myself; Why are they not using bigger stones so the suffering can be over? Why are they not throwing them harder?" Mariah covers her mouth with her hands as she listens empathetically. "But suddenly, the noise stopped, and the stones stopped raining on me. My vision was poor as blood covered my eyes, but I could see some of the men standing as if they had been frozen in time. Poised to throw the next stone but not moving at all. That's when I saw him."

"Gundo?"

"Yes."

"He asked if I wanted to live, but I could not answer. I thought he was the angel of death. But why would death ask if I wanted to live? He wrapped my hair around his hand, pulled me up to expose my neck, bit me and vanished. Suddenly, the men continued stoning me. It was as if they had been paused, and somebody had pressed play again. I could feel the burning sensation on my neck and the venom running through my veins as I faded and died. Except I didn't stay dead. When I woke up, it was in the middle of the night.

"Sand still surrounded me with only my head sticking out from the ground. The stars were shining so bright and seemed closer to the earth than usual. The taliban had left me for dead, but I was more alive than

I had ever been. My senses were heightened. I could hear the crickets crawling around me and the ants feasting on my blood. But something was different. The same sand that held me in place and hours before felt like dried cement around my body, felt like butter. With a strenght I had never known and no normal woman should possess, I erupted from the ground and grabbed the very first man that was within my reach. I drank him dry.

"Gundo has compelled all the innocent people to leave the small town and made sure only those that played a part in my murder remained. I drank them all. Each and every bastard that threw a stone. When I had killed the last one, Gundo appeared again, and threw my parents at my feet. My Father's blood was enough to tame me. Fortunately, he survived, and I never had to touch my mother. I knew that day that I could not go back home. Not when they had seen their daughter massacre an entire town. I knew that the old Tasneem was dead, and I was starting a new life. Gundo erased me from my parents' memory."

"Yep, that sounds like something Gundo would do," Mariah remarked.

"Has he told you about Lord Shaka?"

"Yes. He told me. Nothing good."

"Lord Shaka is the oldest and most powerful vampire I know. A relic of the past who made sure the vampire guild in Africa is one of the most powerful and respected in the world. Vampirism may have its benefits, but it is not for everyone. It was certainly not for me. I had dreams, family, plans and loved ones that lived outside the eternity that came with being a vampire. Every time I closed my eyes, their voices echoed in my mind, and I couldn't forget them. I wanted to be human again. That is when I learned about Angel blood."

"Gundo said there are only four Angels in the world. How did you get their blood?"

"Yes, there are only four angels. One of them is the Angel of Death, and he is a collector of rare souls. You see, everyone, save immortals such as vampires and werewolves, dies of old age. However, some people, if the soul was rare enough, are collected. If the life you lived was interesting enough, or if you had an enormous influence in the world, good or bad, death may decide to not rip you. He may collect you.

"Shaka turned Hitler and a few of his comrades into vampires before they could die. Death had been looking forward to collecting them for many years. The fun he would have with them after all the atrocities they had committed was priceless to the angel. Now that they were vampires and under the protection of Shaka, Death could not collect them. Shaka struck a deal with death. He made the Angel purchase them in exchange for his blood. Lord Shaka knows that vampirism is not all it seems. He used some of the blood to cure the vampire's Death wanted to collect. He used the rest to control vampires that wished to be cured, promising that he would cure them if they served him faithfully.

"Sometimes he would hold tournaments and sports and get them to compete in exchange for a few drops so they can be cured. But he would never keep his promise. Yet many vampires kept hope and continued to serve, hoping he would one day reward them. Vampires that were much stronger and older than me wanted the cure. I knew I could not compete with them. So I avoided showing Lord Shaka, even Gundo, that I wanted to be cured. I did not just blend into the guild, I blended into the main family. I blended into Shaka's heart. I wanted him to love me like a daughter. He ended up loving me like a man loves a woman. It was not what I wanted, but I had to take it. He kept the vial of angel blood hanging from a necklace wrapped around his neck for safekeeping at all times. He trusted me enough to allow the vial of angel blood to hang from his neck and dangle above my head as he made love to me. That is when took the opportunity to clutch the vial between my teeth. I crushed the container with my teeth and swallowed the angel's blood, along with the shards of glass from the broken vial. That is how I was cured. He was furious. I thought he would kill me on the spot. But he loved me too much to kill me and allowed me to walk out of the guild unharmed. He said he never wanted to see me again. From that day onwards, any vampire that speaks of vampirism as a curse or wished to be cured was punished. Many were killed."

Mariah sighed. "So there is no more angel blood?"

"Not unless you can find the Angel of death. Nobody knows how to find the other three angels."

"What if I find a rare soul that death wants to collect and do what Shaka did?"

"Gundo said Shaka tried it again with Margaret Thatcher, Trump, Dave Chapelle and a few founders of apartheid in South

Africa, but death never showed up. I believe his angelic pride will not allow him to be controlled by lower beings again. It is said that the only other instance the Angel of Death has shown himself was for love. Legend has it he gave his heart to a witch, but it ended with his heart being broken."

Mariah hung her head and started wringing her hands. "So there is no hope for me."

Tasneem's eyes softened with empathy. "Sometimes hope returns when we change what we are hoping for. I think it is unfair to allow you to hold on to hope for something that you can never attain. That is why I told you the truth, so you could be free to search for something else to hope for. Maybe then you will find a reason to live on."

"Easy for you to speak, since you are cured and all."

Tas smiled gently. "Yes, it is easy for me to speak, but it doesn't mean I should be quiet when my words could help you. The next best thing is for you to take off that lunar bracelet, walk into the sun and get it over and done with. It's all up to you. Gundo is an asshole, and a good man. I know your history with him. Hopefully, there is something left between the two of you to give you hope for the future."

"Speaking of Gundo, where is he?"

"He is sleeping upstairs. Like most vampires, he sleeps during the day. I suggest you do the same."

"What will you do?"

"I'm going to take a shower and get ready for work. Feel free to do the same in the guest bathroom before you sleep. Some of my clothes are there as well. You look like you are about the same size as me, just a little more booty on you, but my clothes should fit." Tasneem offers as she walks away.

"Tasneem," Mariah calls her before she can disappear around the corner. She turns and waits to hear what she has to say. "Thank you." With a serene smile, Tasneem acknowledged the gratitude and gracefully sauntered away, leaving Mariah alone with her thoughts.

Tasneem's home has an open plan setup. Across the room, Mariah can see the kitchen top where a few chef knives are sheathed into a wooden holder. She stares at them for two minutes before finally standing and making her way upstairs. She finds the guest room, which is plain and mostly white. Including the closets that are filled with some of Tasneem's clothes. She pulls out a pair of blue jeans, a white vest and a purple hoodie. After a quick shower, she is dressed and on her way downstairs, she can hear the water still running as Tasneem is taking a shower. Mariah goes to the kitchen, pulls out one of the butcher knives and makes her way to the second guest room where Gundo is sleeping. Without hesitation, she aims for Gundo's middle finger, on which he wears his Luna ring. She ends up chopping off two fingers instead. Gundo screams and scurries away from the sunlight that enters the room through the window. They both watch as Gundo's severed fingers turn into ash in the sunlight, leaving black stains like charcoal marks on the bedsheets. Mariah grabs Gundo's ring from the ashes, breaks the window, jumps out and makes a run for it.

Gundo steps forward to pursue her but the sun burns him, forcing him to retreat back to the passage. "Mariah, stop." He calls for her, but she is gone. He watches from the safety of the passage.

Tasneem arrives. She has wrapped herself with a towel, and water is still dripping from her hair. "I think it's time you stop undermining her. That is the reason you are on her bad side."

"Do you still have your lunar ring?"

"No, those things are worth a lot, so I sold it to a vampire long ago. Why don't you call Victor to bring you one?"

"We haven't been the best of friends lately."

"Wow, you need to watch it. You are becoming more and more like Shaka. I will try to arrange a new luna ring for you. But it looks like you will have to wait till sunset to go after her. Also, the window is gonna cost you."

"Damnit," Gundo muttered.

CHAPTER THIRTEEN

SUPERNATURAL LOVE

As a New Yorker, Zendaya has a deep love for the bustling city life. Although she and her brother spent their childhood in a countryside orphanage, the pursuit of education and her former career as a detective led her to the city. Having spent many days and nights patrolling the city as a beat cop and rookie police officer, the city had become her habitat. Her dedication, resilience and tenacity allowed her to quickly work her way up to detective. She loves the challenge of constantly pushing herself to the limit and proving her survival skills in the city that never sleeps.

The diverse and rich New York food culture has especially been good for her YouTube channel, where she has built quite a reputation for being one of the best female professional competitive eaters. Her career as a detective is something she never expected would end prematurely, so she never saw a need for a backup plan or something to fall back on. She turned her unhealthy eating habit, which she picked up as a coping mechanism for her depression, into a lucrative career as a content creator. This provided her with a stable income.

Nestled in the Bronx, Zendaya's apartment is a serene haven adjacent to the captivating Bronx Botanical Garden. It offers spectacular views of nature that sometimes make you forget you are in the city. The surrounding trees provide a constant supply of fresh air. Sometimes butterflies and bees visit her small balcony garden. She makes sure it is well kept, so they keep coming back. She tries to add a new flower to it whenever she can make some space.

As the sun rises over the city, casting its warm rays upon the third floor of the apartment building, slender strips of light slip through the slightly parted blinds, gracefully alighting upon Zendaya's bed. The gentle touch of sunlight gradually found its way to her closed eyes and caressed her flawless amber skin, waking her. Her skin wears the rays of the sun as if they were a garment custom made for it.

Without opening her eyes, she turns and stretches her arm. Her hand lands on Jabu's rock hard abs. With a playful gesture, her fingers dance across his sculpted torso, akin to strumming a guitar, before venturing to his chest, where she tenderly caresses its contours. His dark skin color looks like caramel in the sunlight. His afro hair is styled in a fade with a line on the side of his head shaped like lighting. Built like a Spartan warrior, Jabu embodied the mesomorph ideal. His love for working out is the reason Zendaya has been able to eat so much without becoming obese. A personal trainer by profession, he has managed to keep her on a calorie deficit.

As Jabu extended his arm, inviting Zendaya to rest her head on his chest, she entwines her leg with his. She felt a subtle prominence pressing against her thigh. She giggles. "It looks like Rambo is more awake than you are."

Jabu tittered with a smile. "I had hoped we would make love last night."

Zendaya groans. "I'm sorry babe, I got carried away with the investigation. Using my powers also drained me. I must have dozed off on the couch."

"Yeah, and I had to carry you to bed."

"Are you complaining?"

He shook his head, a warm affection filling his eyes. "Nope. If I could I would carry you all the time, wherever we go."

Leaning in, Zendaya pressed a tender kiss on his lips. "I appreciate you so much. In fact, you deserve breakfast in bed."

A low rumble escaped Jabu's throat as he pondered the idea. "Mmm, now that sounds nice."

"And what would you like to have?" Her playful tone carried a hint of seduction.

"English breakfast?"

"Oh, I thought you wanted to have me, but if that's what you want.." Zendaya sat up, teasingly feigning indifference.

"Come back here." Jabu takes her by the waist and pulls her into a woman-on-top position. Their lips meet like two magnets drawn to each other. Jabu possessed an intimate knowledge of Zendaya's body, knowing every curve and secret spot that brought her pleasure. They shifted positions until he found himself on top, the weight of desire fueling his movements.

He began by tracing a trail of kisses from her lips to her neck, her nipples, and then her belly button. His hands gently rubbed between her thighs. She welcomes them by spreading her legs till her knees are close to her shoulders. With the finesse of a gentleman, he used his tongue to play with her clit. When the sensitivity escalated and threatened to overwhelm her, she closed her legs slightly, so her thighs kept his ears warm. The pleasure coursed through her veins like sweet nectar. The room filled with a symphony of her moans and the intoxicating sounds of their passion growing wetter with each passing moment. Every sound only heightened Jabu's desire, quickening his pulse and bringing life to every fiber of his being. Their passion is all the lubrication they need.

When Jabu moves up, he takes the opportunity to penetrate her. He enjoys the tight feeling of resistance he has to deal with before her lips give way and part, allowing him to enter. Her warm, moist walls close in tightly around him. She constantly increases and decreases the tension of her vaginal walls around his man-hood, further increasing his pleasure. A surge of exhilaration coursed through their intertwined bodies. Her eyes roll back and flutter as he pushes deeper into her till their eyes are locked in a passionate gaze.

Jabu starts off with slow, prolonged, gentle strokes in a missionary position. He pays attention to her breathing so he can know whether to slow down or increase the tempo. Zendaya is not one to lie there like a piece of wood and let him do all the work. She wraps her legs around his waist, pulling him deeper into her and starts making circular movements with her waist. She knows she has him when his breaths are accompanied by a low, deep moan.

After a few minutes, Zendaya's body starts shaking. She moans louder as they reach orgasm at the same time. Her climax is the only time she has no control over her magical powers. She experiences half of her orgasm in her own body, before her power kicks in and she involuntarily switches bodies with Jabu. They both enjoy the other half of their orgasm in the other's body. When they switch back, she is in time to catch the remnants of her climax as Zendaya's orgasm lasts longer. Her body is still vibrating as she breaks into a giggle-gasm accompanied by a few squirts. It is Supernatural sex. When witches make love, they make magic. It ends with them falling asleep in each other's arms and another hour in bed before they eventually get up and shower together.

Once they are ready, they head to a Starbucks downstairs for breakfast.

Jabu adds some sugar to his coffee and stirs. "So? What's the plan for the day, Detective?"

Zendaya takes a big bite from her bagel donut and licks a small bead of cream from her lip. She speaks with her mouth full. "Gwendoline Jenkins, I need to speak to her about her Mother."

"The lady that was executed? I don't think that's a good idea. They are still grieving. You don't want to risk coming across as insensitive."

"That's the thing. I don't believe that her mother is dead." Zendaya takes one last sip of her coffee and stands from her seat. "Let's go. I'll explain on the way." They hop into Zendaya's Ford Raptor truck and drive off. It was 11:00 AM, so they managed to avoid the worst of the morning traffic. Thirty minutes later, they pull up next to the driveway of a house in Queens. There are already three cars outside.

"Looks like they have visitors. This may not be a good time," Jabu points out.

"There is no other time. Wait here." Zendaya jumps out of the car, makes her way to the door and rings the bell. A tall, light-skinned man opens the door. Zendaya flashes her old police badge as she greets. "Morning Sir. My name is Detective Zabalaza."

"How can I be of assistance, detective?" the man replied.

"Forgive me, I understand this is not a good time but, could I perhaps have a word with Gwendoline Jenkins?"

"Detective, you said it yourself. Now is not a good time. We are not in a good space."

"I promise I will not be long."

"When you are grieving the loss of a loved one, every second and minute feels long, Detective."

"Who is it, honey?" Gwen emerged from behind her fiance.

"A Detective insisting on speaking to you."

Gwen walks out and steps in front of her fiance. He places his hands on her shoulders. Gwen pushes her long braids away from her face, revealing her light skin tone and eyes that are red from crying for too long. "Can I help you, Detective?" she asks.

"Ms. Jenkins, I am sure by now you are aware of the unusual circumstances surrounding the execution of your mother."

"I am. It's all over the news. It feels like a dark cloud is hanging over my family."

"Well, that is exactly why I am here. I have information which just may be the ray of sunshine you need."

"Ray of sunshine or false hope? You are not the first officer to come to us with strange conspiracy theories."

Gwen raises her hand gesturing to her fiance. "Wait Todd. Let's hear her out. Go ahead, detective."

"Thank you, Gwen." Zendaya takes a deep breath. "The papers for the execution show that your family requested your mother's remains to be surrendered to you intact, instead she was cremated."

"Yes. The crematorium told us it was a mistake, and that they were sorry. We intend to take legal action against them."

"That's the thing. I do not believe it was a mistake. In fact, the remains that were given to you may not even be your mother's."

Gwen's eyes widened. "What are you telling me?"

"Think about it. The crematorium would never go against protocol and remove a body from a crime scene before the Police finish their investigations. The same crematorium seems to have remembered to leave the rest of the bodies that attended the execution. There is no security footage of the area and the main suspect in the case has no recollection of what happened. I believe your Mother is still alive and whoever wanted to hide that fact did a poor job of it."

Todd steps forward. "Detective, I do not appreciate you walking to our door and rubbing salt into our wound. The FBI has been assigned this case and they are the ones who should be informing us about the case. Not you."

Gwen turned to her fiance. "Todd, have you listened to a word she said? We have been speaking to the FBI and nothing they have said to us makes sense. For the first time since my mother passed on, we are being told something that makes some semblance of coherence." Gwens's voice trembles.

"Gwen..." Todd wraps her hands around Gwen's shoulder and pulls her close. Tears form in her eyes.

"Mr. Fields, I have no intention of rubbing salt in your wounds. If I felt I could not make a difference, I wouldn't even be standing here. In fact, if I was not sure that I was right, I would not be here."

A brief silence fills the air, pregnant with contemplation between the three of them. "Alright, detective. What do you need from us?" Mariah asks.

"A blood sample from you and a bit of your mother's ashes."

"For heaven's sake, we are supposed to be scattering her ashes today. That is why our family is gathered here," Tod exclaims.

"They will understand. They will have to. I will not scatter my mother's ashes until I am sure that it is indeed her remains in that urn. Otherwise, the ceremony is meaningless and will not bring us any closure," Gwen insists.

"I lost my brother a few months ago, and to this day, I do not know what happened to him. So, I know how important closure is when you lose a loved one because I never got it."

"I am sorry to hear that, detective. And thank you for doing this." Zendaya goes back to the car and pulls out a medical bag before walking inside with Gwen and Todd. After almost an hour, she walks out with blood samples and the urn that has the ashes.

Jabu raises his eyebrows when he sees Zendaya walking back with the entire urn. Todd is still standing at the door trying to talk some sense into his fiance. "I can't believe you pulled that off," Jabu remarks as Zendaya gets into the car.

"Me neither. She insisted I take the entire thing. For a while, her family was having none of it. I think sneaking into the Police station was a walk in the park compared to this," Zendaya said.

They make their way to one of the wealthy sections of New York in Hudson. After a forty-minute drive, they pull into a parking spot and Zendaya walks into a luxurious apartment block. She requests to see Sofia Grimshaw, wife to Police Commissioner Grimshaw. A butler escorts her to the penthouse suite. When she enters, she finds Sofia sitting on the sofa. Sofia is an elegant and statuesque woman with cascading blonde locks. She exuded an air of sophistication, further accentuated by her unmistakable British accent. Zendaya watches as she folds her hair in a knot and uses a small golden band to hold it in place.

Sofia engages Zendaya before she can even greet. "Detective. Please have a seat. My husband said I should expect to hear from you. I hope you have good news for me."

"As I hope you have for me," Zendaya hands her a cooler bag as she sits.

Sofia's eyes widened with interest as she accepted the bag. "What is this?"

"A blood sample from Gwen Jenkins and the ashes that supposedly belong to her Mother. There is also a comb with Mariah Jenkin's hair strands on it."

"And what do you want me to do with them?"

"DNA tests. With your level of connections, I suspect you can get it done fast."

Sofia sighed. "Getting DNA data from ashes is not easy."

"For your husband, I suspect you will pull the necessary strings to get it done. If the DNA results for the blood samples don't match the ashes, we will know the entire crime scene was a setup."

"Very impressive, Detective. My husband made a poor decision by removing you from the force."

"He made a corrupt decision."

"He made a political decision. No need to be bitter."

"Look, I've done my part. Can I have the information about my brother as agreed?"

Sofia sighs. "Alright. But I must warn you. The people you want to mess with are dangerous. If my husband is giving you this information, it's because you are also somewhat of a loose end he wants tied up. He knows you are unlikely to come back from this." Sofia gives Zendaya a card with GPS coordinates on it. "A group of elite members of society who are in close proximity to everything supernatural in this state will be meeting for a quarterly event."

"What type of event?"

"A type of sport which I believe your brother was unfortunate to find himself involved in." Sofia leaned back, crossing her legs, and leisurely lit a cigarette. The smoke curled and dissipated into the air above her. "The fun starts at midnight. Now, I have also done my part, so do excuse me. I have important matters to attend to." Both women rise to their feet. Sofia gives a brief fake smile and walks away. Zendaya resists the urge to beg for more information. She also turns to leave. "And oh, Detective," Sofia called out, halting Zendaya's steps. "If you make it back alive, it would be wise to keep what you discover a secret. Very powerful individuals are determined to maintain the utmost confidentiality regarding their activities, myself included." She turns and walks away.

Zendaya walks out of the building and reaches her truck, where the tantalizing aroma of cheesy, jalapeno-covered French fries welcomed her. "Wow, babe, you read my mind. I'm famished," she remarked with delight, grabbing the fries and devouring them as Jabu starts the engine and pulls away.

"How did it go?" Jabu asks.

"She gave me a card with GPS coordinates and a date on it," she muffles a response from her stuffed mouth and chews a few times before she continues. "Said some event will be taking place, and that's where I would find everything I need to know about my brother."

"Alright. When is it?"

"Tonight. It's about four hours away. So, I suggest we get going."

"Well, let's hope it's a date with the truth."

"According to Sofia Grimshaw, it could be a date with death," Zendaya adds. She fills Jabu in on everything that was said in her meeting as they make their way home to prepare before they can head out to the location.

CHAPTER
FOURTEEN

BIKER GANG

A chameleon is inching across the highway when it suddenly feels the vibrations of an approaching vehicle, causing it to quicken its pace. Moments later, a gang of bikers thunder past just as it creature makes it to the other side. Five riders on motorcycles, their engines creating a deafening roar, and a black jeep wrangler. Xavi Gonzalez rides in the back seat with his daughter Eva. His son Raphael rides his bike in front of them, followed by the rest of the pack behind them. Raphael sees a roadside pub down the road and lifts his fist in the air. A signal for the gang to stop.

One by one, the bikers pull out of the mostly empty highway and into the pub. Raphael takes off his helmet and shakes his head so his long black hair can hang free. One side of his head is shaved and has a wolf tattoo. He walks over to the Jeep, opens the door and helps his Father and Sister out. The rest of the pack waits at the door on both sides, as if to give them a guard of honor. Xavi walks in first and finds a table to share with his son and daughter. His pack follows. One biker approaches the server as the rest take their seats. He orders multiple portions of raw steak and beer. A server starts serving cold beer to all the bikers while they wait for the meat.

Xavi takes Eva by the hand. "How are you feeling, honey?"

"Excited Daddy. Maybe a little nervous," she admitted.

"No need to be nervous. You are a Gonzalez. You will do just fine," Raphael encourages his sister.

"Raph is right. Your first hunt is always scary. Just remember, everything you need to succeed is in your nature. You are made for this so you have nothing to worry about." Xavi adds. "Your mother will be so proud."

"Maybe we can take some good pictures for her." Raphael suggests.

"No. No pictures. I don't want to risk our activities getting exposed. Besides, if the other alphas see a camera, we will lose their trust. They will think we are reckless. Trust is everything in this business," Xavi said. Raphael and Eva nod in agreement. "But don't worry, my angel. An experience like this is always memorable. It stays with you forever."

"I can't believe my baby sister has grown so much. Just yesterday you were a little bundle of joy, and now you are an apex predator. Ready to earn your stripes and make your first kill." Raphael hypes up his sister but is distracted when he feels the wooden table vibrate under his hand.

Soon the sound of throttling motorcycles fills the area as another biker gang pulls off from the highway and into the parking lot. Fifteen riders in total. Xavi's gang watches silently as the leader walks into the bar. He is a big 6 foot man with a mullet and a horseshoe moustache. More meat than muscle, but looks herculean nonetheless. The words 'Fear the Beast,' are printed on the back of his sleeveless jacket. He stops to look around the room and spits before walking up to the counter and placing his elbow on top to lean against it.

He takes a moment to regard Xavi's gang. "Clear the pub. The fallen angels do not share," he demands of the owner and makes sure everyone in the pub can hear him.

"Yes Sir," the owner replies with a tremble in his voice as he scurries over to Xavi's table. "I am so sorry, Sir. I'm gonna have to ask you and your buddies to order take away instead and wait for it outside."

"I like to sit in while I eat, thank you," Xavi replies.

"Please, Sir, I don't think you understand. I am just trying to avoid trouble for all of us. The big guy there said…"

"Oh, I heard what he said. I may be small, but these big ears of mine can hear very well. I can hear the six rats that are running in your basement and the four in your ceiling. You have two more mating in the kitchen. I also hear the heartbeat of every single person in this pub, so I definitely heard what he said loud and clear."

The owner is perplexed. His brow is wet with sweat. "What? I don't follow."

Xavi smoothly slides out from the table and walks towards the gang leader as he addresses him. "So, my friend, you seem to have an issue with sharing. That is what you said, right?"

"You damn skippy. And I will not be repeating myself."

"Then I suggest you leave and find another pub. This one is taken. Unlike you, we don't mind sharing. We love it. In fact, if you continue to be rude, we may be tempted to share you and your cronies."

"Well well. Little man thinks he is Thorin Oackenshield. I must hand it to you. You've got big kahunas for a midget." Laughter ripples through the pub.

The gang leader's girlfriend steps forward. "Right. I'm hungry.

And I think the beast has entertained your nonsense long enough. Are you filthy latinos moving out? Or would you like us to kick you out?"

Xavi's eyes move up and down as he regards the woman. "On second thought. I think we will opt for take away after all," Xavi responds.

"Good choice, you stinking midget."

"I do not like that word," Xavi responds with a deep growling voice, as if a demon is speaking from within him. His eyes glow red. The gang leader watches as he transforms and within seconds, a black werewolf that is almost twice his size stands in front of him. A large patch of wetness quickly develops around Beast's crotch area as he pees on himself. He wants to run, but he remains paralyzed with fear.

Xavi sinks his fangs into the gang leader's head and shoulder before hoisting him into the air. The pub trembles as the alpha werewolf hurls his prey at the ceiling, splintering the wooden structure. With a vicious swing of his head, Xavi propels the gang leader's body through the window. His decapitated body lands outside. A large portion of his shoulder was also bitten off. A cloud of dust and fragments of pine wood rain down on Xavi. Four rats escape the ceiling through the newly formed opening and disappear under the tables. The sound of crushing human bones can be heard as the alpha werewolf chews the gang leader's head, swallows it, and emits a thunderous roar that reverberates through the air.

The rest of the pack are on their feet. Their eyes ablaze with a mix of colors. Some blue, some green, others yellow. "Let's eat boys," Red eyes Raphael commands. The rest of the pack, save for Eva, burst into a rapid transformation and the massacre begins. A few of the bikers manage to run to their bikes and start them, but before they can accelerate, the werewolves pounce on them and bite off their heads.

Xavi transforms back into human form. His clothes destroyed by the transformation, he was now naked and covered in blood. "Come, my darling. I've lost my appetite. That man left a bitter after-taste in my mouth."

Eva grabs a stack of raw ribs and joins her father as they make their way towards the door. She turns to the owner for a last word. "Mr., maybe to avoid such misunderstandings in future, learn to treat all your patrons equally." She blows him a kiss and they walk to their car where the driver has prepared a suit cover with extra clothes for Xavi.

They wait for the rest of the gang to finish consuming the fallen angels' gang members. Flesh and bone are all consumed save for their clothes. When they are done, nothing is left. As if their victims never existed. Xavi' gang revert back to human form. With their own clothes destroyed by their transformation, hey put on their victims' bloodied clothes, mount their bikes and ride on.

PART THREE

A WICKED SPELL

CHAPTER
FIFTEEN

FAMILY REUNION

Golden pillars of sunshine break through the clouds and rest on the New York skyscrapers as the sun begins to set. For the first time since she was turned, Mariah is on her own and walking the streets of New York. Her hoodie is pulled up, concealing her face, while her fists are balled up in her pockets. She is now used to the orchestra of heart beats from all the people walking around her and the smell of their blood in the air. Though she craves them, it is a craving that is under control.

She remembers how Gwen could never drive past a fried chicken takeaway joint without being tempted to turn into the drive-through and buy takeaway. The aroma from the food as you passed by was the restaurant's best marketing strategy because the temptation that came with it was too hard to resist. Mariah repeated to herself the same words she always used to encourage Gwen to stick to her diet. Just because it smells good doesn't mean it's good for you. *Mmm hmm. Well, in this case, if I feed it wouldn't be good for me or the food*, she thinks to herself.

Now she was walking through what felt like a street full of fast-food restaurants that have legs. Some are walking past her, some in the same direction as her, and others even bump into her. Though that part is mostly her fault as she struggles to keep herself from walking faster than humans do so she can seem normal. She hopes nobody notices the moments when she loses focus and she ends up taking three steps in half a second. *Just because it smells good doesn't mean it's good for you. Just keep walking, Mariah*. She doesn't even realize how many streets she crossed, even though the traffic light for pedestrians was red.

The thought of how Gundo used Gwen to initiate her and suppress her predatory instincts preoccupies her thoughts, stoking a rage in her heart which she fights to suppress. What Gundo did was wrong. A fundamental moral line was crossed, but it worked. As the sun sets, she knows that Gundo will soon be able to come looking for her and has probably managed to find another lunar relic so he can walk in the sun.

From the moment she escaped, she has been struggling to gather courage to go see her daughter. *Will she believe me? Will she accept me? Will she be safe around me?* These are some of the questions racing through her mind. Throughout the day, she walked amongst bustling streets, suppressing her predatory instincts amidst countless human beings, but she still needed to eat. Around lunch time, she had walked into a diner and ordered a steak and wine. Normally she preferred it well done, but this time she ordered her steak rare. She chewed the first few bites for a very long time, but it kept getting easier and easier. Her ability to taste and enjoy normal food had returned and lasted longer, even though it has been many hours since she last fed on blood. She managed to finish the entire meal.

When she was done, she used her vampire speed to vanish without being noticed. She was sure a surveillance camera caught her, but she had kept her hoodie on and her head down. If any camera recorded her, the worst that could happen is for the footage to end up as another mysterious video uploaded on YouTube. Perhaps the diner would even make more money from it than what she was supposed to pay for the meal, she had thought to herself.

Ok Mariah. Enough stalling. She raises her hand to hail a taxi. She jumps in and gives the driver an address for a shopping centre in Queens, about three miles away from her daughter's house. The driver attempted to strike up a conversation, but Mariah remained resolute in her silence, her focus locked on the ticking numbers of the taximeter, especially since she did not have a penny on her. Eventually, the driver gave up.

The sun had almost dipped below the horizon, leaving the world bathed in a soft, subdued darkness. It was dark when they arrived in Queens and pulled into a shopping centre parking lot. The only sources of illumination were the street lights and vibrant LED signs showcasing the centre's name and its various stores.

The driver knows for sure that Mariah can see the twelve dollars that have clocked in the meter but notices how she remains still and silent as a statue. He is familiar with this behavior from previous encounters with problematic passengers who try to make a dash for it without paying. Mariah's head remains tilted down and covered with a hoodie. The driver adjusts the rear-view mirror, hoping for a better view of his passenger. "That will be twelve dollars Mam," he says as he observes her, looking for body signs of her intentions.

Mariah takes a deep breath in and out and lifts her head. "I am so sorry."

The driver locks the doors. "Sorry for what? I hope you are not one of those crazy...What the?" A loud bang emanates from behind the driver and startles him. He ducks and covers his head, thinking he is getting shot at. When he recovers and looks back, Mariah is nowhere to be seen and his entire rear passenger door has been ripped out and is lying on the ground next to the car.

Now that it's dark, Mariah can cover more distance faster. She avoids areas that are heavily illuminated by streetlights and sticks to the darker areas of the road. This is her neighborhood. She knows it well. In no time at all, she is outside her daughter's home. She walks to the door, raises a fist, intending to knock three times, but slowly takes three steps back instead. A hesitation fueled by her anxiety envelops her, almost triggering a panic attack as her breathing intensifies.

Deciding it is best to wait until her granddaughter Mia is asleep, she walks around the property, making her way to the backyard. She is drawn to a tall tree at the back of the property on which they had built a treehouse which is directly aligned to Mia's bedroom window on the second floor of the duplex house. All their names and birth dates are grafted into the bark of the tree. A date of passing has been added under her name, reminding her that she is a living contradiction. She runs her fingers over the words that have been carved into the tree. Taken from us, but always in our hearts, they read. A tear escapes her eyes. Mariah wonders how Gwen broke the news of her passing to her granddaughter and how Mia took it. Did she understand? Was she ok?

After some time, with all her weighty thoughts and questions, she climbs up the tree, reaches the top and enters the tree house. A few of Mia's teddies sit in a pile on the corner. Mariah gathers them to her chest and squeezes them in a tight hug. The rabbit teddy's long ear is used to wipe her tears.

Mia's bedroom window curtains are still open. Mariah's heart skips a beat when Gwen appears carrying Mia and getting ready to tuck her into bed. But something is not right. There are tears running down Gwens face and her heartbeat is racing. Her face is contorted with sorrow and fear. That's when she notices a third heartbeat in the room. Another woman appears behind Gwen. "Lupita. How did they find my home?" Mariah's voice trembles. After Gwen has tucked her into bed, Lupita walks over to Mia, places her hand on her head and immediately she falls unconscious. The window pane rattles as Mariah lands on it, slides the window open and hisses to announce herself. She maintains a crouching posture as she enters with her eyes blazing like blue flames. Gwen retreats backwards till her back is pressed against the closet.

Lupita's hand moved slowly back and forth, brushing Mia's forehead in a soothing motion. "Mariah, right? What a pleasant surprise," she remarks with a subtle smile, her index finger playfully wiggling in the air as Mariah enters the room, cautiously taking a step forward. "Please, don't do anything foolish. If you force my hand, your granddaughter will never wake up again."

Mariah relaxes her tensed shoulders and takes a step back. "Please don't harm her. She is just a child."

"Unlike you, I'm not a monster. Unless people and circumstances force me to become one. She is just asleep for now."

"Mom?" Gwen whimpers.

"Hey baby."

"But…how? What is happening?"

"The good news is, your daughter has already met my vampire mates downstairs, and we already did you a favor by telling her that you are now a vampire as well. You're welcome."

Gwen and Mariah maintain a distance between them. "What else did they tell you, baby?"

Gwen does not answer immediately. She takes a moment to take in and process her mother's presence. From her youthful look to her glowing eyes and slowly retracting fangs. When she has gathered the courage, she finally answers. "She said the vampire they are looking for placed me in some kind of hypnotic trance and used me to tame you. He made sure I wouldn't remember any of it. Is this all true?"

"It's true baby. I spent all day trying to gather the strength to tell you all of this myself." As Gwen took a hesitant step closer, Mariah's heart ached at her daughter's evident fear. A single tear escaped her eye, tracing a path down her cheek. "Take your time, Gwen. I know it's a lot to process." Mariah's voice faltered with emotion.

"Mom," When Gwen addresses her with that name again, the walls of the dam Mariah had erected inside of her collapse and send the rest of her tears rushing down. Nothing has managed to get her to lose her breath since she turned into a vampire. But this flood of emotions has done it. Gwen gives her some time before she ventures into more questions. She hopes to collect more pieces of the puzzle they are in and connect them. "She kept referring to me as her niece. Who are these people? Who is this woman?" Unable to speak, Mariah places her arm across her face and weeps.

"All wonderful questions which I think are best answered when everyone is here for this unexpected family reunion. For now, I have to ask that we all be good girls and make our way downstairs. We have lots to do. Dont worry, your daughter will be safe in her room. Your compliance will ensure that all this is over soon," Lupita smiles maliciously.

Gwen slowly walks past her mother and towards the window behind her to close it before closing the curtains. Mariah's head is still tucked into her arm when she feels Gwen's hand taking her other hand. When she lifts her head to look at her, she is greeted by a smile she did not expect so soon. Gwen pulls her into a warm embrace. Lupita finds it in her heart to be patient with them. Despite her baddie demeanor, she couldn't help being affected by the heartfelt moment between mother and daughter. They are not her enemy. She hopes she will be able to use them without harming them. After a moment, Gwen releases her mother and places her hand on her chick. "You look so young. Almost like we are the same age?"

"People will think we are twins." They both giggle. Even Lupita struggles to block her emotions, but fights to maintain a serious face.

"I am so sorry," Mariah whispers.

"You have nothing to be sorry about, Mom. We will figure this out."

Lupita clears her throat. "Ladies. Time is not on our side." She lets the two walk out of the room first and follows closely behind them. They make their way downstairs, where Dabula, Yaya and Ramsey are indulging in wine, snacks, and a drinking game, of which Todd is the unfortunate victim. Dabula opened Gwen's late grandfather's collection of whiskey bottles and they placed bets on the number of shots Todd can take before he passes out. He is relieved when he sees Gwen is back unharmed. So shocked when he sees Mariah, he jumps to his feet only for Dabula to pull him by the belt and seat him back down.

"Mama Jenkins? Is that you?" Todd wobbles as he stands again. This time, Dabula allows him.

"Damn," Ramsey sneered, his eyes scanning Todd. "If he can still recognize his family, he is still too sober. Give him more shots," he ordered, a twisted smile lined his lips.

"Enough with the games. We need to get to work," Lupita tries to restore some semblance of order. She directs Mariah and Gwen to sit next to Todd. "Listen carefully now, Mariah. The next step is very simple. If you cooperate, we will be out of your hair soon."

"What do you want from me?"

Lupita hands Mariah Gwen's phone. "You are going to call Gundo and tell him where you are. Tell him to meet you here. Make sure you give him a good reason to come quickly without telling him we are here."

"What happens when he gets here?"

"We walk out of your lives forever."

"You are using us to trap him?"

A cold smile tugs at the corners of Lupita's lips. "No honey, you are using him to save your family. I do not think he would object to saving the love of his life and his daughter."

"Daughter? Mama, what is she talking about?" Gwen asks.

Just as Mariah is about to respond, Lupita interjects. "Shush! First make the call, and then afterwards you can tell her everything she wants to know at your own time, not my time." Lupita had already dialed the number. Mariah taps the green button to send the call. It rings fifteen times without an answer before going to voicemail.

"Try again," Lupita orders. After ten seconds of ringing, Mariah lifts her head and looks at Lupita, who responds with a tense look as if to say there will be consequences if the phone is not answered. Just as she is about to give up, the phone is answered, but all she can hear is heavy breathing on the other side of the line.

"Gundo? Are you there?"

After a few seconds of silence, Gundo finally answers. "I am here Mariah."

"You need to come over to Gwen's house." A brief silence. "Your daughter wants to meet you." A tear drop running down her face accompanies Mariah's words. Gwen takes in a deep, quivering breath when she hears her mother's words. Gundo does not say anything, but his breathing gets heavier on the phone. "Well? Should I tell her you are coming or not?" Mariah asks.

"I am on my way," Gundo confirms and drops the call.

"Well done. You are such a sweetheart. Now, I think you and your daughter have a lot to talk about. I will leave you to it." Having no interest in joining her compatriots and their drinking festivities, Lupita walks towards the window that is positioned next to the front door. She wraps her arms around herself and gently rubs her shoulders. Just as she is about to get lost in her thoughts, Dabula approaches silently from behind, enveloping her in a tender embrace. She leaned back, resting her head on his chest. "It's almost done, my love," she says.

"All thanks to you, my angel. We couldn't have come this far without you. And I can't wait to have you all to myself." Dabula squeezes her tighter. A soft groan of pleasure escaped her lips. "Shaka promised we could have some time off to ourselves once we bring Gundo back."

Lupita sighs. "I want to believe that, but Lord Shaka is not a man of his word. Ever since Gundo went rogue, he has entrusted all his affairs to you. I just wish he knew how to strike a balance between demand and reward."

"He is hard to please, but not impossible. I promise, not even Shaka will stand in my way when it comes to you."

"You are starting to sound like a Guild Lord yourself."

"I think I would make a great guild Lord, with you as my queen." Lupita smiles before they kiss.

Forty minutes later, Todd has finally passed out from all the shots of whiskey and vodka. He lies on the floor in a pool of his own vomit. Gwen attempted to tend to him, but the vampires refused. They loved the idea of a drunken pastor lying on the floor in his own vomit. They even placed one bottle in his hand, took a few photos with his phone, and posted them on his social media. His fingerprint allowed them access. Gwen has already had to deal with a few calls from Deacons and other concerned church members that were trying to make sense of the posts. Gwen had simply told them that everything was under control and they would explain later. A few had offered to come over, but Gwen had managed to convince them to stay away. She was even forced to be rude to one Deacon who was insisting on coming over. Eventually, Lupita confiscated the Pastor's phone and allowed Gwen to delete all the photos the vampires had posted to avoid attracting unwanted attention.

Mariah had not been able to say a word to her daughter. She was not sure where or how to start explaining. She herself had questions that needed answering.

Gwen eventually decided to break the ice. "Gundo, huh? That's my father's name?"

Mariah confirms with a nod. "He is a powerful vampire with telepathic abilities. The reason I could never answer you all these years when you asked who your father was is because he used his powers to completely erase himself from my memory. For years, I was convinced that I had somehow been drugged and raped and ended up pregnant. I could not understand why I could not fill in the blanks as to how you came to be conceived. At some point, I almost lost my mind trying to figure out what had happened. Even when he rescued me from the execution chambers, all I saw was a stranger. I could not understand why he cared, or why he saved my life."

"So, how come you remember him now, Mama?"

"Vampires have this initiation ritual where they allow a newborn vampire to feed on a loved one. The blood of the person they love somehow makes the vampire's humanity more dominant than the monster inside of them. It gives them better control over their appetites so they do not become dangerous predators that go around killing humans at random. Gundo had placed you in a hypnotic trance and somehow brought you to the initiation. It was at some club in New York City owned by a close friend of his. They placed you and I inside some type of magic barrier and made you bleed so I would be enticed to feed on you. I think at that point, the monster took over because I blacked out.

Thank goodness the initiation worked. I remembered you. Everything about you. The way your kicks felt when you were still in my womb. The labor pains when I gave birth to you. The first time you latched onto my breast to feed as I held you in my arms. It was so painful it felt like you had teeth even though all you had were little pink gums." Gwen smiles and lets out a giggle. Mariah sniffs and wipes tears from her eyes. "You brought me back, baby. But somehow, your blood also broke whatever spell Gundo had placed in my head to erase himself from my memory. I remembered him. I remembered everything, including the night before he left for South Africa. His promise to marry me. He was an African man that believed in tradition and family. He loved them and wanted to tell them about me. Gundo said he was going home to make arrangements so we could get married. Arrangements also needed to be made so he could move permanently to the United States. He promised me so much. We made love the night before he left. That would be the last time I would see him."

"So he used to be human. How was he turned into a vampire?" Gwen asks.

"Looks like you will have the opportunity to ask him yourself.

Gundo is here," Lupita interjects. Gwen and Mariah were so emotionally invested in their conversation, they did not even realize that everyone in the room was now silent and listening to them as well. The vampires take their positions, making sure they will be out of sight when Gundo walks in. Lupita watches through the curtain as he gets out of the taxi and reluctantly makes his way towards the door.

Outside, Gundo paced nervously a few feet from the door, attempting to muster the strength he needed. It has always been easy for him to walk into any room and be around anyone because he was always in control of their senses. Always in control of what they thought, saw, and even how they behaved. This time, he is not tapping into his power or his senses. He has to walk into the house without being in control of anyone. He needed to be honest with his daughter and Mariah and allow all of them, including himself, to face reality as it is. No manipulation. No hypnotism. Just the truth. This is the only way to earn their trust. And it would either destroy them forever or it would be the start of something beautiful.

Gundo is the same vampire who believed that immortality was wasted on him, because all that he regards as worth living for was non-existent in his life. Now he has a chance to connect with a new reason for living. That alone is worth knocking on the door. That is what gives him the strength he needs. And so he approaches the door and lifts a trembling fist to knock three times. Mariah opens the door and takes three steps back. She takes a moment and regards Gundo. She is unable to utter the words to invite him to come in. Gundo takes off his brown panama hat and twists it in his hands. He hangs his head.

Just as the silence seemed to stretch on, Dabula suddenly appeared from behind the door. "Oh, get inside already." He grabs Gundo by the collar and yanks him inside, sending him into a forward flip. Mariah manages to move out of the way in time to avoid getting knocked down. Tiles crack as Gundo lands on the floor, sending dust into the air.

When Gundo lifts his head and looks around the room, he sees Lupita and the other vampires. He realizes that it is a trap.

"Glad you could join us, my friend," Dabula grins.

"Lupita. Why are you doing this?" Gundo asks as he staggers to his feet.

Mariah notices Gundo's missing fingers. "What the hell happened to your hand?"

Gundo groans as he peels himself from the floor and shifts his position so he is on bended knees. "Oh, you don't remember now. You happened."

"Shouldn't they grow back?" Mariah asks in a confused tone. The vampires and Lupita crack into a gleeful laughter.

Gundo holds out his hand and shakes his head. "We are not lizards. They won't grow back. I could have reattached them if you had not left them in the sun to be incinerated."

"Oh my goodness, Gundo, I am so sorry. I didn't know?"

Gundo rises to his feet. "Yeah, well, it looks like you are not done with me yet. You set a trap for me with these guys?"

"No, it's not like that. They didn't give us a choice. They would have hurt my family."

"And there I was thinking we are all one family," Lupita remarks.

"Lupita, we are family. This is your niece," Gundo points to Gwen. "I am your brother."

"They are your family, not mine," Lupita growls.

"I know you are hurting because of me, Sister, but I am your blood. Not Dabula, not Ramsey or Yaya," Gundo raises his voice as he points to the vampires with half an index finger. "If you just give me a chance. If we can unite as brother and sister. As a family. We can overcome this." His eyes glistened with tears. "You are my baby sister. I love you. I have always loved you and always will." He roars, takes a moment to catch his breath, and speaks softly. "Don't shut me out."

Lupita takes two steps forward and stands right beneath Gundo, who is about two feet taller than her. Tears fell from his eyes, landing on her black and white converse sneakers as they locked eyes. "Unite? Can you unite me with Mama? Papa? What about our brother? No, you can't Gundo." She takes a step back. "You are right. My blood runs in your veins. But how are you able to live with yourself, knowing that their blood runs through your veins, because you murdered them when you drank them dry?" Lupita's lips tremble.

"You do not need to remind me," Gundo shouts. "The smell of Mama's blood has never left my nose. It is a hell I can never escape."

Lupita takes three steps back. "I wish you could smell my blood as well, so you can be reminded every day of everything you stole from me and just how much I detest you. But, don't worry. I am here to give you a way out. If the love of my life was not sired by you, I would have killed you long ago. Regrettably, if you die, he dies. Fortunately, there is another option." Lupita stretches out her hand and the front door is broken down as the levitating coffin forces its way into the house.

Gundo steels himself at the eerie sight of the coffin approaching him at waist height.. "Lupita. I do not wish to fight with you," he pleads.

"Good. You should never fight a fate you deserve," she responds. As soon as her comrades have their oxygen masks on, Lupita closes her left hand into a fist and everyone, save her and her compatriots, collapses to the floor as all the oxygen is extracted from the room. Before Gundo can touch the floor, Dabula has him by the throat. He lifts him into the air and choke slams him into the open coffin. The room is silent except for the sound of Gwen and Mariah gasping desperately for breath. Todd's unconscious body also twitches, fighting for breath. Lupita notices and discreetly adjusts the level of oxygen in the room. Only enough for them to stay alive but not conscious as Mariah and Gwen eventually black out. Gundo uses the little strength he has to lift his head, hoping to see Gwen and Mariah, but he is too weak. The coffin has already started extracting oxygen directly from his body, even before the lid can be closed.

"See you after a thousand years, when I can finally kill you." Those are the last words he hears from Lupita before the coffin is slammed shut, and he slumbers.

***

"Gwen. Gwen, wake up." Gwen is ushered back to consciousness by her mother's voice. Her head feels heavy, as if a ton of bricks is tethered to it. Slowly, she blinked her eyes open. When she looked around, she realized that Lupita and her crew were gone. "Are you okay, baby?" Mariah tenderly brushed her daughter's braids back. Gwen managed a nod. "Good girl."

Struggling to regain her footing, Gwen steadied herself and rushed upstairs to check on her daughter, finding her sleeping peacefully and unharmed. Deciding it is best for her to remain asleep until order is restored, she quietly returns downstairs and finds Mariah attending to her fiance. They carefully turned him onto his back. "Bring me all the empty bottles," Gwen requested.

"Why? He has alcohol poisoning. Shouldn't we take him to the emergency room?" Mariah asks.

"There is no time. Just do what I say, please Mama." Mariah's worry creased her brow, but she complied as she gathered all the empty alcohol bottles, placing them next to her daughter. Gwen places her hand on Todd's chest. When she closes her eyes, blue glowing circular runes appear, encircling both Gwen and Todd. The runes are like a circle inside another, with an array of symbols that look like hieroglyphics. One rotates clockwise while the other rotates counterclockwise. The very air seemed charged with an ancient magical power, as the empty bottles gradually refilled, and those opened by the vampires were sealed shut once more. Mariah clasps her mouth and gasps. "Gwen. How did you...?"

The runes vanish, but Todd is still unconscious. Gwen turns to her mother. "I am a witch, Mom."

"But…how? You heal people?" Mariah's hands are trembling.

"It's not healing. It is restoration. As long as I can remember the way something used to be, I can restore it. A friend of mine, also a witch, said the witches of old call this power; Former Glory." Gwen rises to her feet and walks over to the broken door. She closes her eyes. The radiant blue runes appear around her feet as if she is standing in a spotlight. The pieces of the door start to reassemble and reattach. Soon, the door is reconnected to the hinges and good as new."

"Wow Gwen. How long have you been able to do this?"

"I only discovered my powers back at college. I think it was the best time to discover this part of who I am because other witches were able to find me and guide me."

"I was wondering why it seemed so easy for you to process everything that has happened. How come you never told me?"

"One of the things the witches fraternity at college teaches you is that the best way to keep your family safe from the dangers of the supernatural world, is to keep them away and unaware of the supernatural. Little did I know somebody else had already plunged you into it."

"Oh wow. This is unbelievable."

"What is unbelievable is that you are here and alive. More than alive. I thought I lost you, Mama."

"Undead actually. If I was given options, I would have chosen to come back as a witch instead of a monster. I mean, look at all the cool things you can do."

"You are not a monster. You are my mom. And if fate deemed it fit for you to still be here, then you are where you belong."

Until now, Mariah has wondered if it was right for her to still be alive. She felt like an anomaly that must be corrected. An abomination that must be removed. Her daughter's words are a fortress and an assurance she has been longing for, lifting her above her doubts and fears. *Does this mean Gundo was right to erase himself from my memory?* Mariah wonders. "Gwen. Could you restore me as well? Back to what I used to be. Could you make me human again?"

Gwen approaches her mother and gently takes her hands into her own. "I'm sorry, Mama. You have been a vampire for too long. My power of restoration only works within an hour's window from the time an incident occurred. Not a minute more. It used to be only within a minute, and then five minutes. The time increased as my power grew."

Mariah closed her eyes and quickly concealed the outward signs of her disappointment. "Alright. Don't worry about it, baby." She kisses the back of Gwen's hand.

"I am not worried. If I have learned anything about the supernatural world, it's that anything is possible." Gwen offers a comforting and reassuring smile. Mariah smiles back, but it does little to hide her despondency. "I am so glad I finally got to share my secret with you."

"Me too, baby. Does she know?" Mariah raises her brows to point upstairs.

"Mia? She knows enough for now. I had to prepare her in case her power awakened."

Mariah nods approvingly. "You did well, baby. I raised you well."

They exchange a smile. "Shouldn't Todd be up already?"

"Well, an hour ago, he already had a lot of alcohol in his system. He will need some sleep."

"Former glory, huh? Could you raise the dead if they had just died within your power's time jurisdiction?"

"I believe I could. But it is forbidden. They say it angers the Angel of death and can result in severe consequences."

"The angel of death huh?. Well, best we let the dead rest in peace then."

"I agree," says Gwen. She uses her power to restore the house to order as best as she can.

Even though it is now midnight, sleep is the furthest thing from their minds. They have a lot to talk about. A lot of dots to connect and puzzles to put together. Mariah carries Todd upstairs bridal style and tucks him into bed. She and her daughter spend the rest of the evening talking about Gundo and everything Mariah remembered and had learned about him and the supernatural. Gwen has always suspected that she inherited her powers from her Father's side. Years had passed without Gwen and her mother discussing her paternal side, but when her power awakened, she started bringing up the question again. They finally realized that Gwen inherited her enchanted abilities from Gundo's mother. A grandmother she would never get to know. All she learns about her is what Gundo told Mariah. After much discussion, they decide perhaps it's best they make sure she at least gets to know her father.

"It's all up to you, baby. What do you want us to do?" Mariah asks.

"I have to meet him, mom. We have to save him."

CHAPTER SIXTEEN

VANTAGE POINT

At night, the Balsam mountain becomes a place of reverence where the natural beauty of the surroundings is enhanced by the starry sky, untainted by city lights. As the night sky darkens, a tapestry of stars emerges, twinkling like scattered diamonds against a velvety canvas. The landscape below is bathed in a soft, silvery glow from the luminous crescent moon, casting intricate patterns of light and shadow. The celestial display paints an ethereal beauty that seems to belong to another world, far removed from the hustle and bustle of daily life. The world seems to pause for a moment, as if nature itself was taking a deep, relaxing breath.

As darkness embraced the mountain, the nocturnal creatures stirred from their slumber. The haunting call of a distant owl echoed through the forest, its eerie melody blending with the gentle rustle of leaves. Fireflies flickered like tiny lanterns, illuminating the undergrowth with a captivating dance of light. In the distance, the occasional howl of a coyote added a wild and mysterious note to the symphony of the night.

A cool breeze brushes against the branches of the spruce trees that cover the Balsam Mountain, causing the leaves to rattle. Small twigs crackle beneath their sneakers with every other step they take as Jabu and Zendaya trek through the forest, the sound adding a subtle percussion to the symphony of nature at night. Jabu walks in front and leads Zendaya by the hand, making sure she treads safely in his footsteps. He guides her, so she does not bump into anything or trip.

"I wish you could see what I see," he says.

"Unfortunately, I wasn't born a witch of the forge. I'll tell you one thing. I don't need your enhanced vision to know we are surrounded by mosquitoes." She slaps her thigh to swat one. "They are biting me right through my leggings."

"I told you bum shorts and leggings were not ideal for hiking, but you had to be a fashionista."

"And here I was thinking I was dressing up for you."

"You should have dressed for the mountain."

"Shut up." Zendaya pinches his shoulder. Jabu chuckles.

"Well, take heart, my damsel in distress. We have arrived."

A fire lookout tower built around the late nineteenth century stands before them. It is so big even Zendaya can at least see the silhouette shape of the pillars that form the structure on the darkness. Jabu gives Zendaya their backpack to carry on her back so she can carry her piggy-back style. She wraps her legs around his waist and her arms around his neck as Jabu climbs up using a ladder that is fixed to the tower. He moves quickly without slowing down or showing any signs of fatigue, even with the load he carries. They soon find themselves perched atop the tower's wooden platform, exposed to the open sky above. The absence of a canopy allows them an unobstructed view of the breathtaking night sky and the vast landscape stretching beneath them. They do not want to risk being spotted by humans, so they decide to rely only on the natural light of the full moon above them and Jabu's night vision.

"This tower would have been the perfect spot to watch the sunset.

And it looks like the mosquitoes can't follow us up here," Zendaya says.

"Yeah, pity we had to wait until it was dark. Otherwise, one of the park rangers would have probably spotted us and ruined everything."

As Zendaya settled comfortably on the tower's platform, she transformed her blue jean jacket into a makeshift pillow, making a cozy spot to recline and gaze at the vast night sky. "Such a romantic spot as well. The stars and the moon look so much brighter up here."

"That's because there are no city lights around here, so the natural lights are amplified. Good thing as well, because my binoculars work best in pure natural light."

"Are they ready?"

"Yep." Jabu makes a few last adjustments to his binoculars before reclining next to Zendaya and pointing them to the sky as he looks through them. Except he is not looking at the stars and the moon. He is looking through them. Using his prowess as a witch from the lineage of the forge, he crafted a set of binoculars that use natural sources of light as a lens. The Binoculars have wheels that can be rotated to zoom in, out and around scenery with a panoramic view from above. He does not have to be looking in any specific direction to see a specific point. He just needs to look through the binoculars, adjust them, and find the point he wishes to focus on within a mile radius. As long as natural light touches it, he can see it. The light from the moon is not enough to illuminate anything, so he has a night vision setting engineered into the magic binoculars, allowing him to see even when natural light is minimal. His finger pushes the small wheel on the side of the binoculars, making a clicking sound as the view rotates. This allows him to scan the area. "Thank goodness for clear night skies. These things would have been useless if it was cloudy tonight."

"I like those things better during the day. Sunlight lets you see further," Zendaya remarks.

"Yeah, but they will do the job."

"This would make a perfect spot for a date. Maybe like a night picnic under the stars."

Jabu turns on his side to look Zendaya in the eyes. "All I can think about is making love to you under the stars."

Zendaya smirked. "I think you are getting addicted."

"To you? Absolutely. Is it a bad thing?"

"It's not a bad thing at all," she whispered lovingly and planted several pecks on his lips, finishing with a prolonged kiss. "But I'm gonna have to turn you down. We need to save our energy in case we come across any trouble tonight."

Jabu scoffs. "I hate it when you are responsible. It ruins the fun." He lies on his back and checks the binoculars again.

"Well, one of us has to—"

"Hang on, babe," Jabu interjects. "Looks like we finally have some action." He spots multiple vehicle lights appearing on the horizon, gradually approaching an open plain a couple of miles east of their location. With every detail coming into focus through his binoculars, he identified the vehicles as motorbikes, followed by a conspicuous bus. "Looks like the Commissioner's information is legit."

"Can I see?" Zendaya takes the binoculars, places them on her eyes and focuses on the area Jabu directs her towards. She zooms in, scrutinizing the faces of the figures disembarking from a black SUV. "Hey, I know you. The dwarf is Xavi Gonzalez. One of the most feared and elusive cartel leaders in the USA and Mexico. He is considered untouchable because of his political connections."

"Do you recognize anybody else?"

"I'll be damned. This is actually a gathering of the most elite werewolf families in the country." She zooms into a caucasian man, dressed like a cowboy. She identifies him as Chance Decker, a man that emanates a rugged charm. He is an alpha representing the Texas werewolf clan. Her gaze then fell upon Kasa, a figure exuding strength and tradition, Alpha of the Red Indian clan from South Dakota, along with his powerful and mystical wife, Ketari. Their reputation preceded them, and they were revered as legends among werewolf clans. Ketari is also a powerful werewolf and shaman. They are legends among the werewolf clans in the country.

"Who is the Afro?"

"The guy with the big afro is Hakeem Hamilton. He is the leader of a pack of werewolves that claim the streets of New York as their territory. Also very connected to both the political and criminal underworld. All of these stars were on the list of names that came up before I was forced to drop my investigations and was kicked out of the police force. I'm guessing the extras are members of their respective packs."

"How did you even find out they were involved in...whatever this is?"

"Oh, I didn't know they were involved in whatever this is. I just knew they were involved in something big and shady. After my brother disappeared, the best place to check was the place he was last seen, and that was the prison where he worked. There was evidence that he clocked in for work, but nothing showing he clocked out. Footage from the day was also missing. Long story short, I commandeered a high-ranking prison guard's body and snuck into the warden's office. One of the things I found was a paper with a list of names and contact details. The document was titled project red moon. Every top dog on that field was on the list."

"What part does Grimshaw play in all this?"

"I am not sure, but whatever this is, Grimshaw was clearly part of it and was willing to protect it. Now, he is desperate enough to expose it. I just hope the truth about what happened to my brother will also be revealed." Zendaya zooms into the prison buses. Chained convicts, mostly males and a few females, are being offloaded by the guards. She estimates more or less fifty in total. "Looks like they are getting ready for something. And if the information Grimshaw and Sofia provided is reliable, they are about to use the convicts for some sort of sport." A tense silence hung in the air as Zendaya kept her eyes glued to the unfolding spectacle, almost a mile from their position. After a minute, she notices fifteen more people being yanked off the bus. "What the hell is this? Those people look like civilians. Five of them are dressed like prison guards."

"Prison guards?"

"Yeah. Judging by their resistance, I don't think they are here of their own volition."

"Zendaya."

She takes a deep breath. "I know. Whatever is about to happen to those guards is probably what happened to my brother."

CHAPTER
SEVENTEEN

BLOOD DAGGERS

All the top dogs stand in a circle with a cigar clutched between their teeth. The rest of their pack members surround them in a bigger circle. They wait for Xavi to light his cigar before they light their own simultaneously. Xavi moves to the center of the circle and releases an enormous cloud of smoke into the air.

"My brothers. My blood brothers. Each time we are brought together by this old tradition of ours, I am overwhelmed with emotions. We cherish this tradition because it is an opportunity to embrace who and what we truly are. An opportunity to embrace our true nature. To be the hunters we were born to be. Apex predators. The need to adapt has forced us to spend most of our time walking among sheep as if they were our equals. But not tonight. Tonight, the sheep will scatter because of the wolf. As it should be." The werewolves respond with a loud mimicry of howling wolves.

When the prisoners hear Xavi's words, they begin to groan and mumble amongst themselves as an uneasy feeling takes hold of them. Some feel a chill running down their spine. They have been piecing together all the clues they have managed to collect and do not like the picture it paints in their minds.

"Shut up," a guard orders. The prisoners fall silent.

Xavi holds out his hand, beckoning his daughter as she approaches. She steps into the center of the circle and joins her father. She tries to tuck her brown hair behind her ear, but the wind blows the strands back into her face, so she lets it be.

"Another reason I am very emotional today is this beautiful young lady next to me. My seventeen year old daughter Valentina. She has come of age. Today will be her first hunt." There is howling and applause as Valentina responds with a curtsy. "Now, my friends, please, give her your blessings." Xavi steps back.

The gathering werewolves, male and female, step forward one at a time, starting with the alphas. They place one hand behind her neck and she places her hand behind theirs. They pull each other close and touch foreheads with Valentina while whispering blessings to her. Their eyes glow as they embrace her. Some glow red, some blue, some yellow and others purple.

When the blessing ritual is done, a bonfire is lit and the prisoners are ordered to sit around it. The guards grill beef cuts around the fire. When it is cooked enough, they distribute it to the prisoners to eat, along with some bread rolls and soda. The food is so good they almost forget the questions they had regarding their purpose here. Anxiety has left them. The guards even allow them to chat as the mood turns festive. This is further exacerbated by Xavi and the other werewolves keeping their distance.

After two hours, the prisoners fall silent when they notice Raphael who approaches their position. "I hope you have all eaten and had your fill. You will need your strength. Tonight, your lives will either be changed forever, or they will end."

One of the prisoners springs to his feet and throws a bone from the tomahawk steak he was eating into the crackling fire. "That's it. I may be a prisoner, but I sure as hell know my rights. You people better start explaining what is going on here, otherwise there will be all sorts of trouble in the morning. And I am talking about newspapers and paparazzi type of trouble. Even TMZ."

"Calm down Sir. I am about to explain everything. If only you had not interrupted me so rudely." Raphael shoots the prisoner a stern glance. It's enough for him to slowly take his seat. "We are right in the middle of the Balsam mountains. You may not be able to see it now, but we are surrounded by beautiful lush forest all around. This forest is one of our hunting grounds. Tonight, that is exactly what we are here to do. We will hunt. And whoever wins will be rewarded with their freedom, their life, and one million dollars to make sure they are truly free."

The prisoners break into collective murmurs of excitement.

"Well, well, well. I'll be damned. Looks like I'm in luck. I have more than twenty-five years of experience as a hunter. Might as well give me my freedom, hand me the money and save everyone from wasting their time," a prisoner remarks.

"Shut up Rodgers, we all want a shot at the money," another prisoner blurted out.

"There are more prisoners here than all the armed guards and you bikers combined. Are you telling me that you intend to arm us with rifles and risk being overpowered? What are you not telling us?" A prisoner asks.

"Your fellow inmates are mistaken. You are not the hunters. You are the prey."

A nervous silence fell on all the prisoners. "You plan to hunt us down and shoot us like dogs?" one of them asked.

"No. We do not use guns. We hunt using nothing but our bare hands, our wisdom, our teeth and the strength of our backs."

"In that case, I think all of us should fancy our chances."

"Maybe. The rules are simple. This entire forest is surrounded by a gravel road. It connects to three highways that lead out of this place." Raphael points northwards as light appears atop a lookout tower. "The light you see is a fire on top of the northern lookout tower. There is also a tower to the, South, East and west. Some are further than others. There is a fully functional car at the bottom of each tower with keys in the ignition." A guard began distributing notes and small torch lights to each prisoner. "If by some miracle you manage to make it to a car and drive out of here, wait until tomorrow and call the number on the note. You will be provided with an address where you will be able to collect your money."

"What if more than one person makes it out?" a female prisoner's voice quivers.

"Then they will all get paid," Raphael answers.

One prisoner, fueled by a mix of disbelief and newfound excitement, rises to his feet. His voice is tinged with a touch of rebellion, "This still sounds too good to be true. But you know what? I never expected to be enjoying premium steak around a barn fire tonight, so to hell with it. When do we start?"

"We start now."

"Can we have five minutes to strategise as a group?"

"We are giving you all a 15 minute head start. Use it to run and make ground or strategise. It's up to you."

"Excellent. Everyone one me," inmate Rodgers barks out an order.

"Why the heck should we listen to you? I don't remember anyone electing you to be our leader."

"Cause I used to hunt in this area. Even in this peach blackness of night, I still know it like the back of my hand. But you are welcome to go on your own." Everyone suddenly moves towards Rodgers and huddles around him. Before he can start speaking, he notices two females, a guard and a civilian running westwards as they dash towards the forest. The three remaining prison guards and the civilians run in the other direction as they target the other watch towers. "Bunch of idiots. Anyway, don't worry about them. Our best shot at this is if we stick together." Rodgers speaks as softly as he can, hoping the bikers and guards can't hear him. "Listen carefully. These hunters will be coming after us with nothing but their bare hands. However, there are plenty of weapons in the forest. Find a rock, a big stick, anything you can use as a weapon. Once we arm ourselves, we can change the game. The prey becomes the hunter, and the hunter becomes the hunted."

"That's a good plan, Rodgers. But what about the cars at the watchtowers? Those inmates that got a head start will have taken them before we can get to them."

"If we manage to kill most of these guys, we will be driving out of here in those beautiful range rovers, bikes and Humvees. No need to waste energy trekking in this stinking peach black forest." His strategy drew nods of approval and a sense of camaraderie among the prisoners.

"Alright Rodgers, sounds like a good plan. So what do we do from here?"

"We split into four groups and run in different directions. It will also make it easier for us to find things we can use for weapons. From then on, we wait to ambush them and take them out. When we all walk back out into this open field again, we show them no mercy. I'm pretty sure we have enough skills and experience amongst us murderers and serial killers." He chuckles. The grim humor lingered in the air, but everyone nodded in agreement. "Alright. Is everyone clear on what they are doing?" Everyone gives a signal of agreement. "Good, then let's get started." The inmates split into four groups and move in four directions. Their keen eyes searched the ground for rocks and large sticks, makeshift weapons to wield against their pursuers. Intent on survival, they moved swiftly, guided by a newfound unity.

From a distance, Rodgers watches Valentina, Xavi's daughter with a sinister glint in his eye, scanning her body from head to toe as she walks towards her Father. "I hope that latina girl will be in the group that comes after me. I won't beat her to a pulp, but I sure as hell will have my way with her."

Valentina suddenly halts in her tracks and turns to face Rodgers. She strides towards him with confidence and authority, quickly closing the distance between them. "Have your way with me? A feat no ordinary man has ever managed. What makes you think you could do anything to me?"

A perplexed look envelopes Roger's face. "How did you even hear me all the way from there?"

Valentina drew a deep breath, as if smelling the air. "I have memorized your disgusting scent. You have five minutes left for your head start. I think it's time I warm up. I am coming for you."

"I look forward to it," Rodgers gloats and blows her a kiss.

Valentina growls as her eyes turn blue. Steam issues from her salivating mouth and rises from her body as sweat evaporates from her skin. She drops to her knees and arches her back as her transformation begins. Fingers turn into claws, digging deeper into the dry ground. Her clothes are ripped apart as her body expands and she turns. The inmates watch in horror until Valentina is fully transformed into a werewolf three times her previous size. She raises her head and lets out a loud howl.

The rest of the werewolves, save for Xavi and the other alphas, all transform. Their transformation is much faster. They burst into their werewolf form in mere seconds. It is as if the monsters are exploding out of human bodies. A symbol of their experience. Some inmates are frozen with fright. Others do not stick around to watch the full process. They drop their sticks and stones and scatter. Running as fast as they can in all directions as they vanish into the surrounding woods. Rodgers was gone long before Valentina could finish her transformation.

Xavi walks over to his transformed children. They lower their heads as Xavi places his hands on their foreheads and brushes them. "Valentina. Forget about that inmate. With so little time left, they are easy pickings. Leave them to the others. They will make quick work of them. The real hunting experience will come from the ones that ran away first, headed for the eastern tower. Pick up their scent. It is like a trail of breadcrumbs that leads to a sweet reward. This is the chance to show what you have learned. They will feel a chill run down their spine when you get closer. They will know that death and your fangs are creeping up on them. Make me proud." Valentina responds with a growl. "Raphael, hunt down the two women that were first to run. They were headed west. Go!"

The siblings move out towards separate directions. Valentina stops to sniff the ground. She ignores all the strongest scent trails and focuses on the weakest. This must be from the inmates that were first to run away. As the moon cast its eerie glow, the night became a battlefield where primal instincts and human desperation collided. The hunt had begun, and the stakes were life or death.

*****

"The prisoners have split into groups. I think they are getting ready to begin. Wait a minute." Zendaya gasps with the binoculars still pressed against her eyes. "Something is happening. That girl is changing." Her heart is pounding as she watches the bikers transforming into a small army of werewolves. "I think they are playing hunger games with the prisoners. There is no way any of them will survive this."

"Zendaya. Your brother."

"I know. This is how Zane died," her voice trembles, though it's barely above a whisper. "The werewolves killed him."

Jabu allows her only a minute to process the manner in which her brother may have died. "We need to get out of here. It's not safe."

"No. I need to know why they killed him."

"Babe. You got the answers you needed. It's enough now."

Zendaya stands up and looks down on Jabu who is trying to pack their gear. "Not all the answers. I need to know why they killed him."

Jabu shakes his head as he rises to his feet. "This will never end. Everything we discover will just keep leading to another thing."

"It will end. I will end it."

"Babe. We are no match for a pack of werewolves. Let alone four packs of werewolves."

Zendaya looks through the binoculars and starts searching the area again. "The two female prisoners that got a head start are headed our way. There is only one werewolf that is tracking them. The rest are going after the late runners."

"This is madness."

"We can't fight the entire pack. But we can take one werewolf. And he is headed right towards us."

"This is crazy," Jabu shakes his head as he swings their backpack onto his back. He approaches the edge of the tower and watches Zendaya who has already started climbing down. Jabu jumps from the tower and bends his knees to absorb the force as he lands firmly on his feet. He looks up at Zendaya with a smile.

"Show off." Zendaya remarks. When she is halfway down the tower, she pushes herself backwards and lets go, sending herself plunging down. She lands comfortably in Jabu's arms. "Ok, we need to hurry." She doesn't even give him time to put her down gently as she wriggles herself out of his arms.

"So, what's the plan?" Jabu asks.

"Well, do you think you can take him?"

"Forge witches are strong, but most werewolves are stronger. Especially in their transformed state."

"You have the blood daggers, right?"

"Yes, but we will need to draw his blood before they can give us any advantage. Not an easy thing to get from a werewolf."

"That is where I come in. If you can create an opening for me, I will create an opening for you."

"Dating you is an extreme sport sometimes." Zendaya scoffs at his remark.

They walk until they are sure they have aligned themselves with the potential path of the runners and Raphael. Jabu uses his senses to try to gauge the runners' and werewolves' approach so they can refine their own position.

After a few minutes, he can hear approaching footsteps. One woman appears. They shine a torch toward her as she nears their position. The woman is exhausted and out of breath. She staggers from tree to tree, using the stumps for support. She drops on her knees right at Zendaya's feet. "Water." Her voice is hoarse. Jabu pulls a bottle of water from his bag and gives it to her. She drinks it down rapidly, crushing the plastic bottle in her hands as the last drops of water trickle out.

"Where is the lady you were with?" Zendaya asks, her eyes darting around the dark surroundings. Before the prisoner can answer, they hear a loud female scream emanating from the direction the first woman appeared. Followed by a thunderous, vicious growl. And then a silence that did not exist before that. Even the night insects, once chirping and buzzing, fell eerily silent, leaving only the rustling of trees and stillness that matched the peach darkness. The prisoner grabs Zendaya, using her to drag herself back on her feet and starts running again, leaving the couple behind. She never looked back.

"Jabs. Do you think you can create an opening for me?" There is a sense of urgency is Zendaya's voice.

Jabu dips into the backpack and pulls out a leather holster that holds twin daggers. He wraps it around his waist so the knives hang on one side. He fastens a second belt to secure the knife holster to his thigh. Zendaya hands him the binoculars and he starts adjusting them to scan the area for their target. "Wow, he is huge," Jabu exclaimed in awe of what was coming towards them. He hands Zendaya the binoculars and takes his jacket off, exposing the black vest underneath. Taking up his position, he planted his feet firmly on the ground, assuming a stance of unwavering balance. He has a dagger poised in each hand. His breathing is calm and controlled.

"Be careful, babe." Zendaya says as she takes a few steps back. She switches off her torch to avoid attracting the attention of the charging werewolf to herself. The pitch blackness heightens her own hearing. Her heart races wildly in her chest as the monstrous beast draws closer, its heavy footsteps creating an ominous rhythm.

Once it was within Jabu's line of sight, he hurled the dagger with precision, aiming for its eye. However, the agile creature deflected the attack with a swift motion of its head. Its hide too tough for the blade to penetrate. When it recovers, Jabu finds himself beneath the pouncing beast. He tucks his hand under its arm and uses its own momentum to judo flip the werewolf and send it crashing into the ground.

"Wait." Jabu barks an order when he sees Zendaya rushing towards the beast. She had hoped she could body swap before it recovers, but she is too slow. The werewolf retaliates, lifting itself with one hand and viciously swinging at Zendaya with the other. Jabu's heart leaps when he sees the danger the apple of his eye is in, but in the same heartbeat, his forge witch reflexes allow him to overtake Zendaya just in time to block and grab the werewolf's wrist with both his hands. The force causes his feet to slide in the grovel. The werewolf, unfazed, grabs Jabu by the neck, causing his breath to hitch in his throat. The monster choke slams him to the ground. Raphael's sharp claws pressed menacingly against his skin, and for a terrifying moment, he felt his neck might snap. Just as he thought he was done for, the grip unexpectedly slackened. Opening his eyes, Jabu saw Zendaya standing resolutely behind the werewolf, her hand on its shoulder, before her body collapsed to the ground.

"Just in time," Jabu gasped, relief surging through him as he struggled back to his feet. "Alright babe. Ready when you are."

Zendaya, now in the beast's body, takes a few seconds to acclimate herself to the unfamiliar sensation. She has never commandeered a werewolf before. She emits a low growl, a tentative signal of her readiness. Her nod confirms her determination. Jabu plunges his second dagger into the werewolf's eye with unerring precision. The pain causes Zendaya to immediately switch back to her body, where she writhes in pain. The sensation remains with her for some time, as though her own eye had been ruthlessly pierced. Jabu grabs her from behind and drags her away from the beast. He positions her against a tree for support before retaking his position, ready to face the beast.

Tormented by the searing pain in its eye, the werewolf lets out a roar, mingled with an almost human-like scream. Jabu opens his palms. The first dagger he tossed at the monster levitates back into his hand and firmly nestles back in his grasp. The second retracts itself from the werewolv's eye, causing it more pain as it also returns to Jabu's hand. The werewolf raises its head to the sky and lets out a loud howl before it refocuses its one eyed glance on Jabu. Blood squirts from its wounded eye.

A low menacing growl, and then the werewolf charges. Jabu's movements are a blur as he hurls the blood daggers at the beast. With an uncanny precision, each blade strikes its mark, only to obediently return to his hand like loyal servants returning to their master, mirroring the grace of a boomerang in flight. He deftly juggles the knives between his nimble fingers and the monster's writhing form, delivering successive, crippling blows that ravage multiple limbs and inflict tremendous damage as they easily pierce its skin. The creature struggles to defend itself, using its wrists to shield its face, but it can't escape the relentless assault. It's only two daggers, but the speed of the daggers is such that it feels as if a torrent of blades is cascading upon the beast.

Finally, Jabu ceases his relentless barrage, and the once-fierce creature finds itself pinned against the stem of a colossal tree. Exhausted, it lets out a weak growl that sounds more like the mooing of a dying cow. The involuntary transformation back into human form confirms its defeat.

"Babe, you good?" Jabu checks on Zendaya, who has since recovered.

"I'm good. And it looks like we hit the jackpot. That's Xavi's son. Raphael Gonzalez." Zendaya shines his torch onto Raphel's face. He remains on the ground with his naked form leaning against the tree. The transformation back into human form has partially healed him.

Jabu playfully spins his knives in his hands as he approaches the defeated werewolf. "My friend, this battle was over the moment I drew your blood. These are my favorite weapons. They are called blood daggers. The first dagger I threw at you barely made a scratch on your skin. Your wicked hide is too hard. But once I stabbed you in the eye and my dagger tasted your blood, they could pierce your skin as if its butter. The knives were never gonna miss even if I didn't aim." Raphael groans from a stew of pain and anguish. Jabu nonchalantly tosses a dagger into the air, it's mesmerizing flips akin to a deadly dance. The blade, now infused with its victim's blood, rockets toward Raphael's hand, pinning it to the ground. His anguished cries are piercing, amplifying even further when Jabu recalls the knife to his grasp as he continues to explain how they work. "The daggers adjust their power to the blood of whatever they tasted. That way, they can be lethal to any creature, no matter how powerful it is. A grim destiny sealed by their own blood."

"Don't worry, we won't kill you, yet," Zendaya remarks, her voice laced with a sinister edge that sent shivers down Raphael's spine.

"Babe, you just missed a perfect moment to say, Finish Him!"

"What?" Zendaya responds, confusion etched across her face.

"Come on, haven't you played Mortal Com..? You know what, never mind. I don't even know why I try sometimes." Jabu muttered, rolling his eyes.

"I love you, but sometimes you are so weird," Zendaya smiles as she turns her attention back to the fallen werewolf.

Raphael's breath is labored as he clutches his wounded hand. Blood oozed between his fingers. "Witches again." He spits out blood. "The last witch that interfered in our business ended up dead. The two of you will also be dead soon. That howl before I turned into human form was an SOS to my brothers telling them my position and what we are dealing with. So you see, you celebrated too soon. When they get here, we will rip you apart," he barked defiantly, trying to mask his pain and fear.

"The last witch you are referring to, was he a prison guard?"

With a sly grin, Raphael replied, "Well, well. That explains why you are snooping all over our business. Yes, he was a prison guard. Was he also your boyfriend?"

"He was my brother."

"He was delicious."

A flash of anger flickered across Zendaya's face, quickly replaced by disdain. "You disgust me," she retorts.

"I hope you will be just as tasty as he was," Raphael chuckles but starts coughing as he chokes on his own blood. His breaths grow more labored.

"Why was he involved in this? What did he ever do to you?"

"If your brother knew how to mind his own business, he would still be alive. Most people that join these games are wretches, desperate for freedom and money. But it was not his desperation that earned him a spot in the games. He wanted to be Mr. Goody-two shoes and expose our activities, our tradition and way of life. So we took his life," Raphael lets out a soft chuckle.

Jabu's ear twitches. "Babe, we are running out of time. More werewolves are coming."

"Where can I find his remains?" she asks.

"Well, it depends. Some of him should be somewhere around this forest. Some of him should be in the New York sewers. Depends where we pooped. I mean, we poop everywhere, just poop-poop-poop, here a little there a little," he coughs out another laugh. "He was a pile of shit and wherever his remains are, that is where they deserve to be. The two of you will join him soon." Raphael spits out more blood. His demeanor turns bleak as he realizes the extent of the damage he has suffered. "Curse you both for what you did to me."

As Raphael mocked and threatened, Zendaya's tears flowed

silently. She reached into her pocket and retrieved a small retractable knife. Its blade gleams in the torch light reflecting the anguish in her eyes. Whispering an incantation, she made a cut on her open palm. The crimson blood that flowed formed intricate runes on her hand, as if written in red ink. "What are you doing?" Raphael's panic was evident as Zendaya knelt closer to him. Her palm was open as she blew a breath towards his face. The runes transformed into sand-like sparks, and Raphael unwittingly breathed them in, the last of it triggering another cough. "What did you do to me?"

She tilts her head sideways and moves in closer to his face. "I've cursed you," Zendaya declared, her voice carrying an eerie calmness. "Your soul will remain trapped within your body until the worms consume you. You will feel every excruciating moment as your body decays. The stench of your own rotting flesh will overwhelm your senses. You will feel and taste the bitter bile rising from your wicked belly to your throat. I know for a fact that werewolves prefer to bury their dead. Even when they freeze your body to preserve it before the funeral, you will feel the cold. To everyone, you will be as dead, yet all your senses will remain alive until you turn into dust."

After a minute, Raphael is fully paralyzed. He realizes that he can hear but cannot speak. He can see, smell and even taste the blood in his mouth but cannot spit. Suffocating yet clinging to life. He can think but cannot act. And so his hell has begun. Zendaya stands and takes two steps back before fainting. Jabu manages to catch her as she collapses.

"Babe. Are you alright?" Jabu shines a torch into her eyes to inspect.

"The curse," Zendaya manages a whisper.

Jabu wraps his hand around her waist to support her. "Shh. I know. Now was the worst time to use blood magic. It took everything you had. We need to move. The wolves are closing in." When he realizes that she is too weak, there is no other option. He carries her piggy back style and starts running. Despite the load he carries, the forge-witch is able to cover ground as if he was carrying nothing. He quickly puts distance between themselves and the scene of their battle.

The werewolves soon arrived at the scene where Raphael's lifeless body leaned against a tree. In the distance, the ground trembled as the much larger Xavi and the other alphas approached, their sheer size and strength evident in the way they plowed through trees without a second thought. Their shoulders are like bulldozers. Their hands swipe and cut trees out of their path like machetes swiping at grass. When Xavi arrives at the scene, his worst fear is a reality. Still in his monstrous form, he kneels and takes his son into his arms. Tears glistened on the fur that covered his monstrous body. Eyes that were usually fierce had now softened, betraying the pain that gnawed at the werewolf's soul as he weeps. The forest was alive with the mournful howls that emanated from his throat. Beneath its fur, the werewolf's muscles quivered, a visible manifestation of the emotional storm raging within. The rest of the alphas watch on as they change back to human form.

"Find them," Hakeem commands.

The werewolves sniff the ground. "There are two fresh scents.

They can't be far, go!" Kasa shouts. The werewolves lock into the scent and begin their pursuit.

Meanwhile, the female prison guard, exhausted and disoriented, finally emerges from the woods, but there is no car as promised. She spots Zendaya's truck parked next to the gravel road. Still trembling with horror, she feels the ground and picks up a rock, ready to smash the truck's window.

"Stop." Jabu's voice startles the guard, causing her to scream and drop the rock. The lights of the truck flicker on as Jabu opens it with the remote.

"Please. Help me," she squeals.

"Jump into the back," Jabu replies. The woman does not need a second invitation. By the time Jabu finishes securing Zendaya into the front seat, the woman has reclined in the backseat of the double-cab truck, panting as she struggles to catch her breath.

The werewolves burst out of the woods with ferocity, like bees swarming out of hell. Their growls echoed through the darkness, creating an eerie symphony of terror. They spot the truck. Its back wheels spin and its engine roars as it speeds away. The raptor thundered down the gravel road with remarkable acceleration. For a moment, it seemed as though the werewolves might close the gap, but soon the truck's horsepower prevailed, and it began to pull away, leaving the creatures behind in its wake.

Inside the vehicle, the prison guard watched the horrifying spectacle unfold through the rear window. "What the hell are those things?" she uttered, her voice trembling with fear and disbelief.

"Werewolves," Zendaya, who has just regained consciousness, answers.

"Welcome back, babe. How are you feeling?" Jabu asks.

"Like I was run over by a train. My head is pounding," she replied, wincing as she touched the side of her head, hoping to soothe the pain. Their attention shifts to the guard who is sobbing in the backseat. "Are you okay back there, sister?"

They wait for her to gather herself. "They almost had me. I don't even know how to jump start a car. If you had showed up a minute later, I would be dead right now."

"You are safe now. What's your name?"

The guard snorts and wipes her tears with her elbow. "Michelle."

"Nice to meet you Michelle. My name is Jabu. This is my wifey Zendaya."

"Thank you so much. Your husband saved my life."

"He is actually my boyfriend."

"Well, he deserves the promotion. Especially after all the heroics he pulled off." They all chuckle. Despite the darkness, Jabu's struggled to conceal his blush.

"Girl, I have never run so hard in my life. I don't even remember where or when I lost my wig."

"Brazilian." Zendaya asks.

"Peruvian. But I am just glad to be alive."

"True. A wig can be replaced. Your life is irreplaceable."

"What are you two doing out here anyway? I was sure there is nobody else in the area except us and those thugs...monsters or whatever they are."

"My brother was a prison guard. He disappeared a few months back. We found a clue that led us here. It turns out he was not as lucky as you were tonight. Maybe you knew him?"

"I doubt it. I only started at the prison last month. So sorry about your brother."

"What's this now?" Jabu's eyes follow a prisoner that appears in the path of his headlights as he crosses the road.

"Babe, Watchout." Zendaya shouts, but her warning came too late, and the collision was inevitable. Even though Jabu slams on the brakes, they collide with the chasing werewolf. The impact sends it flying as the airbags in the vehicle deploy. It lands a few meters away from the car. The bullbar absorbed some of the impact, but the engine stalls and smoke rises from the air vents on the hood.

"Everyone alright?" Jabu asks.

"I'm fine," Zendaya is the first to confirm.

"Michelle?"

"I'm good. What was that?" she asks.

"Another werewolf. Jabu pulls out the blood daggers. Wait here." He jumps out of the car and carefully approaches the werewolf with a torchlight in one hand and a dagger in the other. He takes a moment to inspect the creature. Its silver fur coat made it distinct from the others they had seen. From the way it breathes, he can tell that it is badly injured but alive. He plunged the blood dagger into the creature's eye and then curved it up into its brain, ending its life.

"Jabs, we need to get out of here." Zendaya shouts through the window. Jabu returns and jumps back into the driver's seat. Zendaya and Michelle have pressed the airbags out of their way as best as they can.

"I just needed to make sure it wouldn't come after us while we try to get the engine running again. Jabu turns the ignition to start the car. The engine sputters and goes silent. He tries again. It sputters and goes silent. "Come on, come on, come on." He pleads as he tries again and again.

"Oh my goodness, we are so dead!" Michelle mutters.

"Shut up Michelle." Jabu knows better than all of them just how close to death they are. His heightened senses nag him much louder than Michelle's panicked voice. The vibrations of the stampeding werewolves as they charge towards their location transfers through the wheels of the truck and Jabu can feel them through the steering wheel. He keeps it to himself while doing his best to keep calm. Hoping to avoid causing panic.

Zendaya watches on in silence. Her heart is pounding so hard and fast, if it was an engine, they could use it to jump start the car. Moments later, she and Michelle can both sense the approaching pack of werewolves as the force of their stampede causes the dashboard and other parts of the car to vibrate. Zendaya closes her eyes and she nervously swallows saliva. That's when she hears it. The engine sputters twice and roars into life. Jabu's foot slams the accelerator, causing the wheels to spin as they speed off. The engine is smoking and leaking but it is still able to produce all the horsepower they need. Elation erupted in the truck as they shouted and screamed in celebration of their narrow escape.

Michelle gets to catch another glimpse of the werewolves as they gather around their fallen comrade. As the road curved, she saw a few of them transforming back into human form, an eerie and surreal sight etched into her memory. "Nobody will ever believe me when I tell them what I saw and experienced tonight."

"Nobody should ever hear about it. Not if you want to keep yourself and your family safe." Zendaya replies with a firm tone.

"I wouldn't want my loved ones to experience anything like this."

"Then keep it to yourself. Not even the authorities can find out about this, you understand?"

Michelle nods." I won't tell a soul."

"That's my girl."

Xavi and the alphas finally catch up with the pack. His senses lock onto a familiar cherished scent, and there, on the gravel, he spots his daughter, unmistakable by the glimmer of her silver coat. Her own blood is her pillow. A rush of emotions floods through Xavi as he witnesses the lifeless figure of his beloved child, still in her beast form. He turns back to human form. The agony of the moment swells within him, manifesting in tear-streaked eyes that mirror the blood flowing from her lifeless eye. The pain his heart was already enduring is now doubled. He wishes he could see her human face again. When werewolves die, they retain whatever form they died in. And so, his daughter's corpse will remain in its werewolf form.

A mix of excruciating pain and unbridled rage overwhelms Xavi, and his body responds to the tumultuous emotions by involuntarily transforming into his powerful werewolf form once more. His mournful howls blend with the chorus of the pack, all raising their voices in eerie unison as they transform and gaze upon the luminous full moon above. They knew it would be a bloody night. They did not expect their own blood to be shed. The sound covers such a large distance that Zendaya, Jabu, and Michelle can hear them from afar. They discern the grief-stricken wails of the werewolves, but as a cold chill runs down their spines, they are aware that this is not merely a mournful cry; it's a resolute declaration of war.

CHAPTER
EIGHTEEN

NIGHTMARE

After narrowly escaping the werewolves, Jabu and Zendaya generously offered to give Michelle a ride home. She insisted on spending the rest of the night with them. She was hesitant to be alone after everything she had seen, unsure if she could protect herself. What she was sure of, is that Zendaya and Jabu know how to stay alive. She was also afraid of leading the werewolves to her family and putting their lives in danger. Zendaya and Jabu agreed to accommodate her for the night.

Zendaya thought she would be able to use the opportunity to ask Michelle more questions about the werewolves and her brother's murder. Unfortunately, Michelle was exhausted and after a quick meal, she fell asleep on the couch. Zendaya covered her with a small blanket and retreated with Jabu to their bedroom. They too were exhausted and fell asleep as soon as their heads hit the pillow, only to be woken up by the sound of Michelle screaming. For a moment, they thought they were under attack, but were relieved when they discovered Michelle was having a nightmare. She was sweating and in her struggle, had fallen from the sofa to the floor.

Zendaya rushed to Michelle's side, dropped to her knees, and enveloped her in a soothing embrace from behind. She helped Michelle to sit up and in hushed, calming tones, whispered words of assurance to her, attempting to quell the tumultuous emotions that had taken hold of Michelle's fragile state. "Michelle. Calm down, girl. You are alright. It's ok. You are safe."

"I dreamt they were here."

"The werewolves?"

Michelle nods. "I didn't mean to wake you. I am so sorry." The weight of the nightmare still lingered on Michelle's mind and expression, but the comfort of Zendaya's touch gradually eased her anxiety.

Zendaya hugs her tighter. "Ain't nothing to be sorry about. Not after what you've been through." Michelle pinches her eyes, holds on tight to Zendaya's wrists and taking slow deep breaths to calm herself down.

"Maybe the two of you can share our bed for the night. I can take the couch," Jabu offers.

"No. I can't allow you to do that. You've already gone above and beyond for me."

"Michelle, you need the rest. If you don't go to the bedroom, I'll sleep with you on the couch," Zendaya insists.

"Then we both won't get the rest we need. The couch is too small."

"It's not." Zendaya stands up and moves the pillows away from the sofa. She pulls the seat, and the sofa unfolds to transform into a bed big enough to fit two people comfortably. "My brother used to sleep on this couch whenever he would visit. We haven't had to unfold it since..." Zendaya finishes off her sentence with a shrug of the shoulders and goes silent. Just as she is about to sink into depression, Jabu's kiss on the neck and his arms on her shoulders yank her back.

"Let me get a bigger blanket and more pillows for you," Jabu offers. He dashes to the bedroom. In no time, he returns with a blanket and pillows, and soon the bed is set. He kisses his woman goodnight and switches off the light as he walks into the bedroom and closes the door.

The ladies lie on the bed and face opposite directions. Both are silent, with the weight of their thoughts keeping them awake. "I don't even have sleep anymore," Michelle eventually breaks the silence.

Zendaya considers taking the opportunity to ask Michelle questions, but she restrains herself, choosing instead to listen and support. "That's because you are still thinking about the werewolves."

"Yeah. But how can I think about anything else?"

"You have a family?"

"I have a daughter."

As the women turned to face each other, Zendaya lifted her head from the pillow, propping it up with her elbow. "Yeah? How old is she?"

Michelle keeps her head on her pillow and her hands tucked under it. "She is turning eight in July." There is a slight smile on her face. "It's just us two against the world."

"Who is she with now?"

"She is sleeping over at our landlord, Mrs. Shire's place. She looks after her whenever I work the night shift. They get along well, so she is in good hands. I want to walk back home tomorrow morning and just arrive like everything is still normal. Except it's not. I don't even think I still have a job."

"Michelle, if you go back to your job, you will end up in the hands of the same people that put you in this situation, and they will finish what they started."

"I know. But I have a daughter to feed, rent and bills to pay. My life has been turned upside down in just one night."

"How did the werewolves get you involved in their games?"

"Desperation. I am just a cleaner. I earn peanuts and I am drowning in debt. The same applies to many other people that work entry level jobs in the correctional services. They offered us a chance to sign up for an opportunity to win a million dollars if we were willing to participate in some type of sport. They made it sound like the chances of winning are high since you just had to run your own race. Get to the finish line and you win. I figured if I only had to win against myself, I had a good chance. I mean, who could lose against me? But when we got to the national park, all hell broke loose. Instead of running for a chance to win a million dollars, we were running for our lives. A race I would have lost if it wasn't for you and your husband. Oh excuse me, I meant boyfriend."

Zendaya chuckles. "Keep saying that and you may end up speaking it into reality."

"Well, what the hell is he wasting time for anyway? You seem like quite a catch."

Zendaya chimed in with a playful giggle. The ring she found in Jabu's pocket was at the back of her mind. "I don't know. I am sure he will make his move at the right moment."

"Oh, so you are expecting it."

"I am hopeful."

"Well, if tonight has taught us anything, it's that life is short. The best moment is always now."

"Yeah, well, make sure you tell that to him."

"Maybe I will." A brief moment of silence followed, allowing both Michelle and Zendaya to get lost in their own contemplations.

"So you and your boyfriend have magical powers."

Zendaya nods. "We are witches. Good witches."

"So there are bad ones?"

"Yes. But the less you know about our world, the better."

Michelle nods. "I agree. But I wish you had a sleeping potion in your bag of tricks, cause this girl can talk all night. Especially when she is anxious." They giggle.

Zendaya stares at Michelle and smiles. "It's not a potion. It's a spell. And it will help you sleep like a baby."

"I think I could really use that right now." Zendaya brushes Michelle's hair back, tucks it behind her ear and places her hand on her chick as she whispers an incantation. Michelle feels Zendaya's hand changing from cool to cup of coffee warm in an instant. Zendaya blinks once and Michelle involuntarily synchronizes her blinks with the witch's eyes. In slow motion, they blink two more times. But when they blink the third time, Michelle's eyes do not open as she sleeps peacefully. Zendaya turns to face the other way. There is nobody to put her to sleep. She would rather be sleeping in Jabu's arms, but if Michelle has another nightmare, her spell may break.

Zendaya's mind is now infiltrated by images of her deceased older brother, Zane. They had grown up together in the countryside under the watchful and caring eye of their parents who had purchased a farm house. In time, their mother would convert it into an orphanage for gifted children. As the memories flooded back, Zendaya's thoughts wandered to the countless afternoons they had spent playing together in the lush fields under the watchful eye of their parents. Their childish laughter echoed through the trees as they ran carefree. Their footsteps forming a symphony of joy.

As witches gifted with abilities that set them apart from others, their parents farmhouse in the country side offered the perfect location for them to explore their powers without fear of being exposed. Zane would use his elemental powers to turn the world into a playground of wonder and enchantment. In those moments, the bond between them grew stronger, forged not only by blood but by shared experiences that made their childhood truly magical.

She recalled how her brother always stood up for her, even when the odds were against them. When the details of her brother's passing did not make sense, her grief slowly transformed into resilience, and the memories of how he protected her became a source of strength. She refused to accept the conclusion that he was dead just because the Police declared it so without any concrete evidence. Even now, when she has heard directly from the murderer's own mouth that her brother is dead, she is not ready to delete his number as she stares at it on her phone and looks at it through eyes blurred by tears.

There isn't much left of the night, and she does not want to spend it all in the company of her thoughts. She decides to close her eyes and count her blessings as best as she could, hoping to gather strength for the next day. Soon she is fast asleep.

CHAPTER NINETEEN

GRIEF

As the sun gracefully ascends above the horizon, casting a warm golden glow on the Balsam mountains, nature awakens with the delicate morning dew adorning the flowers and trees. Amidst this picturesque scene, Xavi, once consumed by rage, now stands in profound sorrow. After he had turned back into human form, his subordinates tried to cover his nakedness with a blanket, but he ripped it apart. The blanket that covers him now is from their third attempt.

He stands between the lifeless bodies of his two children that have been laid next to each other on the ground. Bloodied clothes belonging to some of the victims from the previous night have been used to make temporary beds for the bodies. The rest of the pack has collected wood and is burning the last of the prisoners' and civilians' dead bodies.

Normally, they would have spent the night feasting on the flesh and bones of their victims. Not on this occasion. Not when two of their own have fallen. "Burn all the bodies," Xavi had commanded. "Nobody eats a morsel until we find them. The next time we feast, it will be on the flesh of the people that did this."

The breeze blows some of the ashes of the dead into Xavi's face. He does not blink, even as some of the residue lands directly in his eye. The ashes enter his eye with the wind and exit with a tear. Nearby, a chopper descends, its blades swirling the air and dust around him, but Xavi remains unyielding, a stoic figure amidst the chaos. He could almost be mistaken for another lifeless body amidst the tragic scene. Or perhaps a statue, so profound is his sense of loss and despair.

His daughter Valentina remains in the beast form she was in when she died. Raphael, on the other hand, is in his human form and can hear every conversation about his beloved sister's death as well as his own. He wants to cry, but he cannot. He wants to scream, but he cannot. He longs to hold and comfort his Father, but he cannot, because his father believes he is dead. He wants revenge, but he can do nothing. Raphael feels the wind from the chopper blades brushing against his skin as it lands. Pack members pull out two black coffins from the chopper and place him and his sister's bodies inside their respective coffins before they are closed and loaded onto the chopper. Their father boards and the chopper takes off while the pack watches on as it transports Xavi and his daughters' home where their mother awaits.

The pack watches in silence and pays their respects until the chopper vanishes into the distant sky. The Red Indian clan alpha, Kasa, breaks the silence. "We cannot disperse to our own homes while death visits our brothers' home and the perpetrators still run free. We must work together to find them".

"I agree," Hakeem of the New York clan remarks. "However, your skills and experience are of no use in this case. I am pretty sure those witches are from the city. And if that city is New York, my pack can find them."

"Are you saying you do not need the rest of us?"

"Nope. Not unless we are tracking rabbits. I don't see how you can be of any help, old man."

"Watch your tongue, Hakeem. You forget who you are talking to."

"Hakeem is right," Ketari steps in. "Besides, you are needed elsewhere." The matriarch commands respect even from her alpha husband as she places her hand on Kasa's shoulder, inspiring restraint. "You and Xavi have been friends longer than anyone else here. I think he needs your company at this time, whether or not he admits it. You should be by his side. That is where your presence can be most useful."

Kasa places his hand on top of Ketari's. "You speak with wisdom as always, my love. Very well. We leave this to you and your pack, Hakeem. Do not let us down."

"Well, if there is one thing I hate, it's witches that don't know how to keep their noses out of my business. So I am coming with you, Hakeem," Chance Decker remarks.

"Okay cowboy. Just make sure you keep up." Chance pinches the front of his cowboy hat as he nods. The two packs mount their bikes, their eyes on Hakeem as he delivers final instructions. "Right. This mountain is our territory. We respect it and it respects us. Every living creature that walks and breathes in these mountains respects us. At least that is what we believed. Last night, intruders entered our territory and challenged our sovereignty. Moreover, they hunted and slaughtered two of our own. That means we are no longer the apex predator on this mountain. I will not stand for that. Now, we do not know who the people that did this are, but we know they come from the city. A place I consider to be my pack's second hunting ground. We will ride into the city and we will ask questions. We saw the vehicle they drove. People will have seen it, especially with the damage it had. Ask around, find out who they are, and find them. We do not deserve to call ourselves apex predators until we feast on the flesh of those that dare to hunt us. LETS RIDE!!!" With a nod of his head, the engines roared to life in unison, filling the air with a thunderous symphony that was as much a declaration of freedom as it was a declaration of war.

One by one, the bikers kicked their machines into gear, the vibrations coursing through their bodies, becoming one with their steel steeds. The smell of gasoline and burning rubber lingered in the air, mingling with the faint scent of the forest as they left the gravel and entered the tarmac, headed towards New York city.

CHAPTER TWENTY

TERMINAL ILLNESS

Zendaya furrows her forehead, her smooth features momentarily creased with curiosity and annoyance as she feels a subtle vibration emanating from under her pillow. Her phone chimes, signaling an incoming message, but she chooses to ignore it, determined to reclaim the fleeting embrace of sleep. However, her tranquil rest is short-lived as the phone vibrates again. This time, it is accompanied by a persistently intensifying ringtone that grows louder every three seconds. Reluctantly, she reaches beneath her pillow, retrieves the device, and answers without sparing a glance at the caller identity on the glowing screen. Her voice, laden with weariness, emits a soft groan as she utters a muted, "Yes."

"Detective. Have you had a look at the results I just sent you?" The voice on the other end of the line is insistent, firm, and demanding of attention.

"Results? What results?" She speaks softly.

"DNA results for Mariah Jenkins."

Zendaya pops out of the blankets and sits up, her drowsiness dissipating in an instant. "Mrs. Grimshaw. I'm so sorry. Just a second please." She launches the email app on her phone, opens the attachment and quickly schemes through the contents. "It's not her. The ashes do not belong to Mariah Jenkins."

"That's right. And I bet you Mariah Jenkins is alive and knows what happened in that execution room. And I think she can be a key witness in proving my husband's innocence."

"Alright. Thank you, Mrs. Grimshaw. I have to go."

"Now hang on, young lady. Not so fast. You and I are not done yet."

"What is it?"

"We both know my husband did not fire you from the police force because you were a bad detective. He fired you because you are a brilliant detective and you were getting too close to his business for comfort. And right now, I need a good detective."

"To find Mariah Jenkins?"

"Precisely."

"Rest assured, if Mariah Jenkins is alive, I will find her. But I do not think I want to bring her to you."

Sofia clears her throat. "Detective, let's not ruin this good working relationship we have going on."

"I already have everything I need from you."

"But I can give you more information. Information that can help you expose and destroy the entire syndicate that was involved in the murder of your brother and so many other innocent victims. It's also an opportunity to prevent more deaths of innocent people." Sofia waits and listens to the sound of Zendaya's breathing as it grows heavy over the phone. "Come on detective. You know you want this."

"Fine. I will be in touch," Zendaya says before hanging up the phone.

"Morning ladies," Jabu enters the room, exuding warmth and charm. With a graceful swing of his foot, he gently closes the door behind him. In his hands, he balances three cups of coffee and a box of donuts. The aroma from the coffee envelopes the room in a comforting embrace. With their sleep vanquished by the phone call from Sofia Grimshaw, he finds Zendaya and Michelle seated comfortably, propped up by luxurious continental pillows. He walks up to Zendaya and kisses her forehead as he gives her a cup of coffee.

"Slept well?"

"Yeah. But not as good as I would have in your arms."

"That's my bad," Michelle remarks as Jabu hands her a cup. "If I was not such a baby last night, you could have slept in your man's arms."

"No worries, I am also just being a big baby. How did you sleep?"

"Like a baby. It felt like magic. Thanks to Zendaya."

"I'm glad I could help," says Zendaya.

"But I need to get back to my daughter."

"Oh, of course, you can use my shower."

"No, that's okay. I would rather shower at my place, if you don't mind. I really need to get home."

"Okay, I understand."

"Well, how about you grab a donut for the road and I take you straight home then," Jabu offers.

The ladies rise from the bed and Zendaya pulls in Michelle for a last hug. "Make sure you stay safe."

"I will, and thanks for everything." Michelle says, as she makes her way towards the door with Jabu following closely.

"Uhm, babe, you probably won't find me when you get back. I need to take a quick shower and make my way to see Gwen Jenkins.

The DNA test came back. It's not her mother's ashes."

"What?"

"I can't explain much now. But I will call and update you later."
Another kiss before Jabu follows Michelle out and Zendaya starts
getting ready to leave.

***

Michelle walks into her apartment building and looks back to wave
goodbye to Jabu as he drives off. Once she is inside, she runs upstairs to
her apartment. Within minutes, she was standing under the soothing
water of her shower, washing away the signs of everything she had
been through the previous night. When she is done and all dressed, she
dashes out again. She did not want to collect her daughter whilst
looking like a mess.

Now she makes her way to her landlord's apartment, located in the
same apartment block, and knocks. The door creaked as it opened,
revealing a gray-haired, wrinkled old woman with worry etched on her
face. "Michelle, Lord have mercy. I've been trying to get in touch with
you."

"I am so, so sorry, Ms. Shire. I got caught up at work."

"No, baby-girl, I'm sorry. Tatiana fell very ill while you were at
work. I had to rush her to the emergency room."

"Oh my goodness, where is she?"

"Bellevue hospital. Let me grab my jacket. I will come with you."

Michelle did not wait for Ms. Shire. Without wasting another moment, she took off, hailing a taxi with the hope of reaching the hospital as swiftly as possible. As she arrived at Bellevue hospital, her heart raced with apprehension. She hurried to the pediatric ward, where she found a nurse and doctor, deeply engrossed in discussion over her unconscious daughter. The room was filled with the mechanical sounds of life-support machines, creating an eerie atmosphere. "How is she?"

"Ms. Emmons. Tatiana is struggling. She urgently needs kidney transplant surgery. Even with the machine's assistance, she won't survive much longer if we don't take drastic action."

Michelle starts sobbing. "I am doing everything in my power to get the money I need for the surgery. I tried a go fund me campaign. I approached different people. I just need you to buy me more time, please."

"We are doing our best, Ms. Emmons. And I am not trying to cause you any grief or anxiety. We just need you to be aware of the critical point we are at right now."

Michelle sniffs. "Ok, I know, I know," says Michelle as the Doctor and nurse leave the room to give her time with her daughter. She walks to the other side of the bed and cries as she gently strokes her forehead. "Oh, my baby. You are such a brave little girl. Just hang on a little longer. Mommy will never let you die."

CHAPTER
TWENTY-ONE

BREAKTHROUGH

In the heart of New York City, amidst the bustling streets and towering skyscrapers, lies a gritty bar that exudes a unique blend of urban charm and rebellious spirit. The establishment is simply known as "Steel Thunder Tavern." Located in a hidden alleyway off a busy avenue, the bar is a haven for bikers and enthusiasts alike, attracting a diverse crowd of leather-clad riders and locals. The facade of the bar is unassuming, adorned with weathered metal signage and neon lights that flicker and buzz, showcasing the name in bold, fiery letters.

As you step inside, the atmosphere shifts dramatically. The dimly lit interior is bathed in warm hues of red and orange, giving it a rugged and inviting feel. Vintage motorcycle parts, road signs, and biker memorabilia adorn the walls, hinting at the bar's authentic biker heritage. The air is filled with the sweet, smoky scent of barbecue and aged whiskey, creating an intoxicating blend that lingers throughout the space. A classic rock playlist pumps through the speakers, perfectly complementing the bar's vibrant energy.

In one corner, a pool table stands as a focal point, attracting friendly competitions among patrons. The clinking of pool balls adds to the lively soundtrack of the bar. Meanwhile, vintage arcade games sit in another corner, enticing patrons to engage in spirited matches. The afternoon light filters in through the narrow windows, casting shadows on the well-worn wooden floor.

Towards the back of the tavern, a corner has been unofficially reserved for Hakeem's biker gang. He sits like a king on one of the leather couches that hugs the wall as one of his subordinates approaches him. "Boss. We combed the city and asked everyone about the description of that truck. So far, nobody knows who it belongs to. It's no use if we don't have the physical descriptions of those witches. Maybe they are not even from New York."

"Oh, they are definitely from here. The New York Yankees sticker on the side of that truck is all the confirmation I need," says Hakeem.

"We don't know what else to do, Boss."

"Hey Hakeem. Does this face look familiar to you?" Chance shows Hakeem a photo on his phone.

"Yeah. This is one of the two ladies that was first to run off last night. She was one of the prison employees that wanted a shot at the money."

"Yep. She just sent me a text asking for the reward money."

"Damn. That reward money doesn't even exist. Nobody ever survives the hunt."

"Well, it needs to exist. Because she wants it in exchange for the location of the witches."

"What guarantee do we have that she won't disappear after we give her the money?"

"We have a complete profile on every person that took part in the hunt and she knows it. I don't think she would risk it. Also, she needs the money for her sick daughter."

"Then I believe we have the breakthrough we need. Call Xavi."

Chance calls Xavi and starts talking to him on the phone. After a brief conversation, he hangs up the phone and types a text requesting bank account details from Michelle. Within two hours, Michelle's phone chymes with a bank notification confirming that One million dollars has been deposited into her bank account.

PART FOUR

IRONWOOD

CHAPTER TWENTY-TWO

ALLIES

Gwen observed the way her mother had wrapped herself tightly in a blanket, creating a cocoon-like shape on the couch. "Mom, you need to eat something. Otherwise you will starve."

Mariah looked up, her tone and expression haunted by a hunger that surpassed mere food cravings. "I'm starving already. But not for food."

"You mean..?"

"I need blood. And my stomach will not hold anything down until I get some." Mariah notices the nervous look on Gwen's face when she hears her words. "Oh, don't worry baby. I won't hurt any of you. Thanks to you, I can control my hunger."

Gwen blinks in rapid succession and lets out a sigh. "I trust you, Mom. But I also want to help you."

Mariah rose from the couch, taking Gwen's hands in her own. "Gundo is the one who has been supplying me with all the blood I need. This is another reason I need to find a way to save him. There is still so much he needs to teach me so I can be able to live some type of normal life and be independent."

The doorbell interrupts Gwen just as she takes in a breath to fuel her response. "Hold that thought, Mom." She paces to the door and opens. "Detective."

"Hello Gwen. I am sorry for just rocking up unannounced, but..." Zendaya's words trailed off as she caught sight of Mariah standing behind Gwen, a look of surprise spreading across her face. "Oh my goodness."

"Now is not a good time." Gwen tries to close the door, but Zendaya blocks it with her foot. "Gwen, I can help you."

"We no longer need your help?"

"She is a vampire, isn't she?"

Mariah steps forward. "How did you know that?"

"I am a witch. My specialty is bending and breaking the laws of souls. I've been around vampires before and I have sensed their souls. They feel exactly like your mother's." Gwen turns to look at her mother. "I also know you are a witch, Gwen. I couldn't sense it the last time I was here, but I can sense it now. It means you recently tapped into your power."

Gwen pauses and regards Zendaya for a moment. "Alright. Come inside." Zendaya walks in and Gwen shuts the door behind them. No seat is offered as all three ladies stand in the middle of the room, forming a triangular formation.

"Hello Mariah," Zendaya greets.

Mariah acknowledges her with a nod. "What exactly does a vampire soul feel like?" she asks.

"It feels like multiple personalities. A human. A predator. And something else which I can't quite describe. Something cold, as if death is beckoning for something it can never reach. Alive but without feeling. Vampires strive to master a balance of these three energies. And right now, I can feel that the human part of you is in control. But you are fighting back the predator."

"She needs to feed," says Gwen. "Can you help us?"

"If you give me a few hours, yes."

Gwen looks at Mariah. "Mom?"

"A few hours are more than good enough. I will be fine."

"I also need your help. The reason I am here is because the DNA results came back, but you already knew your mother was alive. Mariah, I've already pieced a few of the pieces together, but I need you to complete this puzzle for me. I need to know what happened in that execution room."

Gwen and Mariah look at each other. "I think we should sit." Mariah offers. She tells Zendaya about all the events that transpired and finally led her back to her daughter. It is the second time that Gwen hears the account, but she listens as if it is the first time. They also explain how Lupita and the vampires kidnapped Gundo. Zendaya, no stranger to the supernatural world, remained composed yet fascinated by their narrative. When Mariah is done, Zendaya tells them about the police commissioner, his activities with the werewolves and how it is connected to her brother's death.

"Commissioner Grimshaw is an evil man. He abused his power to make sure I end up on death row, even though I was innocent. I was fortunate enough to find some type of salvation. I am so sorry you lost your brother to these monsters," says Mariah. She and Gwen both notice the aura of sadness that has taken over Zendaya since she started telling them about her brother. There is a minute of silence that follows, as if it was dedicated to Zendaya's brother. The stillness in the room is broken when Zendaya's phone starts ringing. She answers and as soon as she places it on her ear, the caller starts talking in a Mexican accent.

"Listen carefully, you filthy witch. I know you and your stinking boyfriend are responsible for killing my children."

Visibly shaken, Zendaya rose to her feet, her composure barely intact. "Xavi Gonzalez."

"It's the grim ripper to you, bitch," Xavi sneered. "And I have your lover boy." Zendaya's chest tightened as she struggled for a deep breath, trying to cement her crumbling composure. Mariah and Gwen, sensing that something was wrong, rose and stood beside her. "After I hang up the phone, I will send you a location. You have one hour to get here. Every minute you are late, I will feed a part of his body to my pack until there is nothing left." Xavi hangs up.

"What's wrong?" Gwen asks.

The horror on Zendaya's face is unmistakable. "The werewolves. They have my boyfriend."

"How did they find you guys?"

"I am not sure, but I have to help him."

"You can't face a pack of werewolves on your own. He is forcing you to walk straight into a death trap." Mariah points out.

"I have to try," Zendaya insisted, her determination unwavering. "Jabu would also come for me."

"Then I am going with you."

"Me too. Gwen adds."

"No. I know vampires are strong, but you haven't fed in a while. You are too weak. And Gwen, you have a daughter to raise. I can sense her soul upstairs."

"Young lady. We are not letting you walk into that death trap on your own," Mariah countered.

"My mom is right," says Gwen. She unbuttons her shirt and starts folding her sleeves. "I can't go with you, but I can do something to help." She holds out her arm, exposing her wrist to her mother.

"Gwen. I can't feed on you."

"Yes, you can. It's the only way you can have the strength to help Zendaya."

"I don't want to hurt you."

Gwen gets closer and looks straight into her mother's eyes. "You can never hurt me Mom. I trust you."

Mariah's heart swells with pride as she gazes into her daughter's eyes, noticing the unwavering fearlessness shining through them. Her emotions well up, and a single tear escapes her eye before she bravely takes Gwen's wrist into her grasp. With a determined yet remorseful expression, she sinks her fangs into her daughter's tender flesh. Gwen winces, the pain slowly intensifying, causing her to let out soft moans as they both sink to their knees. "Gwen, are you alright?" Zendaya asks as she approaches and holds Gwen's shoulders to support her. "Should I stop her?"

"No. I am fine."

"Gwen, I think you have given enough…?" Just as Zendaya is about to pull her back, Mariah withdraws her fangs and applies pressure to the wound, stemming the flow of blood. Gwen collapses to the floor, and Mariah's features briefly contort with fright. Her trembling hands betray her panic as she checks on her daughter. She bares her blood dripping fangs and lets out a hiss. The black protruding veins surrounding her eyes subside and her fangs retract. In a few moments, she is back to normal.

"Gwen? Baby? Are you okay? Oh my goodness, I think I went too far?" Mariah exclaims.

"Just help me up," Gwen asks. They assist her, but she can only get on one knee. "Ok. Step back." She closes her eyes, crosses her hands on her chest and starts chanting an incantation as Zendaya and Mariah take a few steps backwards. An emerald circle of glowing runes materializes beneath Gwen, resembling a radiant carpet. In no time, the bite wounds are perfectly healed. Her pale complexion goes back to a healthy amber hue as her iron and blood levels are restored.

"What a wonderful and rare gift. I think she is bending the laws of reality and time combined," Zendaya remarks. When the runes vanish, Gwen stands to her feet, as healthy as she was before her mother fed on her. "You, madam, are a very powerful witch."

Gwen smiles and curtseys. "Thank you. But you are running out of time. You better go get your man."

"Thank you. Both of you. And I intend to return the favor," says Zendaya. "Once we save Jabu, we will have a team strong enough to save your Gundo."

"We would appreciate the help," says Mariah.

Gwen hugs her mother. "I will stay here and cook dinner. For all of us."

"And we will make sure we are back in time for dinner. All of us," says Mariah.

"Damn right." Zendaya confirms as they walk out. Gwen stands at the door and watches as they drive away.

CHAPTER TWENTY-THREE

ONE FOOT IN THE GRAVE

The sound of the gravel crunching beneath the tyres fills the car as Zendaya and Mariah turn onto the long road that leads to a large plot with black swing gates guarding the entrance. As soon as the truck comes to a halt, Zendaya hoots.

"Baby-girl, I know you saw the big sign that says do not hoot."

"I did Mama Jenkins. I couldn't resist."

Mariah shakes her head. "Talk about starting on the wrong foot."

"Girl, just by showing up we already have one foot in the grave, so I ain't worried."

The remote controlled gate swings open into the sprawling yard beyond as they slowly drive in. "So, you said you have a plan, right?" Mariah asks.

"I do."

"Mind filling me in."

"We don't have time. Don't worry, I will handle everything. And if it goes well, we should all make it out without a scratch."

"And if it doesn't work? Do you have a Plan B?"

Zendaya steers the car around a large fountain, pulling over beside the majestic stairs leading to the foyer. "It has to work. Otherwise we are dead." Two security officers open the doors and drag them out by their elbows.

One of the security werewolves sniffs around Mariah's neck. With a disdainful sneer, he addressed her, "A vampire, huh? We treat your kind like cockroaches around here. We exterminate you. You stay here with us. We can't allow a pest to go into the house." His grip was firm as he pressed down on her shoulder, forcing her to sit on the stairs.

"Zendaya," Mariah called out.

"Don't worry. Do as they say. We will be fine." The werewolves ushered Zendaya up a grand staircase and through a massive door, leading them into a spacious hall adorned with solemn photographs. Each frame displayed the alphas who had come before Xavi. Images of powerful leaders who have led the family in the past. Deeper within the hall, Xavi stood in the middle of the room, his face turned away, fixated on an elaborate family tree adorning the innermost wall. The tree depicted generations of his family, including his wife and children, all intertwined in their proud lineage. Nearby, Jabu kneeled with bound hands and a silenced mouth, clearly distressed.

You shouldn't have come babe, Jabu thinks to himself as he sees Zendaya approaching with the security escort.

"This is my family tree," Xavi speaks, his voice loud and arrogant, never turning to face Zendaya. "Raphael and Valentina were supposed to be next to add their children to this family tree. Now, thanks to you, that will never happen." Slowly, he turned to lock eyes with Zendaya. "I will smear your blood on this very wall as a symbol of what happens to people who bring harm to my family."

"You do not scare me. And I don't regret killing your children, just as you all felt no remorse when you killed all those innocent people," Zendaya retorted.

"Innocent people? You mean all the crooks, murderers, and rapists?"

"Zane Zabalaza," Zendaya's voice erupted, raw with emotion. "That is my brother's name. He was no murderer or rapist. In fact, you assholes killed him because he refused to take part in your sick, twisted games."

Xavi's grin widened, his demeanor smug and arrogant, as he retorted. "Under normal circumstances, I would not know who that is. We do not memorize the names of our food." His words drew amused chuckles from the other Alphas, further stoking Zendaya's fury. "When I learned that you were witches, I knew who you were coming for. During our last hunt, your brother almost ruined everything with his elemental powers, but he was no match for us. Once he was restrained, we were tempted to kill him. But then I remembered, when a witch is turned into a werewolf, they do not become any ordinary werewolf." As Xavi spoke, distant growls echoed in the room, gradually intensifying. Zendaya couldn't pinpoint their origin until Xavi took a few steps back, drawing her attention to a concealed trapdoor beneath his feet. The sounds of struggle emanating from below hinted at something sinister. The air in the room intensified as Xavi elaborated with a glint of excitement in his eyes. "These hybrid werewolves are a force to be reckoned with, almost as powerful as a hellhound. They are vicious monsters, only able to revert to human form during an eclipse or at their master's will. They submit solely to the werewolf that turned them. I couldn't resist the rare opportunity to add such a monstrous creation to my collection. And so I bit your brother and gifted him with a higher existence than the one he had lived his entire life. I turned him into my pet." With a snap of his fingers, the steel trap door creaked open, revealing a terrifying sight. A werewolf, unlike any other, emerged, moving on all fours. Its mouth foamed, saliva dripping constantly, while its menacing growls caused vibrations that rattled the room. Its fur, a pale gray with red patches of bloodstains on it, remnants of victims it has recently devoured. Its size is so large, it can lock eyes with a tall man. Four of Xavi's strongest subordinates struggled to hold the beast back, their grip on the chain leash tenuous at best. "I won't lie," Xavi exclaimed. "This creature scares even me."

Horror and disbelief twisted Zendaya's delicate features, etching a profound shock upon her face as the devastating revelation unfurled before her. "That's impossible. Your son said you murdered my brother," she uttered, her voice trembling like a cauldron of emotions.

"Raphael likely said what he said to pour salt to your wound and hurt you, just as you were hurting him. Also, he told you what was good for the pack. Witches have a tendency of becoming stubborn pests in other people's business. He knew if he told you the truth, you would come looking for your brother. Maybe bring more witches and cause us more trouble." The rabid werewolf, still seething with rage, strained against the restraint of the four sturdy men. "Shut up and sit!" Xavi bellowed in its direction, and the werewolf's ferocious growling subsided as it obeyed, though a low growl continued to emanate from deep within its throat.

"I don't believe you. That monster cannot be my brother," Zendaya protested vehemently.

"Oh, I assure you, that is your brother. See how he obeys me like a loyal pet," he sneered.

Desperate to prove her instincts wrong, Zendaya closed her eyes tightly, delving deep into her innate power, seeking her brother's soul amidst the chaos that surrounded them. With unwavering determination, she attempted to forge a connection with the once familiar energy that defined Zane. What greeted her senses was the overwhelming darkness emanating from the imposing figure of the werewolf standing before her. Doubt gnawed at her resolve, threatening to shatter her hope. Yet, just as despair began to loom, a glimmer of warmth pierced through the shadows, like a distant beacon of light in a pitch-black night. It was a flicker of what once was the reciprocating love between siblings, the unbreakable bond they had shared, and the essence of home that had always been embodied in Zane.

As the realization washed over her, validating her deepest fears, Zendaya's eyes flew open, their vibrant hue widened and red with shock, sorrow, and fury. Tears spilled over her cheeks, their salty trails tracing a path of anguish, while her heart clenched in pain. She let out a gasp, her voice choking with emotion, she whispered, "Zane. No. What have they done to you?" Yet, in the same breath, she steeled herself with newfound resolve, knowing that her brother was still alive and that she had an opportunity—a chance to save him from this nightmarish fate. Her eyes meet Jabu's, filled with unspoken emotions. He seeks confirmation, and she nods gently, acknowledging that the monster before them is her brother. His head hangs low as he succumbs to the overwhelming feeling of their helpless situation.

"As you can see, we never killed your brother. So preach to me again about how you are better than us when you have murdered my children." Xavi grits his teeth as he fights back tears. "Now, you will watch as your brother shreds your stinking boyfriend into pieces. When he is done, he will rip you apart and devour you as well. I will smear your blood on the pictures of my children on our family tree, so their souls can rest knowing that their father avenged them. As for your brother, he will remain my dog for eternity, paying your blood debt."

With a low, haunting whistle, Xavi signaled the rabid werewolf, its jaws salivating in anticipation. Jabu, trembling with fear, choked back a desperate "no" and tried to rise, but Hakeem forcefully pressed him back to his knees. "If you try to stand up again, I will decapitate you," Hakeem warns him.

"If you lay a finger on him, you will never see Raphael again."

Xavi's eyes glow red as he growls. "Are you mocking me? You think this is a game?"

"I am not toying with you. You took my boyfriend hostage, not realizing that I already had a hostage of my own. Raphael is not dead...yet! You forget. We are witches."

"You are bluffing?"

"Then call my bluff."

A tense silence engulfs the air. Xavi and Zendaya lock eyes in a fierce, unwavering stare down. "What are you saying, witch? Speak plainly."

"Your son is not dead," Zendaya's voice resonated with an eerie, chilling conviction. "I cursed him so his soul would never leave his body till his flesh and bones rot and wither away. He will experience hunger, pain and suffer as the worms feast on his flesh. He will even endure the smell of his own rotting corpse. Even now, he can hear us and everything around him. He can still feel when you touch him, but he cannot react. It is a special curse made for evil people like you and your son. I call it death's beckoning. This is what I do to people that mess with my family. And if you harm Jabu, me, or my brother, you will be condemning him to unimaginable suffering. I am the only person that can release the curse."

"Lies. All lies," Xavi erupted, his voice betraying a mixture of fury and fear of the possibility.

"If you are so sure about that, go ahead and kill us." Xavi burst into his formidable werewolf form, gripping Zendaya by the neck, and suspending her midair. Jabu's heart almost stops at the sight of it.

"Xavi, wait," Ketari shouts. "Do not be rash as if we are helpless. You forget. I am a shaman. If the boy's spirit is still in his body, I will know." After a momentary stillness, Xavi transforms back into his now naked human form, releasing Zendaya as she falls to the floor, gasping for breath. "If Raphael still lives, shouldn't you have sensed it before now?" he challenged Ketari.

"It is not as straightforward as you believe," Ketari replied, her gaze steady. "Especially when a curse has been deliberately woven to conceal the presence of life and his soul."

"Very well, Ketari," Xavi relented, his impatience still palpable. "Hurry then. This wretched witch should have met her end already."

"Bring my things," Ketari commands with authority, and one of her trusted subordinates swiftly departs. He soon returns with a finely crafted leather pouch. She opens it and pulls out a clay bowl and essence. Her every move exudes an air of mystique, wisdom and confidence. "If Raphael is still in this body, the smoke will not rise. It will cover his body like a blanket." She explains as she places the bowl on Raphael's forehead and prepares for the ritual.

"Can you maybe put some clothes on in the meantime?" Zendaya taunts Xavi.

"Fuck you, witch," Xavi spits in her direction. Jabu can't hold back a muffled laughter, but soon regrets it as Hakeem punches him in the stomach.

As Ketari burns the incense, the smoke starts moving from Raphael's head and makes its way down, covering his entire body. It does not rise. Even when Ketari tries to blow at it, it is not affected. "She tells the truth. What a wicked curse," Ketari confirms with trembling hands.

"Not as wicked as you people are," Zendaya responds.

Xavi turned to face Zendaya, his eyes now reflecting a crimson hue as tears welled up, tracing a path down his cheeks. His twitching eyebrows arched with a mix of anger and vulnerability as he spoke sharply, "What do you want, witch?"

"You can start by releasing my boyfriend." Xavi turns to look at Hakeem, who opens his palm to extract his claws, effortlessly slicing through the ropes that bound Jabu. Jabu wasted no time, rising to his feet and tearing off the duct tape from his mouth before rushing to embrace Zendaya. They can only afford each other a moment before she refocuses on the mission at hand. "Now, my friend should be just outside the door. Order your men to let her in," Zendaya requested, prompting one of the werewolves to place a call to the security guard outside, who swiftly allowed Mariah entry. As she stepped into the hall, the werewolves' irritation was unmistakable.

Taking a deep breath to compose himself, Xavi spoke firmly, "You brought a stinking vampire onto my premises. You're truly testing my patience."

"No Xavi, I am testing your love for your son," Zendaya retorted. "This is Mariah. Don't worry, she's a friendly vampire. As much as you might want to harm her, you can't. However, I do have other vampires I'd like you to deal with. Once that's done, I'll release your son."

"And who might these vampires be?"

"A group of three vampires and a witch from an African guild. They kidnapped someone that is dear to me," Mariah explains.

"We only need you and the other alphas. We don't need your henchmen. Bring my brother as well," Zendaya adds.

"Your brother? He is lost to me forever. Only I can control him. There is no cure for this," Xavi declared.

Zendaya is quick to retort. "Just do as I say."

"And how do I know you will keep your end of the deal?"

Zendaya's response held a subtle weight of confidence as she took three steps forward. "There is no shift of power here; you are still at an advantage. Especially since you have my brother. When all this is done, we just need to work out a safe way for me to remove the curse from your son with the guarantee that we will be allowed to walk away."

With emotions running high, Xavi closed the distance between them, engaging in another tense stare-down. Zendaya met his gaze head-on, her eyes unwavering despite the intensity of his blazing eyes. A moment of silent understanding passed between them, both aware that neither would give up easily. "I will never let you get away," he growls.

"I know. But this is your only chance to get your son back. As for us, you will have to chase us down another day." After a few more seconds of staring daggers into Zendaya's eyes, Xavi finally broke the intense gaze as he stepped back and walked towards his subordinates. The werewolves move in around him for a group huddle. Zendaya, Mariah and Jabu also move a few steps back for their own group huddle.

"Alright baby girl, I am impressed. But what's next?"

"Well, we have ourselves a pack of alphas to help us rescue Gundo," Zendaya responds.

"But how do we find him?" Mariah asks.

"I think that one is easy," Jabu steps in. "The fastest way to travel around the world is the enchanted subway. One of the greatest feats of magical engineering ever built. You see, it uses the sunrise and sunset as platforms for space-time traveling. If you are on the train when the sun sets on one side of the world, you can fast travel to another country on the other side of the world where the sun is rising. That would be the best and fastest way to transport Gundo from America to Africa. No dealing with airport logistics and security issues. They would have had to wait for the sunset to board and teleport using the sunrise in Africa."

"That's about two hours from now. Do you know where we can find the subway?"

"It's hidden below the Hudson subway station, close to where the old locomotives are. Very few witches know about it, so it's also the most discrete option they have."

"We have about an hour before the sun sets. We need to get moving," Zendaya points out.

"And after the werewolves help us rescue Gundo, how do we get away from the werewolves?"

"One thing at a time Mariah. I promise we will cross that bridge when we get to it," Zendaya assures her. They all turn and wait for the werewolves who are standing in a circle a few meters from them, still deep in discussions.

"What about your brother?" Jabu asks.

"I don't know. We will have to figure something out. No matter what happens, I am not going home without Zane."

All the werewolves have huddled around Xavi as they take instructions from him. "Ketari, I need you to find out if there is a way to break the curse without the witch. And I need you to hurry. If you figure it out, let me know. This witch has trampled on my family's honor. And now she means to use me like a puppet. As if we are pets she can play fetch with. I will not have this. The sooner we find a way to break the curse and free Raphael, the sooner we can break the hold she has on us and make her pay."

"Leave it to me. With magic, there are always options," Ketari assures Xavi as she breaks from the group and immediately departs from the hall.

"The rest of you, stay here and give Ketari any support she may need. Protect our home and our family. Tell my wife nothing until we have saved Raphael. If she finds out what her son is suffering, it will break her further. They think they have a better chance of escaping four alphas than an entire pack of werewolves. They couldn't be more mistaken." The group separates as the four alphas approach Zendaya and the rest of the pack moves back. "Very well, witch. Lead the way."

"Glad you made the right decision." Zendaya whistles towards the werewolves as if whistling to a dog. "Now come on, we need to hurry. Time is not on our side." The alpha werewolves' eyes all glow red as the insult enrages them, but they all restrain themselves.

"Must you provoke them like that? They hate us enough as it is," Jabu asks.

"Mind games babe. It's all mind games."

With their minds set, the pack followed Zendaya's lead, swiftly piling into their trucks as they made their way to the Hudson railway station.

CHAPTER TWENTY-FOUR

IRONWOOD

In the quaint town of Watervliet, New York, where the Delaware and Hudson Railway snakes through the landscape, there lies a hidden secret that few in the supernatural world are privy to. Nestled alongside the active railway line, a disused stretch of track remains obscured from the public eye, veiled by nature's embrace and the passage of time. Forgotten by most, this clandestine underground railroad level harbors a marvel of magic that few in the supernatural world still know about, and even fewer make use of.

Amidst the overgrown foliage and rusted remnants of locomotives, passenger cars, and freight wagons, there lies an inconspicuous broken locomotive, weathered by decades of abandonment. Yet, within the husk of this once-powerful machine, one of the carts, battered and dilapidated, serves as an elevator, its mechanisms still surprisingly functional. Its generous dimensions allow Lupita, Dabula, Yaya and Ramsey to step aboard, along with the coffin that holds Gundo floating closely behind them. With a careful pull of a hidden lever, the broken locomotive's rusty cart whirrs to life, grudgingly descending like an elevator on an ancient pulley system. As it descends, the cart emits a low, eerie hum, reminiscent of whispers from the past. Only the inner part of it descends as its shell remains above the surface so that any prying eyes see nothing out of place.

Once they are below the earth's surface, the group find themselves transported to a hidden world. When they step out, the cart automatically returns to the surface, erasing any trace of their passage.

The platform they step onto is a paradox—a seamless blend of history and decay, preserved in an eternal moment of silence. Dimly lit by faintly flickering gas lamps salvaged from the past, the walls bear the marks of time, wearing the scars of existence like badges of honor. The underground platform stretches far into the distance, its perspective shrouded by the shadowy embrace of the tunnels. Bats flit silently through the air, their wings brushing against echoes of bygone locomotives, and rats scurry along the tracks, drawn by a forgotten familiarity. The air is cool and musty, carrying a faint aroma of old wood, iron, and damp earth. Moss blankets the tracks, and delicate spiderwebs adorn the corners, weaving intricate patterns as if shadowing the powerful ancient spells that were conjured to build the railway and the space time traveling train they now await.

"I told you we were too early. And I hate waiting," Dabula groaned.

Lupita smiled gently, countering, "It's almost sunset. 30 minutes is a short waiting time to experience this magical train."

"I still hate waiting."

"Even when you are waiting with me?" Lupita teased, her eyes sparkling.

"Waiting with you is just fine babe. It's waiting for you that rubs me off the wrong way. Like when you shop for clothes or do your hair and I have to just sit there and wait."

"You don't just sit there when I shop, you are meant to assist me. Tell me which outfits work and which ones don't work."

"Everything works on you babe."

"Such a liar," Lupita tilts her head backward and places her hand on Dabula's chick as she stood on her toes to extend her reach and leaned in for a kiss. "What's wrong?" she asked when Dabula suddenly stopped kissing her, his gaze darting from side to side as if searching for something.

"Do you smell that?" Dabula asks.

"Werewolves," Ramsey confirms.

"What are these filthy beasts doing here?" Dabula asks as their senses identify the direction and tunnel from which the werewolves are approaching. "This feels like an ambush, like they have been waiting for us."

"It doesn't matter. They can do nothing if they can't breathe," Lupita declares, her voice steady but her heart pounding fiercely in her chest. She senses the vibrations of the charging werewolves beneath her feet. Her nerves are on edge. Standing shoulder to shoulder with the vampires, Lupita keeps her gaze fixed on the dark, curving tunnel ahead, where the ominous sounds of the werewolves' approach grow louder by the second.

The vampires begin to hiss menacingly as they catch sight of the sets of glowing red eyes piercing through the darkness. Four werewolves emerge into view, three running with grace on the tunnel's roof and sides, their claws allowing them to cling to the walls and roof of the tunnel. Two more are prowling ferociously on the ground. These creatures are nothing short of formidable. Their massive forms exuding both strength and untamed fury, their breaths visible as steam in the chilly air.

"They are all alphas," Dabula observes, a hint of apprehension coloring his words as he realizes the sheer size and power of these werewolves, far surpassing the average. Xavi and the hybrid werewolf Zane, run side by side on the floor of the tunnel. They are too large and heavy to cling to the roof and run upside down like the others. So powerful the sheer force of their strides leaves deep imprints on the concrete. There is no chain leash on Zane's neck and no werewolves to holding him back, but he is obediently under Xavi's control, sired to him and tethered to his will.

The vampires take three steps back and put on their oxygen masks. Every fiber of their being can sense the murderous intent in the werewolves' eyes. Lupita steps forward as they move into a V shaped formation. She holds her open hand out and closes it into a fist. The tunnel is drained of oxygen, causing the werewolves to collapse in their stride as they struggle for breath. Dust fills the tunnel as werewolf bodies slide on the ground and come to a halt.

Just as Dabula is about to give the order for the vampires to move in for the kill, he instinctively tilts his head sideways to duck a dagger that still manages to strike and damage the small oxygen tank on his mask. Yaya is not so fortunate as another dagger pierces through his oxygen mask, into his mouth, and the blade sticks out through the back of his head. The force sends him into a backward fall. Before he can try to pull it out, the blood dagger retracts itself and flies back to its master, leaving Yaya wounded, disoriented, and unable to breathe. But vampires are rapid healers.

Lupita panics when he notices that Dabula and Yaya have lost their oxygen supply and are suffocating. She restores the oxygen. The werewolves who were about to pass out gasp for air. As soon as they catch enough breath, they renew their assault. Lupita panics and extracts the oxygen again, causing the werewolves to collapse once more. She orchestrates a cycle of controlled deprivation, depriving the werewolves of oxygen at crucial moments, causing them to collapse repeatedly.

Ramsey, realizing that they need to buy Lupita time, takes in a deep breath before taking off his oxygen mask and tossing it towards Dabula, but a dagger strikes it mid air and damages the oxygen tank. Lupita is forced to restore the oxygen once again. The vampires all take deep breaths and stagger back to their feet. They have once more regained their breath and begin charging harder than ever. Once Lupita is sure that all her comrades have pulled in enough breath, she holds out her arms and again withdraws all the oxygen from the tunnel. The werewolves collapse once more. Dust fills the tunnel as they slide on the ground. This time, Lupita holds back the oxygen for longer and it proves too much for the werewolves. Their bodies return to their human form which uses less oxygen, as a coping mechanism. Zane, bound to his beast form until Xavi wills otherwise, fails to transform to his human form.

Lupita meticulously delays the restoration of oxygen, ensuring that Zane, whose beast form requires copious amounts of air, succumbs to unconsciousness. The vampires themselves struggle, their faces contorting, and veins bulging, as they fight to retain their last breaths. Finally, when Lupita is confident that the werewolves are incapacitated, she quickly restores the oxygen, allowing her comrades to recover.

"Kill them before they transform again," Dabula barks an order as Lupita helps him back to his feet. Even in their human form, the alphas are formidable. Their body's waste no time in restoring the vital oxygen they need, quickly amplifying their power. They wrestle the vampires and buy themselves enough time to recover enough oxygen in their bodies. Even without the hybrid, Zane, it's three against three as Chance, Hakeem and Kasa morph once more into their beast form, overpowering Yaya and Ramsey, who were already in their grip.

Dabula picks up Xavi, who is till in human form by the hair and thrusts a fist into his stomach, hoping to punch a hole through it. To his astonishment, it is as though he strikes an impenetrable concrete wall, with Xavi's dwarf body barely swaying from the impact. A wry smile dances on Xavi's lips, reveling in Dabula's feeble attempt, only to respond by unleashing his own transformation into beast mode. In a fluid motion, he grabs both Lupita and Dabula by the neck in either hand, suspending them in the air. The other alphas prove too powerful for the young vampires. Ramsey and Yaya are all decapitated with a bite to the head. Vampire flesh is the only flesh apart from that of their own kind the werewolves spit out. Lupita and Xavi want to scream for their comrades, but Xavi's vice grip grants them no such privilege.

Xavi's gaze locks onto Lupita's, and a chilling sense of impending doom washes over her. She can see the malevolence in the monster's eyes, and fear takes hold of her. That's when she sees a hand reach out from behind Xavi and it rests on his shoulder. Zendaya quickly does a body switch, leaving her limp body to collapse to the ground with Xavi's unconscious soul inside it. Lupita and Dabula are now in her grasp.

Meanwhile, Zane, still in his beast form, starts moving and showing signs of regaining consciousness as oxygen is restored to his body. Zendaya, while inhabiting Xavi's body, discovers its perks. She can feel the power and strength coursing through its veins. The senses that are intensified beyond human comprehension. The scents around her were no longer mere odours, but vivid and telling messages. The sounds in the tunnels were a symphony of secrets, and every movement of the nocturnal creatures around them was a vibrant dance. More importantly, she can feel the tether that connects the sire and the sired. The leash that Xavi uses to control her brother. Using her craft as a practitioner of the supernatural laws of souls, she attempts to break the tether, but it is too sinister and strong. It's like trying to stop the mightiest river from flowing into the ocean. Nonetheless, her connection with her brother is not water, it is blood. And what she cannot prevent, she decides to divert. If she can't stop the river from flowing into the ocean, she will change the ocean to which it flows. Their bond is strong, allowing her to tether his soul to hers instead.

The other alpha werewolves watch in bewilderment as Zane, whom they believed had recovered to bolster their numbers, transforms back into human form as Zendaya wills it. The metamorphosis began with a gut-wrenching snarl that pierced through the air. The hybrid werewolf writhed on the cold floor, its monstrous form contorting with pain. Bones crackle and muscles strain as the beast reluctantly begins its involuntary transformation back to human form. The werewolf's fur began to recede, and its body convulsed as the monstrous limbs shrank and contorted into human limbs. Gasping breaths mingled with desperate moans as the werewolf's once fierce eyes flickered with the fading remnants of its animalistic rage. It clutched at the ground, its muscles spasming and contracting as if battling an invisible force trying to keep it in its monstrous state. And then, at long last, the excruciating ordeal began to subside. The howls faded into pitiful whimpers, and the writhing movements of the werewolf gradually ceased. Like a veil being lifted, the monstrous form dissipated, leaving behind a naked and vulnerable human sprawled unconsciously on the concrete flaw.

"Right. Listen up," Jabu and Mariah emerge from the shadows. "Zendaya just took control of Xavi's body. We are in control now," says Jabu. He takes off his coat and covers Zane's unconscious and naked body.

The werewolves revert to their human forms. Kasa steps forward, his anger evident. "You treacherous sewer rats. I knew you had no intention of honoring our agreement. You will die for this."

"Oh, we intend to honor our agreement," Jabu calmly interjects. "We just want to make sure we leave these sewers alive. If you gentlemen relax and cooperate, you can have your boy back as soon as we are done. But if you choose to fight, we will leave him in the same state his son is in once we are done with his body. Clear?" It takes a moment, but Kasa and the other alphas nod reluctantly. "Good doggies."

Hakeem growls in response to the insult and takes a step forward, but is halted by Kasa's hand on his shoulder. "Patience brother. All they are doing is delaying the inevitable." Kasa tries to calm him. The grin on Jabu's face does nothing to help.

"Wow. We did it," Mariah exclaims in disbelief, her voice tinged with both relief and amazement at their triumph.

"It's not over yet. We still need to free Gundo."

Mariah nods and strides up to Dabula and Lupita who are still suspended mid air. Zendaya in Xavi's body maintains a ferocious demeanor as if she intends to devour them. Mariah turns her gaze to Lupita. "Alright Sister. Now, I know you and your brother have a lot of unresolved issues, but I need you to to open that casket and release him. Otherwise, Zendaya here will bite off your boyfriend's head. And she won't spit it out. I'm sure nobody wants to attend a funeral for a body without a head."

Lupita kicks about and struggles as she attempts to speak. But Zendaya squeezes her neck not too hard so she can't breathe, but also enough so she chooses to comply immediately. Even though she is in the body of a beast, she has compassion for Lupita. Especially when she sees tears run down her face. In her heart, she is urging her to do as she is told so it can all be over. Soon she realizes that a bit more motivation is needed. Zendaya opens her mouth and starts moving Dabula's head towards it. He starts kicking and struggling, but her hold on his neck is so tight he can only muffle a scream. That's when the floating coffin descends to rest on the floor and creaks open. Mariah runs to it and starts smacking Gundo's cheeks, begging him to wake up. After 30 seconds, which feels much longer to Mariah, Gundo takes in a deep breath as his eyes snap open. Mariah pulls him up into a hug as he coughs back to consciousness. She drags him out of the coffin and onto the concrete floor.

"Here, drink this," Mariah pulls out a blood bag from her backpack and gives it to Gundo. He starts sucking on it and even chokes as he sucks in too much blood at once. Zendaya watches on and waits until Gundo regains his footing before releasing her hold on Dabula and Lupita.

Kasa, Hakeem and Chance approach Jabu, Mariah, and Gundo with an air of tension. "You have your man. Now, give us back Xavi. Or we kill everyone." Hakeem demands.

"Oh please, you intend to kill everyone, regardless. Nonetheless, if you choose violence, we fancy our chances way better with a werewolf, two witches, and two vampires on our side," Jabu points out.

"Then how do you suggest we get past this tussle?" Kasa asks.

As they stood at an impasse, the tunnels were suddenly set alive and everyone's attention was drawn to the distant wails of an approaching train. The sound grew steadily, filling the tunnel with an ominous resonance that sent vibrations pulsing through every surface. Even the creatures of the dark, the rats and bats, reacted to the impending locomotive's arrival, scurrying and fluttering in a hurried dance to seek safety in the maze of shadows.

Jabu whistles to regain the werewolves' focus as he playfully spins a dagger in one hand. "Alright, listen up. When the train stops. All of us except for you puppies will board the train. We will take Zendaya's body and Zane with us. When the train has left and is at a safe distance, Zendaya will release Xavi from her spell and switch back to her body."

Chance's concerned voice chimed in, "But what about Raphael?"

"We promised to give you back a hostage, and that is what we are doing. We are just not willing to give you two hostages."

"Xavi will not agree to this?" Kasa points out.

"Right now, Xavi doesn't have a choice. But if he is not happy, he can come looking for us. We will be ready for him."

A staredown ensues and a charged silence fell upon the group as the distant rumble of the approaching locomotive dominated the air. The train emerges from the tunnel and its engine zooms past the platform as the rest of the carts follow. As it came to a stop, the steam hissed with a loud whistle, filling the surroundings with a warm, enveloping mist. It screeches to a halt with the middle most cart stopping at the center of the platform. The machine is a magnificent relic built in the bygone era of the 19th century by witches of the forge in collaboration with the witches who bend and break the laws of time and space. A grand sight to behold, adorned with intricate metalwork and polished brass fittings that would gleam in the sunlight. Though the magic that makes it special is affiliated with the sun and the moon, its tracks move only underground, and so it has never even seen the sun nor the moon. At least not in this realm. Its black smokestack stood tall, releasing delicate curls of white steam that spread around the platform and tunnels like a fog. The lingering scent of coal and grease filled the air, but is inexplicably bearable for those that await on the platform, as if its potency was also engineered for the tunnels, so it is not toxic for passengers.

Gundo's eyes open wide with shock when the train doors open. His breath caught in his throat when he recognized the figure that disembarked. "Lord Shaka," he stammered, his lips trembling with reverence and fear. The ancient vampire stood there, flanked by an entourage of five other vampires. Among them were two regal females and three strong, distinguished males, all adorned in elegant African print clothing that exude power and tradition. Their glowing blue eyes stood out while their dark skin blended with the dimly lit platform. Lupita and Dabula strode quickly toward Lord Shaka and kneel before him as they utter clan praises in unison. "Oh great elephant, chief of immortals, mighty spear of the nation. You who say die and we perish." But Shaka's attention is fixed on Gundo.

"Gundo. Have you already forgotten your manners?" Shaka remarks. Gundo hesitated for a moment, grappling with his conflicting emotions before reluctantly bowing to his knee. Shaka scans the area and notices the dead vampires. "And what has become of my children?" he asks.

"Their blood is on the hands of these werewolves and witches," Dabula responds.

"Not the witches," Gundo interjects. "They only came here to save me."

"Gundo, I did not realize that you needed saving from your own family? Are we your enemies now?"

"No, my Lord, these people are my family," Gundo declared, his heart torn between loyalty to his sire and newfound allies.

"Oh, so this is why you have turned against us. You have found a new family. I suppose this is a good thing then. There would have been no need for all this drama if we knew you were no longer contemplating ending your life."

"I wanted to end my life because I was wasting it on people that do not love me. People that only value me as an asset, a means to an end. They are not a new family. They are the family I always had. I was just too stupid to realize it. Immortality without the ones you love is as good as death. I humbly ask that you release me from your service," Gundo asks with a trembling voice.

"You are too hasty, Gundo. Slow down. Though I am disappointed with your decision, your words move me to compassion. I mean, look at us immortals, royalty, squabbling in the presence of these dreadful creatures and gutter rats." He gestured toward the witches and werewolves. "We are supernaturals. We have spent so much time in this realm of creatures that are beneath us and have allowed them to drag us down to their level. We have forgotten who we are. Nonetheless, if you wish to be tied to them for eternity, you can release yourself by completing one last mission for me. A mission your powers are perfectly suited for. That is why I have taken matters into my own hands and have come to retrieve you." Lord Shaka is interrupted when a phone from among the werewolves rings in the background. When Kasa answers it, Shaka ignores them and continues to speak. "My child. We have discovered the ultimate power. A power that will allow us to change nature itself and a chance for the vampire to reclaim their place in the cradle of all-kind, the realm of immortals and supernaturals. We will change our nature as vampires and become the gods we were meant to be. With this power, vampires will enjoy true immortality without losing the essence of life. No longer relying on the blood of humans in order to experience life. Your powers are best suited for retrieving the source of this power. We know where it is. Back in the motherland. Come with me. Render me this final act of service and you will be free to…"

"EXCUSE ME!" Hakeem shouts from the background as he interjects. Much to Shaka's annoyance. "We have had enough of these foolish games. Fortunately for us, we do not have to play them anymore. We just received confirmation that we do not need the witch to break Raphael's curse. We just need her blood. So we are free to kill you all and end this shenanigan. As from this moment, you no longer have hostages to use against us as leverage. Curse Xavi if you wish to, we will free him with the witches blood as well."

"How disrespectful," says Lord Shaka. The cascading beard that frames his regal countenance swings side to side as he walks three steps past the kneeling Gundo and halts. "Excuse me for a moment, my child," he says to Gundo. First, the flesh on his chick pulls away and rips itself off from his contorting face, revealing the bloody skeletal cheek bones and sinews under it. It is as if an invisible creature is biting a chunk from his face. As the others watch on in disgust and expect the chuck to fall, it instead turns into a bat. As the bat flies around him, the rest of his body follows suit, morphing into a cloud of bats that multiply until they turn into a mini tornado of bats. When the Alphas see the tornado moving towards them, they transform and prepare to defend themselves. They swipe their large paws at the bats as the black cloud positions itself between them. Three long spears with skeletal hands wielding them protrude simultaneously from within the cloud, piercing all three werewolves through the heart and protruding out their backs. In a second, the torrent of bats dissipates and Shaka reverts to his corporeal form. He stands between the alphas as they collapse lifelessly, the spears still firmly lodged within their bodies, held in place by the unyielding grasp of the skeletal hands. "Filthy mongrels," he remarks as he turns his gaze to Zendaya's direction. He quickly morphs once again into the tornado of bats and starts moving towards her. All he sees is another werewolf that must be destroyed. Moreover, he recognizes the body she is in as that of one of his greatest enemies, Xavi Gonzalez.

Xavi's werewolf form crumbles to the ground as Zendaya switches back to her body, leaps to her feet and runs to stand protectively in front of the unconscious werewolf. She raises her arm with her palm facing forward. "Stop, she shouts." The black cloud of bats stops a mere step away from her. Lord Shaka's skeletal form with some parts of him still covered with sinews steps out of the cloud as if he is walking out from behind a black curtain. "This one is mine to kill," Zendaya declares with a trembling voice.

Lord Shaka takes Zendaya's trembling hand and kisses the back of it as the bats return to him and he regains his corporeal form once more. "A beautiful witch that is able to stare death in the face and stand her ground, even as it kisses her. How can I deny you your pound of flesh?"

Shaka's display of power sends a shiver down Gundo's spine, a stark reminder of what they are up against. He makes a decision. "My Lord. Please do not harm them. I will come with you and serve as it pleases you," he shouts.

"No, if you are going then I am coming with you," says Mariah.

"What about your family?"

"You mean our family. When I return to them, it will be with you. That is what I promised our daughter."

Lord Shaka acknowledges their resolve with a hint of admiration. "Splendid. Two vampires lost, but at least one gained. Now, the stench of these rotting werewolves is getting to my nerves. We leave at once." Lord Shaka walks towards the train and enters. His entourage, along with an anguished Lupita and Dabula follow.

Gundo waits for Mariah as she and Zendaya walk towards each other and share a hug. "Are you sure about this?" Zendaya asks.

Mariah responds with three rapid and firm nods of her head, causing the tears from her eyes to drop to the floor. "Tell Gwen that I am sorry, but I haven't canceled dinner. I will be back. Just not today." She blows a kiss to both Zendaya and Jabu as she walks backwards into the train. The train doors close as the newly found friends watch each other from two opposite sides of the window. They barely hold back the tears.

Confusion etched itself onto Zendaya's face as she observed Mariah's emotions shift from sorrow to sheer horror. Something behind Zendaya gripped Mariah's attention, causing her to point behind her with an escalating horror taking over her demeanor. Zendaya can read the words; watch out on Mariah's lips. Before she could even contemplate turning around, Zendaya feels immense pain as something pierces her back and bursts out through her stomach. When she looks down, she sees blood stained werewolf claws protruding from her belly. Jabu watches in horror, frozen like a statue, though Zendaya's blood had splattered upon him like a warm crimson rain. Mariah can only watch on. She frantically pounded against the blood stained window of the train, her screams echoing through the carriage. But the train is called Ironwood for a reason. Even her vampire strength is inconsequential against the enchanted glass door. The train slowly pulls away, its wheels clacking against the tracks, separating her from Zendaya. This is not the goodbye they imagined. Soon she can see nothing but the concrete wall of the tunnels as the platform vanishes into the train's mist and they pull further away.

Jabu pulls out his daggers, his hands trembling with adrenaline, but as he aims for the eye, Xavi swipes at him with the back of his free hand, sending him hurtling through the air. The impact against the walls of the tunnel jarred Jabu's senses, leaving him unconscious and sprawled on the unforgiving railway.

Stupid little girl. How did I ever allow you to get away with so much? Too much. Xavi thinks to himself. With a merciless intent, Xavi lifts Zendaya higher, pushing the claws deeper into her vulnerable body. Her screams pierce the air, mingling with the taste of blood that fills her mouth. As the crimson droplets fall to the ground, a numbing coldness envelops her fading consciousness. Desperate to hold on, she clutches Xavi's claws, her own lifeblood coating them with a chilling moistness. Summoning the last ounces of her dwindling strength, she makes a body switch.

"No. No. What have you done?" Xavi coughs up the words as he realizes that he is now inside Zendaya's fatally wounded body. He is in disbelief that the witch has once again bested him. A few choice words come to his mind, but he has no strength to blurt them out. He begins to fade as he takes his last breath in Zendaya's body.

Zendaya retracts the claws from her own dead body and gently places it on the ground. Jabu has also regained consciousness as he crawls towards the platform, pulls himself back onto it and passes out again while laying face up on the ledge of the platform. Zendaya tries to scream but all she can do in a werewolf's body is raw. It is these painful raws that stun Jabu back into consciousness once more. His head and body are pounding with pain, but his heart pounds more painfully, fearing that he has lost the love of his life. When he sees Zendaya's body next to the werewolf, he too starts screaming. His cries cause Zendaya to stop roaring. Soon she starts transforming back into human form. Back into Xavi's naked dwarf form.

"Jabu. I switched," she utters tearfully. From the way she speaks these few words, Jabu immediately recognizes the unmistakable cadence of femininity. "It's me, babe. I switched. He is dead."

"Zendaya? Oh my goodness," Jabu limps toward her. He gazes at her with profound astonishment, realizing that she has sacrificed everything, even her own body, to stay alive. He embraces her. Forgetting for a moment about the body she is in and embracing her soul. Celebrating that she is still with him among the living. The two embrace for a long time, their sobbing and tears providing the backdrop for the moment.

Amidst the emotional outpouring, a faint sound reaches their ears. The forgotten Zane coughs and stirs back to consciousness. Reacting swiftly, Jabu rushes to attend to him, but Zendaya remains frozen, uncertain of how to face him in the state she is in. "Zane, are you alright, bro?" Jabu asks.

Disoriented and bewildered, Zane's eyes darted around, searching for familiarity. He regards Jabu with confusion and suspicion. "Who the hell are you? Get away from me. Where am I?"

"Calm down bro. I will explain everything?"

Zane's heart quickens as he spots the familiar figure that he recognises as the human form of Xavi standing a few feet from them. "You stay away from me. Stay...wait a minute."

Zendaya knows that if she uses words, Zane will not believe that it is her. She takes advantage of the tether that he took from Xavi to sire her brother to herself. The river that she diverted to an ocean her brother has known since they were children. It is through this connection that Zane senses a familiar energy. An energy that does not feel like slavery, like chains that bound him and a whip that tortures him into obedience and submission. It feels like the warm embrace of love. The same love that pulled him back to his humanity. He has always known about Zendaya's power, and when it all adds up, he knows that the soul in front of him is his little sister. Zane rises to his feet and wraps himself in Jabu's coat. Slowly, he walks up to Zendaya and kneels to embrace her in a hug. At that moment, he catches sight of Zendaya's lifeless body in the background. He understands the source of her misery in the midst of what should be a wonderful reunion. She cannot switch back to a dead body.

Just like his sister Zendaya, Zane is half Mexican and half African, but his Mexican features predominate his face. At the core of his enchanting countenance was a pair of deep, expressive hazel eyes that sparkled like golden embers. His skin, kissed by the sun's gentle touch, exuded a warm, golden hue. Zane's hair cascaded in waves of dark, glossy locks that framed his face. It was a deep, lustrous shade of ebony, reminiscent of a moonless night sky, contrasting beautifully against his golden complexion. The way his hair fell slightly over his forehead only added to the charm, softening the angles of his strong jawline and chiseled features that complement his muscular frame.

After the reunions and introductions, the trio fall silent as they sit with their backs against the wall and start processing everything. Zane and Jabu have many questions about the consequences of this switch, but they are not brave enough to ask them. They are afraid they may not be able to handle the answers, and so they wait for Zendaya to speak.

After a good amount of time, Zendaya finally breaks the silence. "How can I live like this? How can I live out my life stuck in the body of this monster?" she asks.

"There has to be a way to fix it?" Jabu says.

"There is no way to fix it. I can't transfer into a dead body. And I cannot live like this. Even you cannot love me when I am like this."

"Zendaya, stop it. Don't talk like that. I will always love you, no matter what."

"Stop lying. You have to be honest with yourself. Be honest with me. I am not even a woman anymore. I am a monster and I should have stayed in my body and died."

"No. We are witches. There is always a way. We have to find it," Zane interjects. Zendaya hangs her head and starts sobbing.

"What about Mariah's daughter? On the way here, you said she has the power to restore things. She can fix you," Jabu reminds her.

"No, she can't. Her power is limited to an hour from the time an incident occurs. In New York peak traffic, it will take two hours to get to her."

"Oh my goodness," Jabu's eyes widened, as he scanned the surroundings, desperately seeking inspiration for an alternative plan. "Ok, ok, you heard what Shaka said to Gundo. He said they discovered some type of ultimate power. Maybe we should be looking for this power as well. He mentioned a place, a realm of the supernatural. He called it the cradle or something like that. If we can't find help in our realm, we need to look elsewhere. I don't care where we have to go. You always do whatever it takes for others, for me. Now it's time for me to do whatever it takes for you."

"Babe, we don't even know what type of power he was talking about."

"He said it's a power that will allow them to change nature itself and build the life they want for themselves. I say we wait right here for the next sunset and catch that Ironwood locomotive to Africa. It's worth a try. They say it never misses a sunset and always arrives without fail."

"I don't know babe. I mean," she sniffs. "We are supposed to be catching a plane to the Bahamas. Not some strange train to.." her words fade in her mouth.

Jabu kneels in front of Zendaya and wipes the tears from her face. "I don't know either. But I will give my life to help you. Now, I still intend to go with you to the Bahamas. It's gonna happen. You and I have never allowed anything to stop us or come between us. You just need to find the strength for one more fight. That is all I ask of you. Do you think you can do that? For me? For us?" A tear runs down Jabu's face as he reasons with her heart. His pleas are met with a prolonged silence that accompanies the sadness that washes over his face. He had tried to hide it, hoping to strengthen Zendaya, but now he himself needs strength.

Zane rises to his feet. "I have heard about this realm the vampire mentioned. The first time I heard about it was from dad, when I asked him why mom left. He said our mother left to prepare a place for us and the other kids at the orphanage where we could live among other people that were gifted like us. As all the kids manifested their powers, it was becoming too much for her and dad to handle alone. She needed help from people like us. She left with the promise that she would return and take us all so we can be together, but she never returned. He tried to look for her, but didn't even know where to start. Eventually, he gave up. He was not giving up on hope that she would return someday. But he was giving up on looking for her because he needed to focus on raising us. If this place exists and we have a lead as to where it could be, then we have more than one reason to look for it and find it. They call it; The Cradle Of All Kind. They say it is where all supernatural beings and magic itself originate from. Werewolves, vampires, witches and others we do not even know of. If it exists, that is where we are likely to find a way to restore you, and maybe even find out what happened to our mother. Zendaya, you sacrificed so much to save me. Now it's my turn to save you. But I need you to be strong and give us this chance to help you."

There is a prolonged silence as both men run out of words. It lasts until Zendaya breaks it once again. "Mom, huh? That sounds exactly like the person I could use right now. But what if she is staying away from us of her own volition? What if she just didn't want us anymore? What if she is dead?"

"You would have been the first to know about it. You said many times that when you try hard enough, you can sense her soul."

"What if it was just my mind playing tricks on me? What if...?"

"Zendaya. Stop it. You won't find the answers for all your what if's here. We have to try. You are a Zabalaza. Remember what mom told us it means in Zulu. It means to struggle, protest, and fight for what you believe in and what is right. Right now, I need you to fight for what you deserve, because this is not right."

They allow her a moment as she sobs through her contemplations and depression. After a while, she lifts her chin. "Jabs," she sobs. "That night at the police station, I found the engagement ring in your pocket. I have been spending every moment since wondering how you would propose and looking forward to it. Now it will never happen."

Jabu stands up, yanks the coat on Zane and pulls the box with the engagement ring from one of the pockets. He removes his golden necklace and attaches the ring to it. When he kneels again, he puts it around Zendaya's neck. "Since you found this one and the surprise is ruined, I am demoting it to a promise ring. Just wait until you see the engagement ring. The rock will be so big you will sink to the bottom even when you take a bubble bath." They all chuckle. "I don't know how I will propose to you yet, but I promise it will be awesome and a surprise. It will happen. And I will be putting the ring on your beautiful finger as soon as I get you back into your beautiful body."

Zendaya takes a deep breath and sniffs as she runs her elbow across her face to wipe away the tears. "Alright. Where do we start?"

Jabu's face lights up with hope. "That's my girl. We start by putting your body into that coffin. Since it drains all oxygen from its contents, it should preserve your body until we can find a way to restore it." Jabu picks up Zendaya's body and places it in the coffin. When he shuts it close, it hisses as the oxygen is drained from it. A cold breeze from the coffin brushes against his skin.

"Funny how the coffin is here at this moment, as if fate knew we would need it." Zendaya says.

"Perhaps fate also knows that we will fix this." Jabu takes the opportunity to reassure her. The three find a corner and cuddle as they wait for the next sunset, so they can catch the ironwood train, hoping it can take them to a place where they hope to find help. Three days they waited. Three sunsets passed, and the Ironwood locomotive, a train that has never been late and has always arrived without fail, never came.

ACKNOWLEDGEMENTS

Thank you from the bottom of my heart
for supporting my work
and taking the time to read my book.

Zendaya, Mariah, Jabs and Gundo
will be back with another adventure soon.

Please sign up for my newsletter
and follow me on instagram for updates.

www.ingramcontent.com/pod-product-compliance
Lightning Source LLC
Chambersburg PA
CBHW022138170626
46807CB00005B/1979